RENÉ MOON

HER *Guilty* CONFESSIONS

A COLLECTION OF WOMEN'S FANTASIES FROM ACROSS THE WORLD

HER GUILTY CONFESSIONS

RENÉ MOON

A catalogue record for this book
Is available from the British Library.

ISBN: 978-1-3999-7475-2

CONTENTS

ACKNOWLEDGEMENTS

Firstly, I would like to thank my Friend/guiding light Fred Batt for all his knowledge & positivity, without him this book would not have happened.

Facebook/Fred batt

ALL MEDIA ENQUIRIES

CARRINGTON INTERNATIONAL LIMITED.

07860 414194

....

https://www.sdc.com/

A huge thank you to SDC.com for promoting and sponsoring the book...

Thank you to the very talented Mike for taking the amazing shots bringing the book to life.

**Photography by*

www.mikephotography.co.uk

....

Thank you to the beautiful talented Mia & Hannah from the beauty spot for the stunning make-up.

**Make-up by Mia*

Insta. Miamua_101

www.thebeautyspotshop.net

www.facebook.com/theonestopbeautyshop

....

Thank you to my stunning couple
Victoria & James for the amazingly sexy
Shots.

www.empowerinspireawaken.co.uk

....

Thank you to the most fantastic designer & formatting specialist.

Aila Designs

www.ailadesigns.com

....

INTRODUCTION

I grew up in a small medieval town at the foot of the Mendip Hills in Somerset, UK. I had a quiet upbringing with two very hardworking parents. My father was a stonemason and builder while my mother was a housewife, tending a family-owned shop. I have two younger siblings who have both had successful careers.

Basically, it was the ideal perfect family life as one would imagine; the Oxo family dinners, the Werther's Original Grandparents and family holidays in Cornwall.

I got married at 22 and have five children. Throughout my marriage, I had never ventured far from our family home.

Guilty Pleasures is a collection of real women's sexual fantasies I have gathered from across the world and creatively depicted each one, but maintaining each teller's voice retaining even their own preference of English language. Each woman's fantasy is liberating, raw, edgy and a very exciting read. They were written with the aim of putting the reader in each woman's position (*no pun intended*), feeling as if the readers are living the experience themselves. The collection aims to be very liberating to the reader and teller alike.

Some of the ladies' fantasies had been achieved to the fullest while some were just to feed the imagination with no intention of ever doing them. The latter is solely a personal choice.

That's what makes this book great.

There is no right nor wrong regardless of country or religion. This is but an invitation to peek through a small window of another woman's sexual desire without judgement and feel as they feel.

The women I have spoken too, love and are liberated by the idea of reading other women's sexual fantasies. I have collected fantasies from some of the most oppressed countries, aiming to validate what they think and feel as normal in the grander scheme of things. Women, when it comes to sex, are united in their fantasy worlds, regardless of creed, colour, country or religion.

Us ladies love a bit of raunchy fantasy in our reasonably mundane lives of rearing families and juggling work commitments. Our sex lives, including in our fantasy, are a way of escapism from the grind of normality and expectation.

We have all seen chick flicks and read books about this, but after talking to girlfriends and women over the years, I decided to write my book *Guilty Confessions*.

I would like every woman who reads this book to understand that *"there is no normal but all normal."* This book is the one place nobody has the right to have any judgement of our hidden desires—whether you take the step to act on your hidden desires or keep them securely locked away until life allows you the freedom to indulge in them.

I myself love nothing more than to fleet through different scenarios in my head with no judgement, prejudice, guilt or analysing my thought processes. As you can imagine, writing this book has been a very

exciting roller-coaster for myself, the writer, and the women who chose and had the courage to share their fantasies with you, as I have.

Furthermore, if you are a gent reading this book, then, it can only give you ideas of what really goes through us ladies' imaginations, and believe me, this is some very saucy mental wanderings.

CHAPTER 1

A LITTLE OF WHAT YOU FANCY IS NEVER ENOUGH`

MÉNAGE Á TROIS

T, 34, USA

For as long as I could remember, I had fantasies involving other women. I had never considered myself bisexual nor found the courage to act on my desires. I had never discussed it with my husband, so I wondered what he thought I fantasised about. But it was not him nor any other man; I just loved other women.

They looked so beautiful. Their bodies were so delicate and alluring. Something about the way they moved that was sensual. So sexy… They oozed both seduction and grace. As much as I loved men, I could not help, but gravitate towards women sexually.

I was going to let you be part of one of my favourite fantasies. This one got me very turned on, every time.

My hubby and I, were away on a long weekend break in a swanky five-star hotel in Venice. The concierge greeted us in the grand lobby. A crystal chandelier illuminated the room, acting as an impressive centrepiece at the same time. Clusters of plush furnishings loitered the corners, guiding a path with its contrasting, polished parquet floor to a lounge area on one side and a bar full of life and happy, relaxed faces and busy, smartly dressed staff on the other. Tall palms and other exotic potted foliage were strategically dotted about, adding life and warmth upon entrance.

From the grand reception, a porter carrying our luggage showed us to our luxury suite on the fourth floor. On entering our suite, we were greeted by the most delightful classically styled room with antique furnishings, leather sofas and elegant drapes, Murano glass lamps, and an antique coffee table adorned with white lilies and a fruit bowl bursting with colourful, exotic fruits. The bedroom was equally tasteful with its drapes, plush shag pile carpets and sumptuously dressed bed with a view to the lagoon. It was also blessed with a terrace and sun chairs looking onto San Marco square and the clock tower.

It was early evening and after I freshen up, Craig and I went down to dine at the in-house restaurant. As we waited for our order, a stunning brunette woman walked through the restaurant, catching my attention. She had the most beautiful face, and there was an elegant air about her. Our eyes met for a split second, and we acknowledged each other with a smile.

After our meal, we decided to have a drink in the hotel bar. And as Craig found a seat, I went to the bar. I was waiting to be served when I heard a "Hello," and as I faced the greeter, the same woman who caught my attention earlier smiled at me.

"I passed you in the restaurant," she continued. "You caught my attention, but I didn't want to intrude on your dinner. May I join you now?"

Seeing Craig over the far side of the bar in full conversation with a group of men I didn't recognize, I said, "Yes, of course."

Taking seats at the bar, we began chatting, which was very easy to do with Maris as I found out. It turned out she was in Venice on business, alone. We obviously made a connection upon catching each other's attention. So, I invited Maris over to join us at the table, where Craig was still engrossed in a conversation talking about football. Sitting down, Maris and I continued our chat, now even more openly.

And so, it went on for the next hour.

After some time, I leaned over the table, accidentally knocking my red wine all over my white dress. I told Craig I was going to get changed and invited Maris to come with me so we could carry on with our conversation. I was not worried about leaving Craig as he was having a ball talking about my pet hate—football.

In the suite, I asked Maris to come with me into the bedroom to help me unzip my dress. As she did so, she very tentatively brushed my hair from the Knape of my neck, sending shivers down my spine. It was the first time another woman has ever really physically touched me, and I loved it. It was more tender and gentler compared to a man's touch. I had

a white strapless bra on, and Maris skilfully flicked the clasps and released my dainty, little breasts, commanding me to stay still. She would help me freshen-up, she said.

Sauntering to the bathroom, she ran some warm soapy water and drenched a sponge. Coming back to me, she proceeded to cleanse the red wine off my neck and chest, gently brushing the moist natural sponge over my erect naked breasts.

I could feel my pussy igniting, burning with an aching desire. Then, Maris slipped my wine-stained moist panties off as well, leaving me fully exposed. She got on her knees in front of me, gently sponging from my navel to just above my exposed sweetness. She looked up at me with big doe, sexy eyes, silently seeking permission to touch me, of which I granted by stroking her hair.

Gently kissing my treasure, she probed my hidden jewel with her tongue. It felt so different from when a man does it—soft and gentle but very precise. She made me gasp as she explored, opening my legs to give her full access to her desire, and now mine, too. Sucking and delicately licking me to my first glorious orgasm, gifted to me by a beautiful woman.

Standing back to her feet, she turned and asked me to unzip her dress. I watched it slide down her body until she stood before me, totally bare and alluring. Taking my hand, she beckoned me to the bed. There, we both lay, kissing passionately and exploring each other with gifted fingers. I, touching her as I would touch myself, and she, me. My feminine fingers gently ran between her warm, moist, pink lips, feeling the tiny engorged clit as I tentatively teased it with my finger. It made

her moan, as I had, creating more excitement in my wet pussy that was being adored by her.

We both slipped a couple fingers into each other's hot, naturally-lubricated pussies, indulging one another in harmony. We were a hot tangle of femininity, enjoying each other's tender touch.

I wanted to taste her and feel her come in my mouth; to taste her and know I did that for her. Pulling away, I moved down the bed. I positioned myself between her trim-toned thighs, and wrapping both arms around them, I pulled her pussy towards me. Without invitation, I placed the tip of my tongue gently on her exposed clit, just resting it there until she pleaded to lick her. The power sent a surge of energy through my body. It was such a turn-on having so much control, enough to make my beautiful stranger beg for my touch.

As I was sucking and licking her appreciative pussy, I heard the door. Craig walked into the bedroom and stopped in the doorway with an initially shocked look on his face. It soon turned to total desire as I beckoned him in with my hand. While I was preoccupied indulging my new friend with my lips and tongue, he stripped urgently out of his clothes and then sat on the edge of the bed.

Craig started stroking his huge, hard tool at the sight that beheld him; his woman and a stunner he only glanced at in the bar, engaging in something he had only witnessed in a porno. Without invitation, he went behind me. He spread my prone ass, spitting on my exposed crack. A ribbon of drool lubricated my puckered starfish and elegantly exposed pink clam. Lining up his tool, he slid it into my appreciative pussy. It felt different this time. Everything was more intense and urgent.

Thrusting deep, he drew out a stifled moan as I still licked and sucked my sweetness to a glorious orgasm. Maris contracted around my fingers, and soon, she was squirting violently into my face with a scream of ecstasy as I continued to suck enthusiastically on her clit.

I was also on the brink of another mind-blowing orgasm. I felt my pussy greedily clasped Craig's generously engorged cock, convulsing violently and refusing to free his member. Holding him fast, the three of us came, in a sea of total ecstasy.

This was just one of my fantasies involving women, and definitely not the last that involved a ménage á trois.

AND ACTION

R, 39, ESP

I loved attention, and had always had a hidden desire to make a sex tape. You know, the kind that you've read about, like the one that Tommy and Pammy made or Paris. But I had never been brave enough to tell my boyfriend.

Then, one evening, I was out with my oldest friend, T, and for the first time, confessed about my hidden desire. T, crazy as she was, screamed like a teenager sharing her first sexual secrets, causing others in the bar to turn to see what all the commotion was about.

I told her I could never find the courage to tell my boyfriend about my fantasy. After chatting in depth and drinking an unscrupulous number of cocktails while giggling like foolish girls do, I told her I could

do it if she was there. In truth, there was not a lot we hadn't done together over the years as friends, even down to sharing boyfriends. So, I suggested she stayed at mine, which was not unusual and would be no surprise to my boyfriend.

We made our plans as we guzzled the last of our fruity cocktails, before heading back to the tiny town house I shared with my partner.

We fell through the door arm in arm, giggling as we made our way to my bedroom, where I knew he would be asleep or waiting for me to come home. Sure enough, there he was, an amused smirk on his face.

Unceremoniously, T and I both lifted our dresses and dropped our pants, laughing at his expression of bewilderment.

I, then, reached into my bag and pulled out my phone, as T lifted her dress over her head. She clambered onto the bed and seductively crawled towards my partner. I set my phone to video and sat on the end of the bed, filming them as she seduced him.

He was clearly terrified but extremely turned on at the same time; he had the biggest throbbing erection, which came into view as T drew the sheets back, revealing his nakedness. She made her way between his legs and grasped the root of his solid column. Then, she glanced up at him before devouring his hard length within the warm moist confines of her mouth.

I had the most amazing view of her shaven, glistening, pink pussy and puckered arsehole, winking seductively at me. My partner, who was making submissive eye contact with me, got lost in the euphoria of his unplanned union as she took him deeper into her gagging, restricted, warm throat.

He groaned and glanced at me again. As I smiled at him, he gave in, savouring every tiny action her mouth, tongue and gag reflex administered to his now raging sensitive length. At the same time, she teased and caressed his sack, almost bringing him to a climax. But instead, T unsheathed his tool from her oral restraints, leaving him extremely frustrated. She seductively manoeuvred off the bed and took over the filming, smacking me on the bum, urging me on.

Mounting the conjugal bed, I held my partner's gaze. I hesitated as I watched him caress the length of his angry weapon with a firm masculine grip. As he slowly worked his tool, pre-cum glistened on its impressive shiny head

I approached him on all fours, as a panther would stalk its prey. Reaching my quarry, I straddled the wild beast to contain it within my grip. I slid my moist, hot cleft onto him, fitting him like a glove as I sank him deeper into my soul. Clasping my hands around the back of his muscular neck, I anchored on and started to rise and fall onto his impressive appendage. As the speed and momentum built up, I adored every exquisite sensation. I let my inhibitions dissolve, totally forgetting we were being filmed. We were totally lost in our own euphoric joy as we both thrust to meet each other.

I paused to turn around on his piece into reverse cowgirl, but this didn't satisfy my lover. He brutally thrust me forward, forcing me onto all fours but not unsheathing me. Using his masculine strength, he secured me to him and held my hips as he skilfully got to his knees. He was now in control and began thrusting into my spasming quim with no mercy. Like a man possessed, he drilled me to delectable orgasm time and time again; golden nectar erupting from deep within my warm,

quivering cleft over and over, splashing and seeping down my inner thighs.

Looking up at T, who was still filming us, I beckoned her over to join us. Laying down on her back in front of me, her shaven pouting pussy just a breath away from my lips. I could smell her womanly perfume and even though I had never touched or tasted another pussy other than my own, I just had too.

Leaning onto my elbows, I used one hand to part her succulent, dark pink flower. I touched the tip of her clit with my pussy-virgin tongue. She let out a soft moan, which sent shivers of excitement through my body. Taking her clit deeper into my warm mouth, I gently sucked and licked her to her first perfect orgasm. She writhed under my mouth and thrust her hips into my saliva-and-juice-coated face. I slipped two fingers deep into her hot convulsing wet walls and worked on her as I would myself. I could feel the tension building once more in her perfect pussy. She gripped my fingers as I sucked and licked her to climax over and over again.

At the same time, I could feel the euphoric tension building in my own pussy as my partner worked his length deep into me, my pussy convulsing around his engorged tool. My nipples erected, as a tantalising electrical wave swept through my body as I climaxed hard on him.

Changing position, I propped myself up on pillows and took over videoing my partner and best friend fucking like lost lovers. But it turned me on. Laying on her side, T rested a leg on his shoulder as he got between her milky-white thighs and eagerly introduced himself to her. There was no gentlemanly intro; he just drove in deep, drawing a scream from her lips as he incessantly pumped her tight, wet wonder.

They both ground on the union of each thrust. T greedily took everything he had to offer, orgasming in screaming glory time and time again. Until my partner thrust even deeper and harder, roaring a guttural moan as he expelled every drop of his man milk deep within her convulsing walls. A fine film of perspiration glistened over his entire masculine form, clenching his perfect little butt as he absorbed every sensation running through him.

I smiled at my phone's camera I was still holding as my other hand pinched my own nipple.

MAN WITH NO NAME

C, 53, UK

Stu and I had been happily married for a long, long time—almost a quarter of a century, to be exact. We had a happy life, and generally, we were very content. But for some time, I had itchy feet, never seemingly fulfilled with my lot. Although, I couldn't tell why.

I was still a very attractive trim woman with a good pair of boobs. I had gotten implants a few years back when I had a menopausal crisis, so they are still fabulous and perfect. The girls even got a lot of attention from curious ladies and roguish men. I did have that brassy barmaid look about me. I just loved big, bold things and colour, big hoop earrings, red lippy, a layered pixie cut, fitted jeans and a flattering low-cut top to credit my girls.

I was out for coffee and a shopping trip with girlfriends when we started discussing a woman we know who frequented dating sites. Such

bitchy ignorant women we were! Taking a well-earned break from our shopping expo, we found a delightful little bistro café on the high street. Walking through the doors, we were met by the glorious aroma of freshly ground coffee, the chatter of friends, old and new. The place definitely had a French-inspired feel about it with small round tables and slatted chairs. Rows of buns and gorgeous cakes graced the counter where a well-seasoned lady was taking orders and planting them on a nail block next to her for the waitress to prepare and get out to the customers.

Taking our seats in the window, the four of us started chatting about the woman and decided to get the site up and have a nosey at her profile, expecting a good giggle. Well… long story short she looked fabulous, and there was a lot of interest in her. So clearly, she was doing something right, which slapped us down a peg or two.

Finishing our coffee, we set off to our next jaunt of shopping before going home and rush hour starts.

Stu was going to skittles as he did every Tuesday evening after the news. The smell of Boss aftershave permeated the air as I heard him clattering about above me, sprucing himself up. Skipping down the stairs, he popped in the living room and kissed me on the head, saying he was off.

Sat staring at my phone, I decided to have another look at the dating site my girlfriends and I had looked at earlier. But to access it, I had to set up a profile and add a pic, which I did, not even processing what the hell I was doing. As I browsed the site, my phone pinged, alerting me to a site message. Nervously opening the message, it was a man with a random identity— spock22.

The message simply said: *Hi, your beautiful pic caught my attention, if you're bored and want a bit of fun this eve meet me at 4A Summer Bay Villas @ 8pm.*

It was only a short distance away. So, what do you do when you know you're not meant to do something, but…?

Uhhh, you do it. Well, I normally do!

It was 7 p.m., so I ran upstairs and freshened up. I did my hair, touched up my make-up, and put fresh clothes on, along with my red stilettos and a good spray of Gucci Guilty. Then I was grabbing my keys and making for the car; I had no bloody clue what was going through my head.

I was almost at the villas when I had second thoughts and almost stalled the car. I shook it off though, thinking, bugger it! I only live once, so I might as well see what all the fuss is about. Chucking Lenny Kravitz on my stereo to pump me up, I kept going.

Pulling into the villa's car park, I was instructed to park next to a Bentley Continental Supersports, which I had absolutely no idea about. But when I saw it, I almost had kittens.

Clearly, this was no ordinary man.

Pulling up, I turned off the ignition and locked my humble mini. I felt like a scared girl going into a nightclub for the first time. My stomach was in knots, and I was shaking. Tapping on door 4A, a deep husky voice commanded, "Come on in."

Walking through that door was the scariest, headiest experience of my life. I almost fainted and stumbled but was caught by a big, strong

pair of male arms, drawing me in until our noses almost touched and I could smell his minty breath on my face. He held me as if guarding me from harm.

He was so stunning, rough shaven, with piercing blue eyes, golden hair and glowing skin, giving me a big, cheeky smile showing his perfect teeth,

He planted a kiss on my lips, which I instinctively replicated, urgently searching his mouth with my tongue for answers. He started lifting my top over my head, exposing my lovely firm girls. He slipped my bra off with one expert motion; it fell to the floor as he kicked the door shut.

Stepping back towards a freshly-laundered double bed, he sat, pulling me into him and taking one of my hard, threatening nipples into his hot moist mouth. Pushing my breasts together, he swapped his urgent attention from one to the other, sucking and nipping them and making me moan and squeal.

Moving his hand down to the waistband of my jeans, he flicked the button open and lowered the zip. In one smooth move, he exposed my lacy thong knickers. Leaving my breasts, his expert tongue teased a trail down to my navel. Migrating to a soft kiss trail, he moved my knickers to one side. He inhaled deeply as he moved in for the honey, dipping his tongue expertly in the honey pot, savouring the taste of me, lapping and sucking me to my first climax while I still stood over him.

He guided me to the bed and stood, removing his clothes. In no time, he was naked in all his masculine glory. Toned, cut and fit; he was a picture of a man. His penis was circumcised, revealing an impressive

purple, shiny helmet that just screamed, "swallow me." Pulling me to the bottom of the bed, he tilted my head back and introduced his big, hard member to my throat.

I had always been good at deep throat, but this was something else, and every time, I gagged, he groaned with pleasure. My eyes were watering, and tears started streaming down my face. Drool like boot laces hung from my cheeks as he fucked my face deep and hard, holding onto my tits to give him leverage as he thrust into my throat.

Pulling out, he flipped me over violently, demanding to know which hole I wanted it in. I went for my ass as I have always loved the intense feeling you get from sodomy. Taking some of the drool from around my mouth, I lubricated my fingers and slipped them between my fruitful lips. I started massaging my swollen clit in preparation for him descending into the dark side; he was rather larger than I was used to.

Spitting on his tool, he placed himself between my legs, lining his beast up with my puckered desire. I drew in a breath, in anticipation for what was to come as I felt him gently working his way into me, past the golden gates and beyond. I was so full up. He eased himself out again only to thrust back inside with slightly more enthusiasm, making me cry out.

After a few tough minutes, it got easier. I found myself relaxing, absorbing every nerve impulse radiating from between my legs. Faster and harder we went at it, both lost in time and space with our hedonistic sensations, raging through our beings. Until I came with a tremendous climax, squirting all over him as he still pumped into me. Then, with a deafening bawl, he shot his lot deep into me. Staggering backwards, he withdrew from his restricted thallic restraints.

Not one word was uttered between us as we dressed. I found my keys by the door where I dropped them and made my way to my car as did he, swapping a fleeting smile before going our separate ways.

I never even got Spock22. Real name!

SIBLING RIVALRY

H, 41, DNK

My sister and I were the only girls in our family; we had three brothers. We had always shared a room growing up and had a love-hate relationship. Our house was a strict one growing-up, so we tended to keep our squabbles close to our chest to avoid causing family drama. I was always a little jealous of her, if I was to be honest.

She was everything I was not—we were true chalk and cheese.

In our mid-20s, we both met and married the love of our lives and did a lot as couples—pub, day's out, concerts. The boys were best buddies and also did guy stuff together whenever my sis and I went on shopping trips or had girls' nights, watching slushy movies and beautifying each other, consuming copious amounts of wine and junk food.

On one such evening at my house, we were both in our pyjama shorts, relaxing in the living room, painting each other's nails, straightening our hair, face masks—you know, normal girls' night escapades. The boys had gone out together with other male friends. We were that disinterested, we didn't even ask what or where they planned; we just ushered them out the door to do their thing.

We decided to watch the trilogy of *365 Days* after our pamper session, and by then, we were a tad tipsy. As we got into film 2, we started discussing events and scenarios that we found sexually appealing. It all got rather truthful as we got around to talking about our husbands. I supposed the drink had lowered our inhibitions as I frankly admitted I had always had a crush on my brother in-law. Ironically, my sister also declared she had always fancied my partner, which I found funny as I thought I knew her and yet, never had an inkling. It just went to show, I supposed, how deep people could bury things.

As we got more drunk, we got more daring with our sisterly chat. I suggested, exclaiming what if we were to swap lovers for one night, just to experience what the other did. Excited, we agreed that when the men returned, we would go to task and shock them,

We carried on watching our movie, gulping down unmeasured amounts of chilled prosecco. The film only added to the sexual tension that was building within us.

We turned the lights off, and with only the light of the TV, we waited excitedly for the lads to return. Our hair was very similar, and we wore matching pj's I bought us at Christmas. And as we heard the laughing and key in the door, we knew the lads would be well-oiled, so to speak. My sister and I gave each other a smile before we set about our goal, descending on both men in the darkness as they entered the room.

Passionately kissing my sister's partner, excitement surged through me, not knowing what his natural reaction would be when he realised I was not his wife.

To my surprise, as he stepped back and realised I was not, he re-engaged with me, taking me firmly into his arms. He passionately kissed me as I haven't kissed for a long, long time. He searched out every nook with his tongue as if mapping out his bearings.

Glancing over, I was met with a bittersweet sight of my husband and sister in a deep passionate embrace, lowering onto one of the sofas.

Lust flooded through me like an unstoppable boar hitting an estuary in spring; the power was immense and unstoppable. My brother-in-law tugged at the string on my pj shorts. He pulled them down, exposing my fresh pink pussy. All my apprehension and doubt vanished, replaced with unadulterated sexual need and want. No, not want. Demand!

Placing his palm on my smooth, bald mound, his warm fingers descended between my moist welcoming lips. My God, the man had expert fingers and worked me to the point of coming.

But then, he abruptly stopped. He grinned and lowered me to the floor, onto the soft shag pile rug. Throwing off his top, he joined me on the floor, dominantly opening my legs. He descended towards my aching vagina, giving me a seductive glance as he took me into his soft warm mouth. Sucking my lively clit into his welcoming hot moist orifice.

He didn't lick and suck me as I would expect a man to pleasure me but more educated and precise as a woman would. So skilled in his actions, he brought me to orgasm very quickly.

As I lay, relishing my explosive pleasure, he removed his jeans and unbuttoned my top, exposing my alert pert breasts. My nipples stood on ceremony proudly for all that wished to view. Placing himself next to me on the floor and leaning against an armchair, he beckoned me to him.

Straddling him, I felt his gorgeous weapon tease between my fleshy, welcoming labia. I absorbed him deep within my warm, wet treat.

Taking one of my erect nipples into his mouth, he greedily sucked it as I rode his hard, glistening cock like none I had ever mounted before. A pang of guilt ran through me. As if sensing this, he spat on his thumb and placed it expertly on my begging clit in tiny circular motions. I threw my head back, appreciating every last sensation being gifted to me by my borrowed lover.

I hit my peak time after time. My legs were quivering as he expertly lifted me and told me to get on all fours with my ass prone. Doing as instructed, he placed himself between my eager legs. Liberally spitting on his meat, he unceremoniously worked it into my tight virgin restricted hole. I screamed as it gained access.

My sister and husband looked up and both giggled, going back to their business.

The pain began to ease as he slipped his hand around and started stroking my pussy. Pain melted into ecstasy, like nothing I had ever experienced before. The orgasms were harder, tighter, and more electrifyingly intense from deep within my body, and I felt the most amazing feelings as my pussy and asshole embraced his weapon.

I hugged him tightly as we both climaxed: an ultimate reward that I never knew could be achieved or even existed.

After withdrawing from my ass, we just lay in each other's arms, trying to make sense of what had just drunkenly happened between us. But there was nothing to understand. It was too complicated to analyse, so we just let it be and enjoyed our moment

We have had our extended girls night dozens of times now, and it only gets better.

A LITTLE STORY TO START THE NEW YEAR

Anonymous

He let out a groan and shot his cum deep into her. She felt his penis throb as his semen squirted inside her, and she watched his face as his orgasm subsided. At the same time, another man reached the point of no return and shot a thick stream across her breasts.

How many was that? She had almost lost count.

She decided that two had cum in her pussy, four on her tits and two in her mouth. Not bad, considering she had never done anything like this before.

Her husband had told her about the sex club but, though curious, she had never agreed to go there with him. Then, almost on the spur of the moment, she had decided it was now just what she had been looking for. The situation required no less.

She had arrived, dressed in spiked stilettos, lace-top stockings, suspenders and a little black dress, and quickly found herself being chatted up by a number of single men. After a while, they found a private room, and very soon, she was very much the centre of attention.

Her dress was quickly removed, and many hands explored her body. She found this far more exciting than she expected, and was soon ready to take one of them inside her. From then on, they took turns entering her. Those who were waiting took turns to have her suck them or just masturbated over her whilst watching her take one cock after another.

The men politely thanked her, and one by one, they left the room. When they had all gone, she lay back and looked down at her near-naked body. Her pussy was wet and swollen. She was still wearing her stockings, but they were now smeared with semen. Her tits were similarly coated, though now rapidly drying into a daubed pattern of shiny varnish.

Satisfied with her appearance, she took her phone out of her bag, stood under the light to show the evidence of the evening's activities to best effect and took a selfie. She tapped on "new message," put in the contact name, attached the picture and pressed "send."

There, she thought as she put on her dress, *that will teach the bastard to cheat on me!*

FORBIDDEN FRUIT

R, 39, UK

Brad and I had been married for 12 years when our sex life flagged. I found myself masturbating more and more, fantasising about fictional people. I craved to be adored, excited, aroused and desired. Most of all, I needed him to want me more than he had ever wanted me.

Just like every morning, I was preparing breakfast for the hordes and Brad. The filter coffee maker was dripping and spluttering and the toaster pinged toast up, serving as a constant supply to feed the kids as they grab and run for their buses, half-dressed and shoelaces dragging the floor. With bags slung over their shoulders, they were gone with the slam of the door.

An amazing aroma permeated the air as I prepared Brad's travel mug to set off for his first meeting of the day. Brad would be down shortly, descending the stairs into the kitchen, to the aromatic aroma of ground fresh coffee and warm fresh toast.

I was flicking through the paper in a monotonous manner, with nothing catching my eye or grasping my attention. Until I flicked to the back of the paper, and the page opened on the personal section, which I do love to browse through. There, I began to read an article about swingers parties. The whole idea of going to a swingers party or meeting a couple intrigued me, and my head started to wander.

As I was lost in my fantasy world, Brad meandered through the kitchen door, bringing me to my senses.

"Where were you then, love? You looked miles away. What were you thinking about?"

Our relationship was a solid one, and it would never worry me to tell him anything, generally, but I felt oddly guilty, and I knew I must be blushing.

Brad sat down on the barstool next to me and reached for my hand. Looking me in the eye, he said, "You know you can tell me anything love, don't be embarrassed."

There was no point lying to him, as Brad will know instantly if I did. So, I went for it and confessed my deepest desire.

To my surprise, Brad agreed it could be fun and that I should look into it whilst he was at work. The kids would be at friends' this weekend, so we were free to please ourselves…

I did!

Came Saturday evening. The air was charged with electrifying excitement. With the smell of shower gel, Creed and Black Opium, and a tinge of minty toothpaste, the place actually smelt like a top-end brothel, if I'm honest.

Brad was wearing his Boss jeans, Gucci top and his best Tricker's, while I was wearing a cute little black V-neck Gucci dress and my sexy strappy Louboutin's. I had had a lifetime, but had nowhere or reason to wear them until tonight, so I was even more excited and filled with nervous energy.

When we got to the swanky bar, which was part of a hotel in town, I was pleasantly surprised that everyone there was so normal. Though, to be honest, I was not actually sure what I expected.

It was very busy. The atmosphere was alive, and the air smelt of a mixture of expensive perfumes and aftershaves. The lighting was a warm glow, and the music did its hypnotic job along with the creamy, cool piña colada I was drinking. Most of all, the women all looked so stunningly beautiful, and the men were so handsome and well-groomed.

I was glancing around the room in a content haze, but I found myself locking eyes with the same man. He was a very handsome, dark-haired, dark-skinned man with the most stunning green eyes. His female partner was equally gorgeous with long red hair, blue eyes, and her figure was to die for—hips, bum and perky boobs. Like me, she wore a tiny, white figure-hugging dress but with knee-high boots.

Brad excused himself to go to the gents, so I sat patiently, sipping my drink. Suddenly, I felt a hand on my shoulder, followed by a deep husky voice.

"Excuse me," says the man's voice.

Facing him, I smiled. It was the same man I locked eyes with earlier, and on his arm was his beautiful female partner.

"You and your partner caught our eye," the man continued. "Would you care for some company, myself and my wife!"

Janette and Frank, we soon learned, were a lovely couple, and we hit it off instantly. Conversation was flowing as was the alcohol, laughing until 15 minutes before time was being called.

Frank suggested we come back to their hotel room for fun and a nightcap, which seemed very appealing. So, we finished our drinks, and Brad and I followed the beautiful couple to the elevator. We were all quite drunk but having fun.

We all rolled through the hotel room door. A beautiful, huge leather queen-sized bed that looked out over the city welcomed us. It was dressed in satin sheets and draped in a luxurious fur throw and silk bolster cushions.

Janette went to get glasses from the drink's cabinet while Frank got a lovely bottle of wine from the fridge. He poured the wine and handed a glass to each of us, but when he handed me mine, he openly stroked his manly hand across mine and up my arm very tenderly, causing me to shiver.

I inhaled a tiny gasp involuntarily, which Brad caught but to my surprise, he actually looked turned on. That was Janette's cue to lean in

and kiss Brad. Initially, I was shocked Frank pulled me into him and started kissing me passionately.

I glanced at Brad and Janette, but they seemed oblivious to us now, kicking their shoes off and removing each other's clothes in a frenzy of lust. I felt so betrayed but yet so turned on. As if sensing my mixed emotions, Frank stood and picked me up, carrying me to the bed. He put me down gently on the fur, which felt divine on my toned bare legs.

Frank sat on the bed, bending to stroke my face, and then, tenderly kissed me. At this point, I wanted to kiss him back. Partly because it was turning me on so much, but also, as a revenge for the hurt, seeing Brad kiss another woman.

Brad's kiss hurt, a physical pain but at the same time, it was making my pussy flutter with excitement. Frank was one of them kissers that could awaken your soul with the touch of his soft lips. He touched my cheek, so softly, down to my neck and finally, to my breast; my nipples were already erect from the mental stimulation and anticipation.

Still feverishly kissing, our tongues exploring each other's mouths, he slipped his hand into my panties so expertly and glided a finger across my clit, making me groan. He searched for the warm secret I guarded between my legs and slipped two fingers inside whilst his thumb ran over my clit in a rhythmic motion. I could feel my pussy gripping his fingers, and orgasm building, until I squirted into my panties, soaking the fur throw, which I presume is a hazard of hosting a swinging party at your hotel—beds got wrecked.

Kicking off his jeans and throwing his shirt over his head, Frank got to work disrobing me. He literally tore my pants off and then lifted my

dress expertly over my head. He flicked off my bra with one hand, leaving me totally exposed.

I glanced over to Brad and Janette; they were fucking like a pair of teenagers after prom. It was actually a real turn on to see my husband nuts deep inside another woman. Janette was riding him like she was about to take Beecher's Brook in the Grand National, and he was loving it.

As Frank slid out of his boxers, I could see what a magnificent man he really was. His manhood pointed to the ceiling, proud as punch. It was ample in length, but my god, it was a thick specimen, and I knew I was in for a treat that would make me squeal at first.

Climbing between my legs, he nudged his way inside my warm moist pussy, and boy, did I squeal, indeed. I felt so full but as I relaxed into the rhythm, my pussy started weeping in admiration. My orgasms soon became contagious, catching one after another.

Frank flipped me over, and I saw Brad thrusting his rock-hard column between Janette's cheeks; both were delirious with euphoria.

Behind me, Frank not-so-gently forced his member home, bringing me back to him. As he pummelled my beautiful pouting pussy over and over, orgasm after delicious orgasm, I felt the ultimate reward building. As his speed and tempo built, holding firmly onto my hips with gratification and purpose with his definitive thrusts.

And then, my vagina started to spasm around his cock; discharging her harvested energy all over my quivering body in an undulating blanket of ecstasy.

BLACKOUT ROOM ENCOUNTERS

R, 39, USA

My fantasy was quite an unusual one. My partner and I had been together for 15 years, and we were both career-minded so we did not have children yet. My partner, who we would refer to as Jake, would love a family, but to be honest, I loved my lifestyle so much I was now too selfish to consider having kids, thinking of all the implications of becoming a mother.

My beautiful toned body, for one. I had always been so proud of my gorgeous, perky boobs—only 34B but faultless in appearance. I couldn't even imagine having a child ruin them. Then there was my toned core and tum that I had worked so hard to perfect. Lastly, there was the enchanting, tight moistness between my perfectly-toned legs. The idea that such a perfectly-formed portal that had so much power, manipulation and control would be brutalised by childbirth, was already traumatising to me.

As for my fantasy… Jake and I had dabbled with the swing scene for several years now but this particular fantasy is one we are yet to experience, but boy, do I aim to.

And it got me every time I thought about it. In my fantasy, it would go like this…

We had been invited to a party at a swing acquaintance's condo. I put an extra bit of effort into my grooming; I want to appear perfect for my fellow partygoers and prospective mates of the evening.

Jake and I were both bisexual and had no trouble interacting with either sex. In fact, we were probably greedy and just couldn't get enough

of the unpredictable sexual liaisons, encounters and the excitement that inevitably went with the scene.

Just the thought of it got my pussy fluttering. Like when you popped a pot of pringles, once you popped you couldn't stop, and that went for popping my puss.

We were dressed to impress and did so everywhere we attended, looking like a power couple. No detail was missed. Even our fingernails and toenails were manicured to perfection. Jake's were perfect man's hands—big and strong, yet so gentle and immaculate. Mine equally perfect, but long with coral acrylic polish with toes to match. And we smelled heavenly, wearing only the best scent.

No underwear, of course.

As we pulled up in our taxi, stunning men and women poured into the condo, arriving in sports cars, taxis, private lifts and even chauffeur-driven limos. The sheer volume of people was quite intimidating but I was also very excited. I have been looking forward to this one for a long time.

No expense had been spared nor detail missed in the place, I noticed as we entered the main door, and ascended up some vast steps of an open-fronted glass condo. It was really quite stunning. The thought that had been put into the architecture was amazing, to say the least; a very different world and lifestyle to ours.

Reaching the door, we were greeted by two beautiful women, who both looked classy and dressed in black skirts, white blouses, and stockings and heels almost, resembling air hostesses. They took our coats and gave us a digital code to be collected at the end of the night.

Entering the condominium, we could see the party in full swing through the main doors, which was also attended by two more beautiful, smiling women. Not a finger did I lift until we reached the stunning glass bar, and that was only to be handed two flutes of champagne by the bar staff.

The place was full of stunning bodies, sipping complimentary champagne, conversing, touching each other in a suggestive manner. Some were dancing to the music that was emanating throughout the condominium.

Greedily sipping on our bubbly treat, Jake and I gave each other a knowing glance and then set off to investigate the party. We entered the adjoining room and were greeted by proud, naked bodies undulating and kissing. A blonde beauty was snorting cocaine from another blonde's breasts. Men were kissing and caressing one another unashamedly and basking in the glory of having a captivated audience. Naked women worked two poles, tantalising the hungry eyes that savoured their craft. The physical power of their naked bodies was so astonishing that my pussy was so spoiled and wet. It was like nothing I had ever been a part of before, I had been missing out.

Approaching another closed door, another equally gorgeous couple ushered us inside. The moment we stepped in and the door closed behind us, it went pitch black. Not a chink of light permeated the intense room.

My senses went wild, and suddenly, I had no idea where Jake was. I could sense people, *lots* of people. My hearing was super acute as I listened attentively; heavy breathing coming from every orientation of the room, soft moans, periodic giggles from men and women, sighs, slurping and purrs of contentment.

And there was a very distinctive slapping sound, as two naked bodies fuck unceremoniously.

I could smell sex. That very distinct smell of moist pussy and cum, perfume and cologne. I could smell the person next to me—a man—but I knew it wasn't Jake. I could smell his scent and from his choice, I knew it was an older man. Still pleasant but it was a more refined smell.

I felt soft hands take hold of my hips, drawing me in, and soon followed by a warm, soft mouth, expertly taking my aching, ridiculously moist pussy. He parted my pristine love lips with his tongue, delving deep within like a blind master seeking my engorged clit. He sucked me, devouring me to my first glorious orgasm, which I wanted to go on for eternity.

Taking me by the hands, he drew me to him. Now, down onto my knees, he sought my slightly parted lips with his tongue. His kiss sent shivers through my entire core. His natural smell did something to me; I craved him.

Taking the invitation, I sought out his cock with my hand. On grasping him, I felt numerous piercings—something I had never experienced before. Lubricating my hand with spit, I tenderly grasped its base. It had to be 6" around. I started to work his cock, slowly, precisely and rhythmically, drawing a soft moan from his lips. Even as we carried on passionately kissing, seeking answers from each other's mouths.

His hands were actively busying themselves. One was slipping two expert fingers in and out of my creaming pussy, and the other was playing with my nipple ring, and soon brought me off once more. Each orgasm was more intense than the last, taking me to a higher and higher plain with each stroke and nip.

Taking my hand, he lay on his back. Suddenly, I could feel other hands and lips caressing my body. Where they naturally landed, there was no pre-planning or observation, just instinctive touch and taste.

I lifted myself to straddle his perfectly toned torso, and then, used my hand to nestle his impressive glands between my aching vagina lips. Beckoning him inside me was an intense experience, sending waves of delirium through me as he introduced himself unapologetically to my most secret place.

As I rose and impaled myself deeper with his monstrous bejewelled manhood, a tongue explored my virgin, sacred, puckered hole, and it felt absolutely glorious, bringing me off time and time again. Electricity surged through me with each thrust and soft invading lick of my puckered treasure.

Two more people joined and took a nipple each, ravishing them, suckling, licking, and nibbling as I orgasmed repeatedly. I felt another man line his cock up, with my forbidden entrance, gently deflowering my forbidden fruit and drawing a gasp from my lips.

My body was overwhelmed with sensation. I was violently shaking as the orgasms built to a level I'd never experienced before. As the orgasmic surge peaked, my ass and pussy convulsed around both cocks; the force causing me to unmercifully squirt my nectar over the entirety of my anonymous lover, whose name will remain a secret of infinite time.

Rolling off my new friend, I just lay in the dark, relishing all the feelings radiating throughout my body. And was not even giving Jake a thought.

GIRLS JUST WANNA HAVE FUN

S, 33, USA

I had been smack-bang in the middle of the hardest time of my life now, so please excuse this bitter woman that might shine through this fantasy.

I was in a local bar in town, drowning my sorrows, feeling bitter and sorry for myself. Having a husband who is a total tool, I believed I deserved so much more than he could ever give. I was working through my fourth double Jack and Coke, slurping the cool fiery mixture through a straw for maximum impact and starting to feel a lot more content. The hurt and disappointment were draining away to mere shadows in my mind's eye, a Jace Everett track was strumming away in the background, as my eyes carelessly wandered around the bar.

A few couples were dancing, and a man in his 70s was toe-tapping to the rhythm of the music at the other end of the bar, a half-full bottle of whiskey next to him. Next, I noticed a beautiful brunette, playing pool across the bar. Looking her way, our eyes briefly met.

I spun back to lean on the bar, thinking nothing of the brief eye contact and that way it made me feel. Something about her intrigued me; her expressions, movements and body language had me mesmerised, which was strange as I have never looked at another woman that way. I actually felt my pussy come to life with a surge.

Over the next hour, I just could not hide my infatuation, looking her way once in a while. And she noticed, giving me a cheeky smile whenever our eyes clashed, which was a lot. I felt my nerves building as I realised she was coming over.

After introducing herself as Cassie, she invited me over to the pool tables to join her; her friend had a sudden engagement to attend to and left.

Chatting, giggling and dancing came easily with my newfound friend. It was as if we had been friends forever, sipping cocktails and playing pool, which she was a pro at unlike myself. Cassie asked me if I would mind, she could text some friends and invite them over as well as it was so much fun. She thought I would love them.

Waiting for them to arrive, we continued drinking cocktails and playing pool. She even showed me how to handle my pool cue properly. In doing so, she approached from behind, spooning me and leaning into me, whispering in my ear how beautiful I was.

Getting closer and more familiar, she put her arms around me. Then, turning my face to look at her, she planted a feathery kiss on my lips. Her lips tasted like cherry chapstick—just like the song—and her tongue was soft with hints of peppermint gum that laced over mine.

I invited Cassie back to mine as I knew my partner would not be home; he did anything to avoid me now. We carry on making and drinking cool fruity cocktails. We giggled and danced provocatively, kissing and caressing freely. Until the doorbell rang.

Opening the door, before me stood two stunning women, both grinning suggestively at me. I let out a nervous giggle as their eyes examined the prize—me! They looked like a pair of lionesses about to devour me.

Inviting the ladies in, we all continued dancing, drinking and conversing openly whilst laughing a lot. One of the women started

sensually examining her friend's mouth with her tongue. As if motivated, my bar friend Cassie then joined in and pulled me by the hand. She started kissing me seductively.

We were kissing and caressing each other passionately when one of my visitors suddenly stopped kissing and looked at me. "I want to taste you!" she said.

The other two women agreed as I laughed nervously, unsure I could handle all three women. Moving into my bedroom, they told me to trust them and tied me to my four-poster bed. With my silk neck scarves from my wardrobe, they bound my arms and legs, star fishing me across my bed.

They took turns kissing my soft lips and that delicate part of my neck, just below my ear. One was sucking my erect, proud nipples with lustre while flicking her moist middle finger across her pussy. My bar friend Cassie took my pussy in her mouth, delicately parting my lips with her gentle fingers and started eating me so gently but expertly.

I couldn't stifle my moans of ecstasy. At that exact moment as I let myself go and relished in my new friend's knowledge of female anatomy, so expertly performing cunnilingus as only a woman could, my lying, cheating husband walked in on us.

Initially, he was clearly shocked at the sight of his wife being ravished by three gorgeous women in his own marital bed. But then, he has the nerve to ask if he may join in and help. All three of my new friends stopped and looked at him declaring, "No!" in unison. They glared at him, eyeing him up and down with distaste.

Without another word, they all resumed their duty and carried on licking, kissing and sucking me, occasionally swapping places. It

turned me on to such a degree I couldn't stand it any longer and needed to be part of the action and not just prey.

I struggled breaking free from my restraints, and taking my bar friend, I forcefully slammed her on the bed. I kissed her with urgency as I worked my way down to her sweet, pouty pussy. I had never eaten pussy before, but the act came naturally to me. As I parted my friend's dark pink lips to reveal her treasure, I licked and sucked her moistness until she came in my mouth with an extreme convulsion. Her musky womanliness tasted so good.

One of the other beauties wanted a piece of the action declaring, "It's my turn!"

So, I moved my attention to her sweet flower, skilfully slipping two fingers inside her hot, moist hole. I searched for her g-spot while licking her like a moorish lollipop.

The other beauty positioned herself behind me, parting my peachy cheeks and exposing my puckered secret. She expertly licked, sucked and rimmed me as I wailed in total euphoric delirium.

So lost in my orgasm, I didn't realise the bar beauty had slipped on her strap-on, which must have been in her bag. Ordering me to lay prone with my butt totally at her mercy, she placed a palm on each cheek and parted them. Introducing the tip to my tight hole, which was amply lubricated by my own juices and their copious amounts of slimy spit, she ordered me to spread my cheeks.

"Yes ma'am!" I said, allowing her full access.

One of the others positioned herself beneath my face and ordered me to lick her clean. So, I planted my face in her beautiful pussy. On the

other hand, the other girl lay herself underneath my free pussy from behind and proceeded to lick and suck until I had orgasm after orgasm.

This heaven went on for hours. We swapped positions and roles over so it was fair on us all and we were all fulfilled. And at last, we all unashamedly collapsed on the bed as one big pile of satisfaction, lounging there in our total female bliss.

Who needs a man!

MASQUERADE BALL

T, 26, USA

I had always been intrigued with masks, even from a young age. It intrigued me how they were used throughout the world by different cultures for different ceremonial purposes. And how masks totally obscured the wearer's identity along with their facial expression, leaving other people slightly in the dark, so to speak. We humans relied on facial expressions because they tell us a lot about circumstances and situations. This, in turn, could prove extremely alluring to the onlookers, hence them being used in cultural sexual ceremonies across our vast planet.

This was my favourite fantasy, and it was one I masturbate to when I was alone or in the bath.

In my fantasy, I was married to a rich successful plastic surgeon. I was his PA initially, that's how we met.

We were taking some well-deserved time off in a very prestigious private estate in the Highlands of Scotland.

We were having a late dinner prepared for us at the Manor House, and whilst sat dining, I noticed my husband make a suggestive gesture at the waitress, who responded with a very flirty, sinful, little giggle.

Enraged, I slammed my cutlery down on the beautifully-laid table, anger welling in the pit of my stomach. I gave my husband a definitive glare, excusing myself to get some fresh evening air. I was planning to re-evaluate the situation when the red mist whirling in my mind had settled.

As I walked in the cool fresh night air, through the manor grounds, the dark veil of the night descended on the spectacular surroundings. The air was filled with the smell of fragrant wildflowers and heather. Insects hummed around my head, and in the distance, I could hear a faint sound of beautiful, classical music and what sounded like chanting. As if entranced, I followed the path for what seemed like an age in the direction of the enchanting sounds, with no clue as to where I was, what I was doing, and not even caring that people might be looking for me back at the manor house.

As I blindly followed the enchanting music, I could see a majestic building towering over the whispering silhouette of the trees. It had magnificent elaborately carved columns and huge leaded windows, shrouded in grand crimson and gold drapes that someone had expertly drawn, for privacy.

I approached with excitement buzzing around in my head, feeling like a naughty child up to mischief. Seeing the smallest crack in one of the drapes, I couldn't resist the temptation to peek inside, full of intrigue. Inside, clusters of beautiful women, all dressed in their finery. Their feminine forms were shrouded in black satin cloaks, and adorned with

the most stunning hand-painted masks. The elaborately adorned masks obscure their identities, making them totally anonymous to the eye.

The music had a seductive, ominous heady rhythm, which radiated through my whole being. I felt oddly aroused, confusing me a little. I descended through the impressive red door, and to my alarm was greeted by a gentleman, in an evening suit and plain gold mask.

"Good evening, Madame, let me take your coat for you," the man warmly greeted, handing me the most beautiful gem-encrusted mask, which I instinctively put on. He helped me drape a cloak over my exposed shoulders. Then, he gestured me towards the internal door—my only physical restriction to whatever was going on in that grand ballroom.

But I wanted to be part of it!

As I entered the magnificent room, I caught my breath. The stunning vaulted ceilings, scalloped architrave and glorious marble floor with beautifully-carved statues around. The only light source was hundreds of white church candles, illuminating the impressive ballroom. The air was filled with a hypnotic scent I was familiar with as a teen—marijuana with a sweet undertone of jasmine, sandalwood and cinnamon.

All the women simultaneously turned to look at me briefly, but were captivated once again by what was going on, that was yet to come into my view. I walked between the women standing attentively, enchanted by what I was about to become part of, and something I would never forget.

In the centre of the ballroom stood a High Priestess, veiled in a blood-red cloak. Her face was totally obscured by the most amazing gold

and gem-encrusted mask, the only thing visible were her enchanting dark eyes. She was chanting what I could only guess is Latin and rhythmically oscillating an impressive incense diffuser, swaying from brass chains and releasing its heady contents into the air for all to ingest. In her other hand was an ornate staff with a brass tip.

Around her, in a large circle, stood a number of men all veiled in crimson cloaks, secured with satin ribbons around their necks. As the gent who greeted me, plain gold masks hid their features and identity. They all looked like young virile, impressive specimens of our species, quite a delight to the eye.

All the women in the room seemed to come alive in apprehension of what was coming, while I was nervous; I had never experienced anything like it, nor knew what to expect from my new adventure.

With a loud clash of the High Priestess's staff on the marble floor, all the men dropped to their knees and plunged forward, outstretching their arms towards the priestess in unison. As she hypnotically chanted, there was another clash of her staff, they all sat bolt upright, disrobing their cloaks and allowing them to drop to the floor.

The hypnotic chanting continued over the music as the men raised to their knees, as if beckoned by some invisible force. I had never seen such an impressive sight, such amazing brutes to represent mankind. They were bare-chested, muscles rippling in the candlelight. Some had divinely hairy chests, others smooth and clearly regularly-groomed, and others had tattoos. It was like a chocolate box of male beauty, but which do I choose?

I didn't choose any. The High Priestess made the pairing, as I witnessed her walk in front of one of the men and clash her staff onto the

cold marble, indicating she had chosen. The masked man would stand, pointing to one of the women who would walk to the priestess. The High Priestess would then place the pairs hands together in union, and they would walk off out of sight.

This went on as couple after couple were paired, until to my surprise, she beckoned me over.

Apprehensively, I walked to her, not having any idea of the events that will follow nor what the purpose of the ceremony is. I was scared, excited but scared. As she placed our hands together, my partner must have been aware of my fear as he securely and dominantly squeezed my hand ever so delicately, indicating he knew and had me.

As we walked away into another exquisite plushily-furnished room, there were naked bodies, undulating and caressing, feverishly fucking like a scene from the Kama Sutra or a Sultan's harem. There were couples draped over soft furnishings and floors, foursomes in a sea of twisted limbs, as a man was buried to the hilt in his chosen partner, with another amazing specimen of a man, buried to the hilt in his fellow man's ass..... there was a vast ocean of debauchery in every direction.

Men fucking men, while the women watched, caressing pert nipples and teasing each other's clits with their delicate touch, that only a woman knows. They were oblivious to everyone around them and lost in their own euphoric world, where nothing and nobody else matters, just pure exquisite carnal lust.

My delightful partner whispered, "Relax and enjoy. You are safe!" His sole purpose at that moment was to cater for my every sexual whim and provide me pleasure and safety.

He undid the ribbon around my neck, and I heard him draw in a heady breath as if he was familiarising with my scent. As it dropped to the floor, he moved behind me and unzipped my evening dress, helping me to step out of it and leaving me vulnerable, as I had no underwear on. Us ladies hated a panty line!

He then dropped his trousers, presenting me with something that resembled a Greek god. My pussy fluttered involuntarily and my nipples became erect. My body was covered in an electrically-charged blanket of goose pimples. His amazing column of cock already stood to attention in anticipation for his reward.

He lifted me off my feet, as I spread my legs, allowing him to lower me with ease onto his perfect thalis, my own body weight impaling me as deeply as I could accommodate him. He lifted me with ease, up and down whilst still thrusting deep into me, as I wrapped my lithe legs around him, absorbing as much of him as I could. As my first exquisite orgasm pulsated through my body, he lifted me off, placing me across some cushions on my belly, eagerly mounting me from behind.

Oh, my Lord… I was in heaven as he pumped in and out of me so expertly, my pussy was creaming down my legs. He decided to tease me, flipping me onto my side. He lifted a leg over his shoulder and drove deep for a few thrusts, and then paused, nestling his warm, throbbing tower just between my lovely moist lips. I let out a disappointed whimper, which he answered by driving it home with vigour for what seemed like timeless ecstasy. Over and over, until I had another explosive orgasm forging through my soul.

My charge for the night rolled onto his back, lifting me down onto his still engorged beast. We instantly found our own natural carnality

tempo, coming together as one being, something I had never experienced. Hands clasped together as age old lovers would, terrified they would never hold one another again. Ecstatic rapture building within our beings, to the point neither one of us could contain it and we both, as one being, hit that magical plateau.

He let out a huge bellow as he released his soul into me, as my inner love embraced his column to absorb every molecule of energy within my body. I crumpled forward onto his heaving sweaty torso. We both lay there, motionless & chests heaving, absorbing every delectable euphoric, heady over-indulgence ... .both fully aware, neither one would experience again in this life.

As I expected a little of what you fancy could do you a world of good!

SAVING IT WITH A SEX SCENE

S, 28, UK

Most people had fantasies, right? I mean, we were all adults; we all have different pleasures, and our bodies, minds, stimuli and needs were different. I was thinking lately, more than ever, of the usual life stuff on repeat, groundhog day. The cycle of family, work, never-ending washing piles, bills to be paid, kids… and it went on!

Curriculum reminders and commitments, and of course, what to cook for dinner. The never-ending cycle we all felt trapped in at one time or another. Our relationship became work—home, kids, money, grabbing food and sleep where we can.

We need *us* back, so as I was sitting, waiting for the washing machine to finish so I can hang out yet another load of odd socks and pants we've almost ran out of, I stared at my phone pointlessly, scrolling through endless meaningless crap posted daily by everyone pretending they all have their shit together. I pulled my partner's name up on my phone and typed:

> *"Hey Boo, just a message to say I hope your day is going well. Let me know if there is anything special you want for dinner, unless you want me to choose something for you?*
>
> *Do you fancy coming to kidnap me in the car and take me to some secluded remote beauty spot to ravage me, that's more than fine with me."*

As I pressed send, I giggled to myself mischievously. *Did I just do that?* I thought to myself, and also hoping he realises I was fully okay with the idea. Although, I knew he would have assumed I was joking.

Well… I was carrying on with the housework when my phone pinged. It was a text from Hubby, saying, "Stressful day at the office, don't mind about food, I'll sort dessert"

35 minutes later…

I heard the unmistakable rattle of my husband's key in the door—metal against metal. Our dog leapt to attention and scurried off to fondly greet her master, wagging her little tail.

"I'm home love!" a familiar voice echoed through the house.

I have a routine of running him a bath as soon as I hear him coming through the door. So, I got up and made my way to the bathroom. I saw him about to climb the stairs but caught me crossing the hall. And as our eyes met, he paused briefly, then sharply stepped towards me. He took my hand and led me from the house towards the car. He was grasping my hand firmly but still sensitively.

Glancing at him, I instantly recognised his expression, one that I hadn't seen for some time. I felt that rush of warm fluttering between my legs, engulfing my body from head to toe. The tingle radiating from my clit, almost pulsating with desire.

He took his place in the driver's seat and pulled away. I was looking at him in disbelief, but I wanted him so badly my pussy was aching with want. Totally disregarding me, he drove on with his soul focused on his planned mission.

Destination unknown, aroused but bewildered, I gripped my thighs firmly as he drove. He trailed his fingers up the inside of my bare thigh, just enough to get my juices flowing. He teased me to distraction, knowing every action and reaction of my body.

This is the man I have missed—the sexy, spontaneous, wild, unpredictable man, smug in the knowledge I need him. My heart pounded in my chest, breathing shallow as I was trying to control my reaction to his precise touch. My eyes seductively locked on him, analysing every inch of the man that made my whole being crave that touch that every woman wanted and deserved.

The light was dwindling, and darkness was fast approaching. We pulled to a standstill in a small gravel car park, nestled away in a small

beach cove and surrounded by rocky outcrops. Waves could be heard breaking on the rocks below. The brisk warm summer's breeze tantalising the course grass, caressing the sole tree that stood firm, like it guarded the beyond and we had no right to be there.

Making our way through the grass and sand dunes to the awaiting beach, we tasted the salt in the breeze as it brushed my lips. I was being escorted firmly by hand, and we walked in the dimpsy dark until we reached a slightly raised, sheltered nook of the beach. It was out of the direct breeze and with minimal chance of the water catching us unawares.

Rich took hold of me with urgency and started kissing me passionately, lowering my body to the dry firm sand of our secret bay. He kissed my neck, bringing every nerve alive. He caressed the entirety of my body over my clothes, causing every part of me to erupt into a sea of goosebumps and raising an involuntary whimper from my lips.

My chest heaved as he touched me ever so delicately. Then he slipped his fingers under my panty, seeking the path to my desire. He parted my warm moist cleft with his fingers, seeking my screaming clit. I thrusted my hips to meet his precise touch, moaning with unrestricted pleasure.

He slipped off my wet panties, then flicked his fly button and zip open, allowing his jeans to fall around his knees and his gorgeous weapon to erupt in its full glory. Positioning himself between my accommodating legs, I drew him between my warm labia lips. He thrust deep within me, using his thumb to caress my engorged clit with definition and purpose.

So absorbed in our moment, we didn't notice the waves lapping closer. As I wrapped my legs around Rich, taking him all the way in, we both thrusted wildly in an unstinting show of carnal need.

Brushing that ultimate goal for at least an hour, I felt my shaking body overcome with mounting ecstasy. And I exploded with sensation as a wave crashed over us with every nerve ending screaming as we both climaxed. As both our bodies twisted in our natural intended form as one entity.

Collapsing into the surf, both our bodies screamed with overwhelming emotions and fulfilment. I caught a cheeky smirk and twinkle in Rich's eyes. His unplanned goal of the day had been accomplished with honours.

Now, guess who spent the hour driving home looking up secluded beaches and beautiful natural scenery?

Sometimes, we just need to release ourselves from the expectations of daily life for total fulfilment of the mind, body and soul.

Send those messages and hopefully, you will have a pleasant surprise!

EUPHORIA

R, 46, USA

My husband and I had always been very interested in trying out a sex club. We had been looking into them, but hadn't had the nerve to go yet. Still, it was on the cards as we really wanted to experience the

hypnotic erotic atmosphere. My husband would really get off on watching me getting fucked by other guys and I found the idea was super hot as well. I think part of the fantasy was knowing other men find me attractive—he got off on the knowledge I am being turned on and sexually satisfied. We had talked about different scenarios many times.

We finally found a sex club, which was located down a gloomy back alley in the centre of town; the only identifying factor is the neon "EUPHORIA" sign. We walked apprehensively through the main doors, which were guarded by big burly security guards; they were smartly dressed with the standard black suits and arm bands, intimidating hunks of men, and I would go as far to say man-mountains but they were very friendly guys with big welcoming smiles.

The atmosphere was very warm and welcoming as we stepped through the door. The decor of the foyer was red with gold beading, big proud pillars and beautiful elaborate architrave with a plush blood-red carpet, giving it a very opulent air.

We didn't have coats as the weather had been glorious and the night breeze was very warm. Passing by the beautiful classy but scantily clad young woman in the cloakroom, we made our way upstairs, apprehensive as to what we were about to walk in to. Entering the main room, we were greeted with a sea of leather, latex and soft bare skin.

Beautiful men and women were chatting, drinking, dancing and making out. Bodies undulated and moved in unison with the deep house music that was playing; the sonic stew of the bass, tempo and vocals pierced your very soul, frisson causing chills and goosebumps only added to the hypnotic euphoric experience laced with liquor.

The lighting was a soft warm pink. Neon strip lights illuminated the bar and features of the room on a backdrop of white walls. In the centre of the room was a black-and-white chequered dance floor, which was also illuminated from underneath, held captive by white cage bars, encasing its occupants.

Over at the far side of the vast room was a more subtilty lit area surrounded with beautiful ivory drapes. Through the drapes, I could see people making out on stunning tiger skin beds with cream mattresses. The whole ceiling was mirrored, and various large potted trees and foliage adorned the area, adding warmth and life to the room. Plush cream leather seating areas scattered around the edge of the room, each with a beautiful table, all occupied by smiling happy people who were getting acquainted.

Jim and I got our usual spiced rum and coke on the rocks and made our way through the expanse of bodies. We ended up at a vacant table and chairs near the draped bed area; all the rest were occupied. Sipping our cool drinks while taking in the view, both our eyes gravitated to the beds where two gorgeous men—one handsome blonde surfer dude and a dark Italian stallion— and a brunette Hispanic woman were playing and fucking.

It was such a perfect scene it could almost have been the gods making out. The blonde was being ridden by the beauty and she, sucking greedily on the Italian's huge column. After about 20 minutes of being engrossed in this scene, we must have caught the blonde man's attention because he signalled to us to come join them.

Needless to say, of course, we did!

Slipping beyond the drapes and dropping our scanty garments to the floor, we both climbed to join the stunning trio. The woman smiled and passionately kissed us both in greeting; the men slapped hands. Beauty, as I called her, gravitated to the Italian man, who I guessed was her life partner. Passionately kissing my new blonde friend, his lips explored my mouth with his tongue, so tenderly. I sucked and licked it back in appreciation.

Jim started stroking his hardening cock, enchanted by this glorious, carnal scenery. My new friend slipped his hand between my legs, seeking out my exact point of pleasure, targeting it with definitive strokes and caresses. Pussy juice coated his finger as I moaned with satisfaction, reaching my first climax.

I briefly glimpsed our brunette friends, fucking like rabbits on all fours and clearly lost in their own world of gratification.

Kneeling before my new friend on all fours, I took his cock, swallowing him deep within my welcoming throat and then let my mouth rise and fall onto him. He was leaning back on his powerful arms, head thrown back, enjoying the sublime sensations as I periodically gagged on his meaty tool, saliva and stomach fluid adding to his joy.

Jim was tugging his beautiful cock at the sight of his wife gagging on another man's cock. He ran his soft palm over my peachy butt, occasionally brushing a finger over my screaming clit, which sent charged shivers through my pussy.

Position change had Jim on his back. I straddle him, parting my soft fleshy lower lips with my fingers and giving my new friend the best view in the house as I expertly slid my husband's rock-hard cock into my eagerly awaiting magical portal.

Jim parted my peachy cheeks to allow blondie to line his beast of a cock up with my pretty little pink star. I relaxed, knowing the easiest way to accommodate two big hard cocks at the same time was if I didn't have any resistance. Even though I knew the initial penetration would be uncomfortable, the following euphoric satisfaction would be worth the discomfort.

Lubricating up his tool and my deep dark desire generously, Blondie rested the tip against my puckered hole, slowly slipping it inside. Searing pain took my breath away, and I let out a cry, but Jim held me as my friend fed the entire length of his cock mercilessly into me; slowly drawing back out, back in again, the pain lessening with each stroke.

I spit on my fingers and slipped my hand down to caress my pussy as the pleasure continued rising in my loins. Both men are pumping feverishly now. Even after numerous orgasms, my climax was building even higher and more intense. Every muscle of my anus and warm wet pussy gripped both cocks as they rode me to an epic, all-imposing triple orgasm. The three of us reached our harmonious concord, collapsing on poor Jim in a perspiring, gasping multiplicity of anatomies.

This was our first visit of many to sex clubs; just pure, unadulterated indulgence!

CHAPTER 2

DEEP, DARK DESIRES... AND BOY, DO I MEAN DEEP!

HOT WIFE

B, USA

Last year, my husband revealed to me that his biggest fantasy was me being a Hot Wife (HW), and fucking other men. He said it turned him on imagining me with another man's cock in my holes. And a few months ago, I finally gave in to his wants, and it was the wildest Saturday of my life. So far.

He took me to an upscale five-star hotel in Dallas. First, he booked an in-room massage for me. The masseur was a beautiful well-built black man. As I laid on his massage table, he unceremoniously slipped out of his clothes. I swear, his cock hung almost to his knees.

At the end of the massage, he started delicately massaging my now aching clit, slipping his finger inside me at the same time. He brought me off several times. He moved closer to my head, and started rubbing and massaging my tits. He was gently tweaking my beautiful, hard pink nipples as he flicked the pad of his middle finger skilfully over my love bud.

With his semi-hard weapon just inches from my eager mouth, I took hold of it, engulfing it between my warm pouty lips. It made him as hard as cold steel. Grasping my head, he forced his way into my restricted but willing throat. He groaned, savouring the glorious sensations as my throat and gag reflex massaged his enormous organ for an age.

I felt his massive member engorge as he exploded his glorious salty cum, lining my throat as I accepted his gift with greedy appreciation.

After he departed, I texted my husband telling him to come up to the room. I thanked him profusely as I was stepping into the shower to freshen up; I smelt of my new sexy friend. All the while, J was laying out my outfit for the evening.

When I had finished my immaculate make-up, I slipped on the dress. J chose a stunning electric blue silk dress. With nothing but three chains across the back, it left my body too exposed; it was obvious I wasn't wearing panties or bra and going commando. You could clearly see my proud erect nipples and areolas. And the dress was too short, only three inches below my voyeuristic pussy; my pussy loves to be peeped on. A sexy new pair of stilettos accompanied my gorgeous dress.

Reception belled our room, notifying us that there was an uber waiting outside to take me to a fancy cocktail bar four blocks away. J

instructed me to sit at the bar when I arrived and order a drink, and he would catch up with me in a half-hour or so. Having no clue what to expect, I nervously climbed into my Uber. As I slid into the seat, the doorman got a good view of my exposed pussy as my dress rode up my thighs.

Our sex life was indeed beginning a new chapter!

Walking apprehensively into the bar, I felt every guy's eyes caressing my curves. I took a seat at the bar and ordered a much-needed Manhattan. It didn't take long for the first guy to take the seat next to me. And within minutes, the stunning, chiselled Hispanic man asked if he could buy me a drink.

Gingerly, I agreed.

The guy's name, I learned, was Jorge. He was making light conversation about being a business owner, which, to be honest, I really was not interested in. But he really was very handsome with his olive skin and jet black, well-groomed hair. And he had the most attractive deep, brown eyes, framed by glorious black lashes.

As we chatted, Jorge subtly inched his chair closer, until eventually, he placed his hand on the naked soft flesh of my thigh. He was eyeing my body from head to toe, seducing me with his eyes, which spoke without words.

The dress caressed my bare skin beneath, revealing my swaying big bouncy breasts and invasive erect nipples. I was wearing my gold necklace that nestled just above my cleavage, and he lifted it as if to look at it. As he did, his hand brushed over a nipple.

I knew exactly where this was going as I caught sight of my husband, walking through the door.

The three of us, Jorge, my husband and I, had a lovely dinner. We did some drinking and dancing until Jorge asked if we fancied getting out of there. Knowing what that meant, I eagerly agreed. So did my husband.

The three of us went back to our hotel room. As Jim poured us drinks, Jorge started caressing and nibbling my neck passionately as I stood admiring the beautiful Dallas skyline and lights through the open drapes of our fifth-floor room. Then, he slipped my dress off, letting it float to the floor, but requested I kept my shoes on, which I did. I stood naked in front of the window, totally at ease with my nakedness, hoping prying eyes from onlooking windows would be watching.

My new friend was trailing moist soft kisses across my eager body, awakening every nerve within me as I watched our reflection in the highly polished window. He pressed me up against the cold glass; the bare skin of my big bouncy breasts pressed firmly, sending a shiver down my spine. But I didn't care as the cold was counteracted by Jorge's warm breath and soft tender kisses.

I parted my legs in anticipation, knowing what he desired as I felt his throbbing hard cock nudging between my soft peachy cheeks and teasing my moistening lips.

Jim escorted me to the huge king-size bed, which was also next to the window, and I ushered Jorge to sit on it. Getting on my knees, I started inspecting Jorge's lovely uncut cock. I took him in my hand, feeding him deep within my warm moist mouth. I ran my tongue over and around his rock-hard throbbing rim, darting my tongue in his jap's eye and then enthusiastically sucking him.

In front of the window, for the world to see, I started off at a slow and methodical pace, but as my rhythm quickened, it hit a feverish pace.

Jorge was groaning in sheer indulgent ecstasy, having his life force sucked from him. He grabbed my head with both hands, thrusting to meet me, exclaiming, "Oh yeah, baby, you suck cock good and hard. Take it right down."

And I did.

I took every inch of his cock, occasionally gagging as it hit the back of my throat, and my spittle adding to his joy. I cast a fleeting glance at him, and then to Jim, who stood at the other side of the plush bed, tugging purposefully on his beautiful hard cock as he admired the sight he was beholden. I gave both men a cheeky little wink as Jorge emptied his salty load against my tonsils; this was my second load today.

Jim seized his opportunity to lean across the bed and beckoned me to lie down. Becoming impatient, he literally threw me back on the plush bed and dived head first into licking my creaming pussy, licking it so intently.

I felt my second orgasm building within my wet walls as he expertly tongued my tinder box and asshole to the point of ignition; waves of static euphoria were undulating over my hot sweaty body.

Jorge was ripping a condom open with his teeth as Jim moved to my massive tits, sucking and licking them as I recovered from my powerful orgasm.

"Stop!" I told Jorge. "I want to feel your raw cock inside me!"

He obliged, and soon, his hard bare cock was sliding in and out of my precious pussy. The whole time, he whispered obscenities in my ear,

declaring how tight and wet my pussy felt as I absorbed every inch of him with each thrust.

What a naughty girl I am for taking the cock of a man I just met!

Flipping my position onto my hands and knees, Jorge continued slamming in and out, dominating my sopping pussy.

"Yes, fuck me! Fuck me harder!" I screamed as another epic orgasm was building in my pussy. "Don't stop! Give it to me!" I pleaded, looking at his beautiful, deep brown eyes, and then, "I'm going to cum!" I cried out, letting a momentous orgasm engulf my whole being.

Holy Shit! How amazing it felt!

After one last epic thrust, Jorge came deep within my unprotected hot pussy as it hugged him deep within its spasming embrace. Jorge collapsed on top of me with an animalistic bellow. His breathing was so laboured as if his lungs were on fire. Droplets of saltiness showered my entirety; his full body weight pinning me to the damp mattress.

"God, you're so sexy!" He growled in my ear.

We laid together in silence, basking in the afterglow of our epic lovemaking being observed by Jim, until he climbed on the bed with us. Jim laid on his back with the most impressive erection, and I crawled to him wearily. I took his cock into my mouth, sucking it like a lollipop.

"Ride me, please," Jim whispered.

I straddled Jim, gently absorbing my familiar friend into his rightful place between my thighs, into my sticky warm pussy.

Beckoning me forward, Jim wrapped his firm strong arms around my torso, pinning me fast, exposing my ass.

Jorge lubricated his finger with saliva and slid it slowly into my vulnerable free hole. I steadied my pace and slowed my erratic breathing, knowing what was to come. Biting my lip, I felt Jorge position himself between my cheeks. His rock-solid cock nudged my asshole ever so dubiously. He worked the tip into my puckered hole, drawing a gasp from me as it made its way through the ever so familiar barrier.

I let out an involuntary, "Fuuuck!" as Jorge eased his cock out, only to work it back in with slightly more vigour; it was a much more girthy cock than I was used to. I love anal sex, but this was different; I was so full. But once I was used to the glorious stretched full feeling, I held on for the ride of my life.

Boy, oh boy!

With both cocks slamming into me, I felt the most historic orgasm of my life building. It was coming in hot, electrically-charged waves of euphoria as my pussy and ass greedily clamped onto both cocks.

I wailed like a Banshee as Jorge and Jim picked up the pace. Both were really battering my holes and hitting each other's thighs as they moved in unison, filling me to the hilt with lashings of warm cum.

It was the best Saturday of my life, counting the masseur. I took two loads in the mouth, two in my perfect pussy, and one in my shy but accommodating ass.

After Jorge left, Jim and I drifted into sleep in each other's arms, content. I had the sweetest of sleep.

MY BBC MASSAGE
C, USA

J and I had been married for 41 years, but over the years, our sex life had been up and down due to numerous jobs, children, grandchildren and just life in general. We were married for 39 years when we finally agreed to consider swinging and having sex with other people. After our first encounter with another couple, I realised I really enjoyed the alternative lifestyle. And almost overnight, I became a sex machine.

People called me insatiable or nymphomaniac.

One of J's fantasies was to see me being pleased by a Big Black Cock or BBC. He found a way to make this happen, and here was how it played out.

I had blonde hair and blue eyes. I stood around 5'9" tall and wore size 16 to 18 clothes after having two kids. Most men thought I had a nice ass. My nipples were extraordinarily sensitive and sometimes, I could come just by playing with them. Everyone I met seemed to lust after me.

But I'd been very self-conscious, because I never felt I looked that good.

One Friday afternoon, while I was at work, my husband texted me, saying he had a surprise for me when I arrived home. I was told to shower and shave my pussy, and that he would pick out my clothes.

As I had the most exquisite hot shower, he laid out a very sexy short black skirt, a yellow semi-sheer top that emphasised my beautiful full breasts and gorgeous four-inch slingback kitten heels—no underwear.

As we travelled to town, about 15 minutes away, my husband informed me about the sensual massage he had arranged for me with a young black man at his apartment.

I was nervous but excited at the same time.

At the apartment complex, J and I had to climb two flights of stairs to the masseur's second-floor apartment. I had some difficulty with my heels, so my husband stayed close behind me to ensure I didn't fall. It also allowed him to look at my bald pussy as my skirt was really that short. My skirt was so short it would ride up to my waist if I crossed my legs when I sat.

I looked back at my husband with a smirk on my face and asked, "Enjoying the view?"

We knocked on the door, and a tall, black young man, who introduced himself as Christopher, answered wearing scrubs. I sat next to him on the sofa, and we chatted for a while, discussing my massage session. He told me I would be receiving a full body massage, and he hoped I would enjoy it.

When I excused myself to the bathroom, J told Christopher my full expectations. My husband explained to him my fantasy, telling him I wanted a super therapeutic massage. And that when I was fully relaxed and aroused, Christopher was free to do anything he wanted to me within reason. My husband further explained he would be taking photos and videos.

Christopher agreed and handed my husband his camera, saying, "Please, take some for me."

When I returned from the bathroom, Christopher showed me to his massage table, inviting me to make myself comfortable. I looked at my husband who was making himself at home totally naked.; he just aimed on spectating and filming from a distance. As I disrobed, he glanced up at me and winked, which sent a shudder of excitement through my core.

Then, there was Christopher, who was also already naked.

Shocked, I watched his flaccid cock of at least nine inches, bouncing between his thighs as he moved around the table, getting ever closer to my face.

Christopher stood at the head of the table, bending right over me to massage my back in long firm precise strokes. As he reached forward to massage my peachy ass cheeks, his big cock brushed my cheek. For the next 30 minutes, he expertly massaged my back, neck and shoulders.

Oh my, what bliss!

The firmer he applied pressure, the more relaxed I became in his expert hands. He then moved to my legs, slowly moving up and down and getting closer to my aching pussy. He could tell I was relaxed as I cooed softly in appreciation.

Moving to my side, he started stroking my leg and arm simultaneously; his big black monster of a cock lay on my arm. I couldn't resist. I took hold of his cock and slowly started massaging its length. Then, I kissed its glistening head.

Moving to the foot of the massage table, he spread my legs so slightly, gaining access on both sides. He gently stroked my thighs, and then calves, advancing to my inner thighs. He massaged me there for a glorious age; I could feel my pussy coming alive with each tender touch.

Occasionally, Christopher's expert fingers would brush over my now moist pussy and sphincter. I would gasp and moan lightly whenever it happened.

When he finished massaging my legs, feet and arms, he bent forward and suddenly plunged his tongue into the cleft of my naked pussy. Intuitively, I pulled my legs up to give him unrestricted access. Christopher used this to his advantage, running his tongue over my pouting lips and butthole. He massaged my clit with a finger as he worked on my star, licking and fingering me to an impressive orgasm.

As I relaxed once more, he invited me to flip over.

I turned onto my back, and Christopher put his focus on my upper body. First, he worked on my shoulders and stomach, making periodic eye contacts and grinning in a cheeky seductive manner, like a cat that got the cream.

He moved to my right breast and traced around my areola. As he did, my nipples hardened even though he hadn't actually touched them yet. Moving around to my left side, he did exactly the same pattern; both my nipples were now fully erect.

Christopher drizzled some warm oil on them and started massaging them. My stomach started twitching, and my hips rose as he focused on my alive nipples. He teased my nipples, lightly pinching and tugging them. Moving down my legs, he worked on my feet and upward to the inside of my legs. He teased my thighs open to give him full access to work on my inner thighs, intentionally brushing my pussy lips as he did.

He then worked on my pubic bone and to both my hips, allowing his thumb to work from the point of my asshole to the point of my hips and back, titillating my ass and pussy and getting me so hot under the collar.

I wanted him then, there and now, but he sensed this and decided to tease me more by moving to my head again. Working his fingers through my hair, he massaged my scalp. Feeling his cock on my shoulder, I reached over and easily took it into my mouth.

Obviously, the therapeutic magic massage was over, so I took hold of his leg and had him climb onto the massage couch, putting us into the 69 position. His impressive monster of a cock brushed against my lips, and I reached up and took hold of the beast at the base, bringing my hungry lips up to meet my treat.

Putting it between my lips slowly, I realised how large it was. I thought I would have a heart attack when I took the tip; it might've been more than 10 inches long and 5" around. But I never flinched as I absorbed it into my awaiting warm wet mouth.

Christopher was expertly working on my pussy and star, nuzzling between my moist inviting lips. His tongue darted over my swollen clit and teased my relaxed butthole, causing me to come violently in his mouth and then lapping me clean.

I withdrew his rock-solid cock from my mouth , he position himself between my

legs.

His huge hard shaft nudged the gateway of my very wet willing pussy.

Christopher asked if I was ready for him, and I just smiled, slowly working the huge bulbous head into the entrance of my most prized possession. Teasing his cock through the opening, I gingerly introduced

its head as I grimaced a little. Six inches in, and I felt a heady combination of pleasure and pain deep within my warm wet pussy.

He slowly slid his hard cock in and out, allowing my pussy to adjust to his size. The pain started to fade, and when he was almost fully inside me, he stopped and withdrew his cock with just the tip remaining in my screaming pussy. Then, with no warning, he drove back home, balls deep, causing me to scream as his helmet hammered my cervix. But the pain soon faded once more, and all I could feel was total pleasure as my pussy stretched around him, his cock filling me completely.

And I loved it.

He whispered in my ear, and we both climbed off the massage table and moved to the freshly laundered bed. Positioning myself on my back, I lifted my legs high in the air.

Christopher donned a condom as he didn't want to risk an accident inside me. Pinching the rubber nipple, he teased it along the length of his shaft. Then, climbing between my warm thighs, he thrusted in one powerful motion deep within me. He pumped his cock in and out with such force and momentum; I was matching his thrusts.

I reached my second glorious orgasm, which I had never done in one session. Christopher just kept going like a machine, pulling his cock all the way out to the very tip, then pommelling it back inside me. After half a dozen strokes, I came with force again, but this time, I squirted all over my new lover's cock. It was one more thing I had never achieved during intercourse before. I couldn't help but laugh in my head, knowing I had ruined the bed.

Christopher then withdrew and unceremoniously flipped me onto my stomach. He resumed fucking me deep and lustfully from behind as cum oozed from my full pussy, dripping onto the already sodden bed.

Finally, I felt Christopher got extremely hard; his cock started to quiver as he burst his load inside me.

When we had recovered enough, Christopher helped me freshen up and dress. As he was buckling my slingback stilettos, he leaned in and kissed my bare pussy, nestled under my tiny little skirt.

As I walked away, I whispered in his ear, "Next time you want bareback? I regret not feeling your cum inside me!"

Christopher grinned like a Cheshire cat, beaming from ear to ear.

As we made our way back to the car, I told my husband, "I'm glad we have leather seats. I'm going to be leaking all the way home!"

In the parking lot, there was a guy working on his car near our vehicle. As I climbed into our SUV, my skirt had ridden up, and the guy got an eyeful, including the cum dribbling down the back of my thighs. I winked at him, smiling at myself as J started the car, and we left.

THREE IS A CROWD

R, 46, USA

I'd been very much into Consensual Non-Consent (CNC) Play. It was a big turn on for me, and most of my fantasies are based around it.

My fantasy went like this: my husband and I met two guys at a bar when we were out for a casual drink. We were having such a blast that we invited them back to our place for a nightcap after the bar closed.

At our place, we enjoyed a few drinks in the living room, which had an airy open-plan feel with its French doors and big skylights. It had wooden floors and beautiful deep pile rugs. A solid oak sideboard was against a wall, a massive matching coffee table stood in the middle of the room and huge cushions were scattered about. state of the art ceiling lights beamed gloriously down onto us, and the smell of jasmine permeated the air.

My husband got us a bottle of Jack, liberally pouring the fiery liqueur into the glasses and handing one to each of us, which we savoured greedily. Since we were all already tipsy, it only took a few more generous glasses, and we were openly chatting.

I sat with one of the guys on the sofa, and on the armchairs on either side were my husband and our other new friend. Deciding to try my luck, I turned to the guy sitting next to me and kissed him tenderly on the lips. If he rebuffed me, I thought, I could shrug it off as a mere friendly gesture. But to my surprise, he returned the favour.

We were passionately kissing when the other guy got up and bent behind me. Brushing my hair aside, he started licking and kissing my neck.

After a few moments, reality hit me—I was making out with two strangers. I questioned what I was doing, and I wanted to stop. So, I pulled back and said so. But the guy next to me just pulled me back to him.

They carried on, ignoring my objections. Trying to push them off me seemed to make the situation worse. They started getting rougher with more urgency. I struggled while trying to look at my husband,

urging him to save me with my eyes. But he was clearly very turned on seeing his wife being ravaged by two strangers against her will.

Writhing and squirming with every ounce of strength I had, I tried to break free but the two men overpowered me. They devoured me like their prey, dragging my clothes from my body and exposing me in my natural form.

One pushed me onto my knees, on the hard, cold wooden floor while the other kicked my coffee table out of his way with no effort at all. One firmly grasped me from behind while the other forced his big hard cock into my mouth, as far as he could physically force it down my throat, forcing my head back and forth as he thrusted deep.

The other guy got impatient, and they swapped places. Thankfully, he was not as long but his cock's girth made me gag, and my jaw ached in its unnatural position. Their cocks kept getting bigger and harder with every thrust of defiance. The guy behind was pulling my hair, sending excruciating pain through my entire being.

As the engorged weapon went deeper within the restrictions of my throat, I spluttered, and tears streamed down my cheeks. I was filled with terror because it became harder to breathe.

Slapping my face, the guy behind me urged his accomplice. He eagerly had my arms locked into his, rendering me at their mercy; I was totally helpless!

When the cock was pulled out of my mouth for a moment, the guy behind pushed me onto my hands and knees. Uninvitedly, he forced his humongous member between my pussy lips, making me scream aloud. He rammed me to the hilt so hard my whole body was being tossed

forward with every stroke, and the guy with the girth restricted my breathing once more, making me gag and cry. Salty droplets coursed freely as I urged on his rod. The guy buried deep in my pussy, grabbed my shoulders, forcing himself even deeper, and leaning forward, he sank his teeth into my neck.

The guy in front of me withdrew his meat gag from my mouth, and lay down on the soft shag pile rug, demanding it was his turn. I was dragged by the hair and was instructed to straddle him, as I lowered my swollen pussy onto his thick saliva-moistened cock; his arms clasped around my body so I couldn't escape.

The guy with the bigger cock then degraded me once more. He grasped the back of my head, and his immense appendage powerfully gained unrestricted access deep within my throat, causing me to regurgitate the slimy contents of my stomach. This seemed to arouse him further as they spewed out of the creases of my mouth, lubricating his way to my lungs.

My husband was generously greasing up his lovely cock as he approached from the side, making his way behind us. He bent his knees and slowly eased his ample dagger beyond the restriction that guarded my asshole. He proceeded to build a rhythm in unison with the guy buried deep in my swollen pussy.

I had a cock in every orifice, and I was struggling. I tried to let out a scream of protest and resentment, but nothing came out as my throat was restricted by an uninvited cock.

Soon, they all withdrew from their chosen warm moist orifice and pushed me down onto my back. At least then, I was on the rug and didn't have the cold hard floor biting into my knees.

One guy climbed over my chest and knelt across my shoulders. He forced his still-loaded weapon between my lips with such vigour, and I violently gagged as he pounded my face.

The other guy with the bigger and longer cock, spread my thighs wide and slammed deep into my battered pussy.

My husband got my vibrator from the side of the sofa cushion, where I left it. Turning it to full speed, he held it on my big juicy swollen clit, making me come violently. The combination of pleasure, pain and oxygen deprivation brought me to the most intense orgasmic experience of my life.

I lay there in my delirium, while the three men stood over my trembling body. They stroked their cocks to a frenzied climax until they blew their loads all over my quivering face and nakedness. Then, each guy kissed me tenderly in turn….

PAST CONQUESTS

C and T, 36 and 41, IND

My husband and I had been together several very happy, contented years with next to no fighting. We attributed this to the openness of our marriage. Our fantasies were ghosts of our past and previous lives and relationships, that simply had left their legacy as memories.

Many couples shared their past conquests but then ended up resenting each other. But we, as a couple, were so united and strong. We used this information-sharing as an ultimate bonding experience that had kept us rock solid through the years; I'd love to hear every sordid

intricate detail of my husband's past sexual experiences with ex-girlfriends, and he, mine while we were having sex.

One of my past experiences that my husband loved to tease me with was my memories of Siddh, who was a very attractive athletic guy I dated from another state.

I returned from work as a make-up artist, early one evening, though it was considered late for me to finish the day. As I walked through the door, I heard Hubby calling me from the terrace the second he heard the door click shut.

We were lucky enough to own a beautiful rooftop apartment in India with its luxurious private terrace and panoramic views of the city. The weather was amazing most of the time, which meant glorious sunrises and beautiful burning sunsets.

As Hubby greeted me with the usual tender kiss on the lips, he whispered, "Siddh wants you!" He breathed into my ear, and gave the soft flesh of my lobe a tender nibble. Instantly, I felt quivers between my hot smooth thighs.

He handed me a glass of crisp chilled white wine and took my hand, escorting me to the sun lounger—my favourite spot in my spare time. I obeyed his instruction, lifting my open-fronted skirt and feeling the warmth on the back of my legs. Sinking back in the sumptuously soft seat, I raised my feet and spread my legs to allow the breeze to tease my warm, moist, musky treat.

I allowed myself to relax while my husband wandered back into the apartment. Taking big, cool mouthfuls of the fruity treat I so deserve, I mulled over what my husband whispered fondly and smirked to myself.

I felt a piece of silk being slipped over my eyes from behind me, followed by another whisper.

"What would Siddh, and his big black cock do to you? Tell me... every filthy detail?"

Silence followed. Soft lips kissed and delicately licked my toes, until I felt that divine feeling of a warm mouth taking a toe and sucking it with such relish.

A voice once more urged me, "Tell me what he would do to you?"

At this prompt, I allowed myself to be mentally transported back to Siddh.

As he took my toes and enveloped them with his voluptuous soft lips, I started narrating Siddh's pattern of seduction...

With his gorgeous soft lips and tongue, Siddh would lightly kiss and nibble his way from my toes to my insteps, then to my ankles, and from behind my knees, he would trace an imaginary path up the inside of my thighs.

Then, when he reached what he wanted, he would pull my panties aside, and Siddh nuzzled his way with those wet warm lips of his between the moist petticoat that masked my true desire. His firm tongue was precisely on mark, urging me to involuntarily arch my back and cry out, with pure desire and appreciation. I would meet each wet caress as Siddh rewarded me; the more descriptive I was, the better the reward. He would feverishly suck and lick me to a statically charged reward, resulting with me grabbing two greedy handfuls of his hair, Siddh would groan loudly.

Not giving me time to catch my wits or breath, Siddh would take both of my hands, pulling me blindly to my feet. We stepped forward and I would be instructed to drop to my knees, which I did willingly and knowingly.

Siddh would lower himself next to me onto the beautiful Turkish rug and instruct me to straddle him. I must lower myself onto his magnificent anaconda of a BBC, without using my hands and have to guide his majestic beast to his warm lair with the skill and dexterity of my warm, wet yoni lips, alone.

As I rolled my hips and nuzzled him into position, I could feel my pussy pulsating and beckoning him in. And with one firm impaling motion, my greedy, welcoming yoni captivated the entirety of his BBC to the hilt. As I started to ride him mercilessly, Siddh took the opportunity to seize both of my nipples in a pincer grip, making me moan harder and louder. I revelled in the delicious bittersweet sensations that flooded my entire body as I rode him for the win—faster, harder, and deeper.

My yoni was almost frothing from the friction, stirring up our mingling juices into a gene frenzy. I reached my high, time and time again; each was more intense than the last. He would grip my arse cheeks, driving deeper and harder, until we both released our souls, colliding as thunderous as a tsunami meeting the breakwater.

I couldn't imagine what the neighbourhood heard or visualised, as I recalled my past conquest, but one thing I was sure of, I missed that BBC as much as I loved my husband.

PROHIBITED LOVE

S, 28, USA

I was born and raised in conjunction with one of the many interpretations of the Christian Bible. I would not dwell too much on my religious fortitudes, but it was drilled into us, from a very young age, that interracial relationships were forbidden. Therefore, it was taboo to even discuss it with others.

But…

In the Old Testament, Moses took himself a bride who was a Cushite, and Cushites were Ethiopians. This indicated that his wife was Black. Moses' sister, Miriam, became very angry and upset that her brother had married a Cushite. Miriam reprimanded her brother so strongly that because of her response, God judged her and gave her Leprosy.

So, that told me that God frowns on racists.

I thought the taboo factor had played a massive part in my fantasy from a very early age and was the foundation of my secret obsession with black men.

My fantasy went on like this…

I worked in a large corporate office, doing basic secretarial duties. There were probably 30 workspaces on the floor where I worked. Each workspace had a pc, and was littered with papers, trinkets, and personal memorabilia. Trainers were under the desks and coats were strewn across swivel chairs. The air was stuffy and smelled of paper, stationery and cheap perfume and aftershaves, all mingling into one sickly pungent

acrid smell. The clicking sound of keyboards filled the room along with the chattering of people making polite conversation about their mundane lives, the normal tedious office whitter regarding a printer or stapler with the odd squeal of office chair wheels on cheap corduroy carpet once in a while. We had been short in the office lately, so the workload had been crazy and tensions ran high with half a dozen spare workstations.

On Monday morning, I plonked myself down in my chair at my workstation. Slurping my latte that I picked up on route via the drive through Costa, I flicked my trainers off and left them where they fell. I slipped my feet into my compulsory 4-inch black heels all the women were required to wear for aesthetic reasons.

I glanced around the room. The frantic scurrying had already started around me. It was typical every Monday as we knew we had work to catch up on from over the weekend.

At the far end of the office, in one of the workstations closest to our stationery area, I could see a new face. I looked with intrigue. But then he glanced up, and our eyes connected in an embarrassing whoopsie on my part with my eyes lingering just a little bit too long.

Ha ha! Busted!

He was the most enchanting black man, clad in an amazing ebony skin that glistened in the sunlight beaming through the window, like a trail of diamond chips. I was totally mesmerised and found it very hard not to stare. He gave me a cheeky seductive smile as he sat down at his station, acting as if he knew what was in my mind. He was everything I envisaged in my deepest desires.

I was trying to concentrate on my task, but my mind kept wandering back to that first vision of him, standing there and looking very cool and totally confident in his new environment.

And that cheeky grin… *Uhh!*

Soon, our hectic but uneventful day was coming to an end, and I knew I would be the last in the office: I had to restock the printers with paper and check our stationery stock.

As the office briskly emptied, I started with the task of filling the printers with fresh paper for tomorrow. I walked across the empty office to the stationery cupboard and stepped inside. I was not yet flicking the light on, when the door shut.

The light flicked on, and standing before me was my infatuation for the day. He was literally just a breath away, I could smell his scent. He smelled so good, and not like the cheap aftershave I was used to smelling in the office. He was giving me the cheekiest, seductive grin.

Without a word, he stepped forward and took the clip that held my hair in a pleat gently from my head, letting my long, auburn hair tumbling over my shoulders and cascade down to my waist like a waterfall. He stroked it tenderly.

Slipping his hand around the back of my neck, he drew me in for a kiss. His soft full lips touched mine tenderly, and I didn’t want to resist.

Returning the gesture, I caressed his lips with mine. Our kiss became more passionate as we explored each other's mouths fervently.

Cupping one of my huge breasts, he removed his lips from mine only to kiss me down my neck to my now heaving chest. He planted a

kiss on my breast bone before unbuttoning my blouse. In one swift action, he scooped my breasts from their safety net, setting them free. Bending, he held them both and suckled them with urgency, flicking his knowledgeable tongue from one to the other.

As he was feeding urgently on my breasts, I undid the button and zip of my skirt, letting it drop to the floor. My panties followed suit.

Sweeping me off my feet, he planted me on the printer and pushed me back. Drawing my legs up and apart, he descended into my now silently screaming pussy, diving straight in for the kill. He ravenously licked and sucked, devouring me to bring me to the most intense orgasm, causing me to explode my golden rain all over his face and the printer.

It was his turn. Sliding off the printer, I feverishly kissed him while unbuttoning his trousers and fly. His garments dropped to his ankles, exposing his red-hot throbbing rod of total gorgeousness.

I had to taste him.

Dropping to my knees, I took him in both hands and introduced him to my parted lips. I glided the tip of my tongue around his glorious angry looking head, before swallowing him deeply within the restricted confines of my throat, using both hands, I massaged his shaft and sac at the same time, almost bringing him to the point of no return. But I abruptly stopped, which seemed to frustrate him.

He flipped me around, face down on the warm printer, and parted my cheeks to guide Excalibur home. His deep, purposeful thrusts made my legs tremble, and my pussy hugged him tightly.

As the orgasm started to build up, so did the ferocity and the urgency in his thrusts, until an explosion of electrifying euphoria swept over me.

My pussy held on to him desperately to claim her ultimate payment in kind as he, too, screamed loud, hitting his prize.

Sid and I regularly stayed back now, to do the restocking. It was better than any pay rise the firm could offer, and an exclusive bonus for us.

CHAPTER 3

GUILTY PLEASURES OF THE GIRL NEXT DOOR

MAGIC HANDS

C, 32, USA

Being the chief editor, I had a very demanding role at work. I did not get a lot of time to myself between work and general life. I found it hard to unwind at the end of my busy day, and I even tended to bring work home with me. So, I was my own worst enemy.

I suffered a lot with shoulder and upper back problems, due to leaning over my computer day in and day out. I had made the decision that every Wednesday afternoon, I would have a full body massage. A work colleague had recommended a massage therapist, and I had made an appointment.

It was now Wednesday, and I was finishing early to get to my appointment for 3 pm. The office was its usual busy self, but my workload was up to date, so I had said my goodbyes for the day and left.

I had made the appointment online and was expecting a man as my masseur named Sam.-I had no idea why I expected a man since Sam is a unisex name. The treatment room was in a huge, classy Period terrace property, next door to a high-end solicitor building. I was greeted by the most beautiful blonde woman I've ever seen. She was about 5'8" tall and slim with big breasts, peachy butt and legs to die for.

Sam was very professionally dressed in a medical tabard, classy, black knee-length skirt, stockings and black stilettos. She was wearing a YSL scent that I also wore so she smelled fabulous.

She greeted me warmly with a big white smile and invited me into her treatment room, which was a warm welcoming space. Potted plants draped throughout the room or stood to attention in a corner. Beautiful deep red leather topped the writing desk, and on either side were matching brown leather chairs for practitioner and client. A green table lamp and papers littered the desk.

Sam invited me to sit before taking hers on the other side of the desk. She asked me several personal and health questions, scribbling my answers in a notepad. When we finished, she asked me to go behind the beautiful peacock room divider, disrobe and make myself comfortable on the massage table, covering myself with a huge soft warm bath sheet. And she would be with me very shortly.

I spent a few minutes getting comfortable and relaxing as I waited for my well-deserved treat. Sam finally entered the screened off area,

greeting me warmly with that same gorgeous smile. I instantly relaxed in her presence.

She wheeled over a trolley with probably a dozen of different bottles of oils and a bottle warmer. Then, she squirted lashings of warm base oil into a wooden bowl and added what she said was neroli, lavender oils; the mixing created a heavenly-scented oil to ease my aching muscles.

Dipping her hand into the bowl, she drizzled the delightful oil across my tense shoulders. Then, placing the bowl down, she placed her hands onto my back and started moving upward in tiny circular movements. Reaching my neck, she gently pincer gripper on either side. She returned to working on my shoulders.

Sam's hands were so soft and delicate yet so skilled, and I felt myself melting into the comfy massage table. She moved to the small of my back in precise flowing strokes, dissolving my discomforts away. Slipping the towel from one leg and butt cheek, she applied firmer circular movements, manipulating my gluteus maximus and occasionally brushing a finger over my arsehole. At the time, I thought it was just the hazards of the job in hand. From there, she worked down my legs to my feet.

Jesus Christ! It was intense yet so good.

Asking me to turn over, she placed the toasty warm towel back over my body, then started the process again. This time, she started with my arms and hands, massaging each finger. The close contact of a woman playing with my finger was an intense surprise. I felt a fanny flutter as she firmly caressed each finger, almost as I would have my husband's cock. She was gently twisting and pulling the full length of each finger; it was very erotic.

Moving around to my head, she towered above me; my face was inches from her concealed pussy. Drizzling more aromatic warm oil on my chest, she caressed each breast at the same time as if not to make the other jealous, catching my nipples between her fingers from time to time. Leaning forward, Sam mirrored her hands as they tenderly traced over my rib cage and across my stomach. And I thought her partner must be one lucky person getting this treatment on a daily basis.

Moving to the side of the bed, she drizzled oil over each. She firmly massaged the length of each one in turn, including my feet. On finishing, she covered me with a warm towel and whispered she wouldn't be a minute.

"Please relax," she added as she walked to the sink to wash her hands.

Thoroughly content and ridiculously chilled, I lay there, relishing the sensations.

Turning back to her trolly, Sam picked up another bowl and squirted more warm carrier oil into it. Folding the towel back over to expose my legs again, Sam lubricated both of her hands and generously drizzled the decadent warm oil over my stomach, hips and vagina.

Moving back to the foot of the table, she got to work on my hips, brushing across my bi-curious pussy with her soft warm fingers as she did. Her expert touch trailed over my pussy lips, hovering for longer with each stroke until I felt her deliberately ran her thumb up across my oiled, throbbing clit.

Now, her sole focus was my engorged clitoris. She slightly increased the pressure as she ran one pad of her thumb then the other

over my screaming bud. Keeping her finger on my clit, she moved to the side of the table and introduced a second finger. With long definite strokes, her fingers invaded my creamy cleft.

I was in heaven and knew I was about to come.

Sam's expert touch mimicked what I would do to myself when I masturbated. She knew how fast and firm it should be, and what to touch to bring me to an explosive conclusion, squirting fine juice all over the massage couch. As my pussy convulsed, and my legs uncontrollably shook, my nipples were solid and alive.

Covering me with the towel again, she said, "I will leave you for five minutes to gather your senses, then you may dress and meet me back at my desk. But take as long as you desire."

Well, I had been having weekly massage appointments for two years now. It cost an arm and a leg, but it was my de-stress. I even claim it from work as an occupational hazard.

Shh!

OH, THOSE GIRLS! YES, GIVE ME THOSE GIRLS! FUCK, YES! ANONYMOUS SEXPERT(Original)

He wanted to kiss every inch of her body like she was the roadmap to everlasting, beautiful, bold, badass bliss!

His body, oh my god! So sexy. So salty. So sweet. She wanted his manly meat. All of it!

"Give it to me babe," she whispered in his ear as he nibbled on her hard nipples

He flicked his tasty tongue on her soft, sweet, tight tits. So round and real.

"Oh, my fuck!" he exclaimed. "Where have these been all my life!"

"Right here, babe," she teased as she stole a quick kiss on his lips.

He kissed her with his hot mouth and tongue. So wet and ready. He kissed her collarbone, her neck and made his way slowly and sweetly to her belly, stopping right at her mound.

"Mmm," he murmured.

"Fuck, yes!" She arched her back as she spread her legs wide—as wide as they would go. "Yes, baby! Don't you fucking stop! Holy fuck me!" She felt his cock so hard and hot under his shorts. So sexy and sweet.

He ripped his shorts off, exposing his package proudly. He helped her lower down until her face was right in his cock.

She slowly took it in her mouth.

"Holy shit!" he moaned with such delicious delight. "Yes, baby, yes! Shit!"

She took all of him in and made the loudest "ahh" sound she'd ever made in her life, which only made him fucking harder.

As she was blowing him, she spread her legs wider so he had easier access to her pussy from behind.

"Oh, honey! You are dripping! Fuck baby!" He flicked her lips and clit, then finger fucked her until she fucking squirted all the fuck over his legs.

"Shit!"

She mounted him so strongly, so sweetly, feeling the tip of his cock as it gently caressed her pussy.

"Shit, baby! Holy fuck!"

Her body shook, and her sweet and salty sex quivered like it had never quivered or shook before.

"You ready, babe? I got you. You are safe. I'm here with you… not letting you go." He could not fucking *wait* to be fully and freely inside her all the way! "God! That tight Polish-pounding pussy! Like fucking Heaven!"

CABLE GUY

J, 49, USA

Hello, everyone, my name is J.

Several years ago, when I was younger and still a single, independent woman of 42, something happened that I couldn't forget. I lived in a very respectable high-rise in downtown Houston. This story happened around that time.

After a very long day of running errands, I returned home around 3 p.m., laden with bags of groceries and a few other oddities that had caught my roving eye during the day. Entering my building, a smartly dressed concierge approached me with a welcoming smile and offered to help me with my vast array of bags.

"No, thank you," I said. I did not feel I had very much, but maybe to the onlookers, I looked like a mad bag lady and could have done with a hand.

I bumbled my way into the waiting elevator that was full of residents; most were professionals, doctors, lawyers and other professional bodies. Struggling, I pushed the button for the 7th floor and waited patiently for the door to close.

On the third floor, the elevator stopped and a cable guy got in the lift. Although he was supposed to be going down, he decided to enter the elevator instead of waiting for its downward journey. You know how it was usually in an elevator—nobody makes eye contact with you, generally. But with this cable guy, we immediately made eye contact, and didn't break eye contact for several seconds.

Strangely, it didn't make me feel awkward.

He was young, maybe 23, 24 years old. He had well-chiselled features and red wavy hair—almost golden—with piercing blue eyes. He had the most athletic, fit, young body, even in his boiler suit with its top tied around his waist, exposing bronzed skin decorated with the most beautiful tribal tattoos in his grubby muscle vest.

The sexual energy between us was unreal, like electricity bouncing between electrodes. I thought everyone in the crammed lift could smell the wetness between my legs.

Arriving at my floor, I jostled my way out the hot stuffy lift, which was ridiculously hot even with the building's aircon. Somebody else followed me off but I was too laden to even bother looking. But I sensed the person was close to me and turned around…

To my surprise, it was the hot, young red-haired guy, and without warning, he kissed me passionately. The lift erupted with a huge cheer. Shocked and slightly embarrassed, I pulled away and hurried to my apartment.

I had never been so intimate with a perfect stranger. My perfect stranger walked away grinning in the opposite direction.

Fumbling with my keys and juggling groceries, again, I sensed a presence behind me. I opened the door with haste, but strong hands grabbed me around my waist. I was helpless, feeling the familiar bulge most women know of—an aroused man up behind me, pressing his obviously ample, rock-solid rod of pleasure, possibly 8-8.5 inches long, between my pert cheeks. My pussy was dripping wet with anticipation and excitement.

I dropped the groceries just inside the front door as he flipped me around to make my now-willing lips once more accessible for him to devour. Kicking the door shut, I led the way to the bedroom. We went through the door like a cat-5 tornado, enthusiastically discarding clothes in a trail of fabric mayhem, carelessly discarded where they fell to the floor.

Both now in our natural naked glory, I pushed him back onto the bed forcefully. I climbed between his muscular thighs and instantly inserted his hard member between my luscious willing lips. Swallowing him with relish, I sucked and licked that fantastic eight inches of glorious muscle almost to his limits.

He was so desperate to release his load I could taste his salty pre-come as I withdrew my mouth. Lowering my lips to take his warm, soft

balls gently into my mouth, where I nestled them safe from harm, I ran my tongue so gently over them, making my blue-eyed boy groan with pleasure.

He couldn't and wouldn't come yet; I won't let him until I have felt that magnificent fleshy steed between my thighs.

Mounting my steed, I slowly lowered my eager wet pussy, watching his stunning face as I swallowed his hard flesh into my warm, wet abyss nestled between my legs. I started rising and falling as my tight welcoming pussy enveloped him in her warm wet embrace.

We fucked like wild animals for around 15 minutes and didn't stop until I felt my climax building deep from within. My pussy wildly unleashed her full glory from his chest to his balls, and golden rain swept over him as my body gave her full permission and opened my love gates. As my pussy contracted around his cock, he was ablaze and he, too, climaxed his creamy liqueur inside of me with a roar.

We lay there on the bed for a good 20 minutes, dazed and unsure of what had just happened with us not even knowing each other's names.

We got dressed without saying a word; there wasn't really anything to say. Afterwards, he gave me a cheeky wink and smirk before leaving my apartment. We had never even introduced ourselves, and to this day, I had never seen him again

But I had had numerous similar encounters with other men since. They were far more exciting than any lifestyle encounter I have ever had; it was almost an addiction.

EDEN

O, 38, UK

Every year, I attended an age-old horse fair called Appleby Horse Fair in Cumbria, which idyllically took place by the River Eden. whose name was derived from the Celtic word "*ituna*" which meant "water."

During the first week of June, thousands of people attended from across the globe. It originally began as a drover's fair for folk to sell cattle, sheep and horses, and was chartered by King James II in 1685. It was later adopted as one of the biggest annual Gypsy and Traveller gathering event worldwide. It has become one of the most important events in the Gypsy and Traveller calendar, where family and friends gather and strike deals, conclude disputes, sell their wares, find love, get christened and even get married. Everybody looked forward to Appleby—gypsies, travellers and common folks alike.

If we were very lucky, the weather would be glorious and if not, there would be a sea of happy, smiling, spackled people from far corners of the world, enjoying the atmosphere of the fair. There would be beautiful women with immaculate makeup, manes of stunning hair draped around their shoulders to their waists, wearing their finery and dripping with solid gold jewelleries and with mud up their legs.

Of course, there would be stunning men running horses, soaked to the skin with refreshing rain cascading from their mullet-style hair down their bronzed muddy faces, seemingly prepared for anything nature threw at them and still going about their business.

My fantasy would start with my normal routine. Once we pulled onto fair hill, we set up camp and descended to the town on foot, and

through the droves of thousands of people, children and dogs. Horses would be flying up and down, either pulling sulkies, drays and exercise carts or taxiing people to and from fair hill where most camp to the river, shops and pub.

Hundreds sat on the banks of the Eden, watching the horses being swam and bathed. Shirtless lads showed off their skilled horsemanship while bareback in the river, smiling and catching the admiring attention of beautiful girls, who were usually in family groups with an older sister or cousin, taking on the matriarch role and supervising.

Sitting down on the bank of the river with the sun beating down on my bare shoulders, I could feel my skin burning. So, I slid down the bank, and as I slipped on my derriere into the freezing running water, my toes gripped the smooth pebbles on the riverbed to steady myself; it was total bliss.

A horse ridden by a gorgeous example of a man came flying past me, soaking my upper body with ice cold water, and straight out the Cumbrian hills, it had a bite.

I screamed in shock and fell backwards, alarming the horse in turn. The beast shied, unseating his rider, and made off towards the other horses further down the river near the bridge.

Erupting from the water with a bellow was the most stunning young man I had ever seen. He couldn't have been any older than 18, but what a man he was with his muscular, bronzed chest and black hair, green eyes and well-groomed beard. Thinking he had harmed me, he cut through the knee-high water and scooped me up in his big warm muscular arms. But realising I was laughing and not crying, he scooped a handful of cool

water and splashed me again. He still held me with his other strong arm as if reluctant to release me and joined in my laughter.

Our eyes met as the giggles subsided, speaking unspoken words as I felt the familiar ache between my soaking thighs. My nipples were very obviously erect, but I could shy that off as the cold biting water nipping at them. We smiled at each other, and I turned to scramble up the steep bank. Suddenly, I felt strong hands around my waist, and they effortlessly lifted me on to the grassy bank. As I found my footing, a sharp cheeky slap landed on my bum, drawing an involuntary giggle from me.

I turned to make eye contact again. We both grinned before he strode off through the river to retrieve his loose animal.

Meeting up with friends and family, we enjoyed a few drinks from the inn. We revelled in the atmosphere of the fair in full swing. It was just a landscape of happy, laughing faces under the glorious sunlight.

The day flew, and I made my way back up the hill just as dusk was falling. I was slightly tipsy but very content; I totally forgot about the incident in the river.

Reaching Fair hill, all the trailers had lights on already. Campfires burned and surrounded by content people, chatting over the day's events and news. As I meandered through the warren of trailers, trucks, horseboxes and bow top wagons, and almost back on my trailer when I heard someone approaching from behind. I didn’t even turn around as there were souls everywhere, enjoying the beautiful warm evening. But then, I felt a big, strong pair of hands grasp me around my waist, pulling me backwards and almost taking me off my feet.

I turned my head, and there in the flickering glow of a campfire was my handsome lad from earlier. I was more than twenty years his senior, so I was a little confused but something about him got my blood pumping and my fanny fluttering.

From the expression on his handsome face, there was no mistaking his intentions, and I knew it was a fair thing and never to be repeated but enjoyed.

“Come with me, woman!” he whispered in my ear, and I couldn’t help but obey my handsome stranger.

It was a very neolithic carnal encounter that I really couldn’t explain. He just made me melt and my feminine instinct told me not to protest. Feeling like I was 18 again, hand in hand, I followed him to a beautiful bow top, and tethered next to it was the horse from the river. A small campfire illuminated the door of the beautifully painted green and red wagon, with ornate carvings and gold leaf; it was like being transported back in time, and one would say, perfect.

He beckoned me up the steps into the gorgeous dwelling fit for a king; there was a queenie stove, stunning built-in dressers and bench and mounted above it all was an ornately dressed double bed, with lacy, big, sumptuous pillows on it. Above the bed was a gorgeous leaded window, dressed with stunning handmade curtains. A lantern dangled from the floral lattice ceiling, giving everything a timeless feel. It was such a relaxed positive space.

Moving in behind me, the man slid his vest over his head, exposing the stunning god-like bronzed body I recalled from the river; warm light teased his naked flesh.

He turned me around and asked my name, which I answered with a whisper.

"That be a beautiful name, woman. I'm Sonny… Now, dat will be a name you will never forget after tonight, I promise ye dat!"

Gently sweeping my long blonde hair to one side, he traced soft kisses down my neck to my shoulder. As he did, his hand moved around to the front of my jeans and skilfully flicked the buttons. He slid them over my womanly hips, ``allowing them to fall to the floor, and urged me to step out of them. One of his hands slid up my top to my breast, taking my hard nipple in his fingertips. His other hand found the outside of my thong pants and started tracing the cleft of my pussy. He had no trouble locating my engorged love button, and he gently teased me until he drew a soft moan from my lips.

This was his que to proceed, slipping down my thong to access my vulnerable pussy, he slid his finger between my moist lips causing me to gasp. Massaging my clit and sliding deep within my warm walls while rolling an eager nipple between his finger and thumb, he brought me to my first exquisite orgasm.

Drawing my cotton top up over my head, I stood relishing the afterglow of that first sweet treat. He picked me up as he had earlier in the river. Draped across his arms, he effortlessly lifted me onto the bed.

I lay there, watching him remove his jeans. I saw what a truly gorgeous example of the male species he really was. He had big, strong muscular legs from walking and running his horse in the wagon up hills, and complemented by his tight toned butt. His perfectly erect cory met a perfect masculine torso with just the tiniest amount of body hair, emphasising his assets. Looking at him made my mouth and pussy moist.

He climbed the steps onto the plush bed and buried his face skilfully between my slim thighs, making delicate contact with my pink pussy. He was licking and lapping her hills and valleys so expertly it wasn't long before I felt another charged climax brewing deep within.

But he did not allow me to climax.

Lifting himself up onto his strong arms, I felt his length nudging at the entrance to my honey pot. He looked me in the eyes as he drove his impressive manliness deep inside of me. I arched my back and raised my hips to meet his thrusts time and time again, orgasm after tantalising orgasm, our bodies united as one.

Climbing off, he rolled on to his back, and I cocked my leg over him and squatted on his big, hard cock. Alternating shallow tight thrusts and just taking his head to slow deep thrusts, I took him to the hilt and brink of cumming. But I wasn't ready for it to end.

I swivelled around on his meat and turned into reverse cowgirl. With his help, I rode the life out of him. He felt so good deep within me. As he grasped my hips to help me ride him vigorously, sweat poured from us both. I could feel the most electrifying orgasm radiating from my pussy and arse; it radiated from my feet, fingers and head towards my pussy.

When the charge earthed through my tight wet screaming walls, I was in a state of writhing delirium, creaming on his magnificent column of flesh. He soon followed suit, filling me with his love liquor. I just collapsed back onto him. As we both panted, bathed with sweat, he wrapped his strong arms around me.

That was the last thing I remember as we both drifted off into the magical world of slumber.

IT'S IN ON THE CARDS

K, 41, CAN

My partner and I had always had a very colourful sex life, trying no end of fantasies. We were both very adventurous.

Once, I was reading an article "How to spice it up" when one paragraph stopped me in my tracks. It had a suggestion of buying a pack of blank playing cards. The playing cards would be divided between participants, i.e., a couple. Each person would write a fantasy on each card, and when all the cards were full, they would be shuffled thoroughly and placed in a safe place until you as a couple or group decided to draw one.

We both had the weekend off so Thursday eve, we decided to pluck a card from the stack with a full intention to live it out. I went first on this occasion. Taking a card, I turned it over to reveal its intent.

"MAKE LOVE ON A SPANISH BEACH"

I wondered about how I was supposed to make this happen; I had some serious organisation to engineer. I told Stacey not to plan anything this weekend, and I got to work finding us an all-inclusive package to fly out the next day. I hit the jackpot with an all-in two nights in Menorca and a full day on a luxury yacht with the option to boat into the tiny little bay of Cala Mitjana.

It took me most of the morning planning, and when everything was confirmed, I called Stacey. Of course, she was thrilled; these spontaneous trips are the best.

We both had work on Friday, but we finished at 4 p.m. The flight was at 7:35 p.m., so we had plenty of time to grab a few bits for our adventure.

The plane journey was uneventful, and we landed in Menorca at 9:20. There was no shortage of taxis at the airport, and flagging one down, we made our way to our gorgeous hotel. It had a luxury studio suite and a terrace facing the marina.

The dark night sky was illuminated by thousands of stars, dusted as far as the eye could see. As if the mesmerising Milky Way dominated the sky with its oranges, pinks and yellows, exploding into the expanse of the universe. It was so beautiful it brought a tear to my eye, which Stacey noticed. She kissed me tenderly on my eyelids in an empathic gesture of love.

We chose to have a bottle of wine and a seafood platter on our terrace as we relished the breathtaking view. The air was warm with a hint of blooming flowers and what smelt like caramel.

After our very manic day, we decided an early night was in order as I had planned a day to remember for the following day. Cuddling into my beautiful, radiant woman, I caressed her ribcage across the landscape of her body to her thigh, she groaned and wiggled her cute peachy butt into me as if an invite, and of course, I accepted.

Gliding my fingers between her legs, I gently searched out the object of her desire, massaging it gently as I would myself. Rolling over to face me, she reciprocated, mimicking my every action until we were both creaming on each other's delicate fingers, stifling our moans as the terrace doors were open. We kissed tenderly, and soon both fell into a content slumber.

Morning came; exotic birds sang and squawked. We could hear the hustle and bustle of breakfast service in full swing. We had slightly overslept. so we ordered room service to the terrace. The sky was a beautiful baby blue with not so much as a wisp of candy floss clouding visible. It was already getting hot, so we both vouched for bikinis and sarong with wedge mules, topped off with a big floppy sun hat; we both looked at a picture.

Finishing our continental breakfast, we made our way to reception to get our taxi to the yacht. On arrival, we were greeted by the most attractive captain in his full boating regalia. The yacht was as impressive. She was called Athena and had five crews, including the captain. It had a huge sun deck, bar, BBQ and dining area with seating area to relax, water sports toys, hydraulic swim platform and to ice the cake, underwater lights for the evening.

We were one of five couples, all around 30-45 in ages. Taking seats in the relaxation area, we were warmly greeted and handed a flute of bubbly. As we sat, the captain explained we were heading for a very remote bay.

"Perfect for lovers," he joked, due it only being accessible via foot or paddle board.

And so, we set off on our 12-hour yachting extravaganza. The blue water was crystal clear and warm; tiny fish swam freely with no fear. The views as we meandered through the still waters of the Mediterranean Sea were spectacular. Looking back towards the island, there was nothing but blue sky and turquoise sea. Luscious vibrant green trees and foliage littered the outcrops of sandy cliffs, framing well-stocked beaches and fringing the glorious coast.

The atmosphere was very relaxed and jovial as there were laughing and smiling people in every direction you look on the boat. Even the crew were loving life, giving the vibe that what more can you ask for but a job you love.

As we rounded a corner, tucked away from intruding eyes on the southern coast, a bay called Cala Mitjana was nestled quietly. Crystal waster teasing craggy sandstone cliffs and golden beach, shaded by beautifully fragrant pines and blooming shrubbery.

Idyllically, the beach was only accessible by foot or boat, we were again told as the captain addressed his guests. We were instructed we could either kayak in or snorkel, and the yacht would moor just offshore and at hand the whole time if needed. We were each given a whistle for emergencies.

I recalled to my partner what the captain had told us on boarding—it was the perfect place for a lover's tryst.

We chose to kayak to the beach, and enjoyed the warm water, lapping at my hand as we ambled to the beach, taking in every detail. The crew had packed us a lunch and a bottle of fine wine with two plastic glasses, which I put in my rucksack.

Reaching golden sands, we dragged the kayak up onto the beach. With the divine warm sand between our toes, we deserted our only route off the island to investigate the idyllic landscape. The place was hot and hypnotic. Walking paths that many lovers had traced before us, we found a tiny little recess where land met the sea. It was shaded by shrubbery and the perfect spot to relax, eat and drink.

I looked into Stacey's eyes; we both knew what the other was thinking as we read each other's mind. Off flew the clothes, no

ceremony, just beautiful naked flesh at one with nature. Giggling, we ran into the warm sea hand in hand. We both relished the warm waters lapping at our bodies, teasing and tantalising our senses. We came together as one, seeking each other's soft fruity sun-blocked lips with our tongues exploring and devouring one another.

My pussy was alive, radiating tingling heat from deep within. Stacey's fingers found the gate to my loveliness, teasing my clit and drawing a whimper from me. Her expert fingers played me like an orchestra cellist—delicately yet so precise—bringing me to my first mind-blowing orgasm.

Recovering, I took her hand and playfully led her back to the warm sand. Laying her down, I descended between her amazing legs, spreading her wide. I engulfed her warm but salty clit, licking and kissing her to distraction. I devoured her savoury morsal as if it was the last time and was making it count. Holding my head, she started thrusting to the rhythm of my lapping and gentle suckling, almost crying with delight. Emotion was overtaking her as hormones surged through her body. She gripped my head with her strong thighs as she claimed her prize.

Moving up her body, I straddled one leg over hers, so we were engorged clit to clit. We both started gyrating and rubbing our salty creamy pussies.

Oh my God, it felt so wet, warm, and intense. It was like no scissoring we had ever done before—epic. Fever and sauce building deep within the pair of us; we're in a glorious state of delirium as we both let out a siren-like cry. Our hot pink pulsating pussies purged us of our beautiful, warm liquor. Puffy, warm and alive, we milked every drop from within.

Falling back onto the warm sand, we once again embraced each other; the sand felt like it was giving us a warm hug in our vulnerable content state.

I cannot wait for the next card.

AS NATURE INTENDED

G, 45, ESP

It had always been my fantasy to entertain my lover on a secluded beach. My husband and I were the same age, and had been married for 16 years. We were both very open-minded but also devoted to one another. We had done most things sexually but not this, and the idea just turned me on so much.

In my fantasy, we were going on a holiday, and Ibiza was our chosen destination. This time, I wanted a more reserved secluded destination; Es Bol Nou, Ibiza was the joint decision.

On arriving, we walked to the villa we rented for the week. Located in a gated resort, it accommodated adults only, which suited us as we had no children and were not overly fond of them if we were to be honest. The villa was spacious, bright, and had a lovely, fresh and homely feel to the place. It had minimalistic yet welcoming white walls with vast windows providing fantastic views of the sea, rustic red clay coastline dusted with green foliage, and turquoise seas as far as the eye could see.

Leaving our luggage after a brief look around, we decided to have a quick freshen-up and go for food and a couple drinks before hitting the

beach as it was only mid-morning. It was warm but clearly going to be a scorcher.

After eating and a few cool refreshing drinks, we made our way to the beach on foot. We were pleasantly surprised to see a sign pointing to a nudist part of the beach around the corner, tucked in a small cove away from delicate souls. Walking along the main beach to our destination, we chatted and laughed, which we did a lot. We discussed the idyllic scenery and warm, fine red sand that was caressing our toes as we ambled along hand in hand.

As we walked around an outcrop of rock shielding the nudist beach, we were witnesses to men and women of every shape, creed and colour, frolicking in the warm clear seas. Some were covered in red clay, resembling tribal people from other continents. They were either liberally coating themselves in the red oozy gloop, laughing and cavorting with friends and partners, or stretched out on the sand, glazed with red slip as you would an earthenware pot before firing. Some were semi-dry, while others were cracking as they made their way to the sea to wash the earthy benefits of their bodies—snorkelling, swimming, or just blissfully floating like sun fish in the tempered crystal waters.

With loud giggles, we both discarded our clothes where we stood and eagerly ran into the glorious crystal-clear water. There, we embraced each other and kissed passionately, our tongues searching out the other's. Naked people around us uncompromisingly cavorted; the atmosphere was electric, so liberating & free.

Moving to the shallows, we sat, allowing waves to sweep over our legs and scooping handfuls of glorious ooze and seductively and lovingly coating each other's bodies and faces. We stood, giving each other's legs

and buttocks equal attention until we were both unrecognisable. Hand in hand, we made our way up the beach and lay in the softness of the fine red sand, baking in the molten rays of the sun and becoming slowly immortalised in clay. We lay, basking at one with nature and totally uninhibited.

A number of hours passed, hot and stiff, we made our way back to the crystal ocean. We lowered our cracking, baking bodies into cool, refreshing waters, allowing our confinements to melt away. Our clay encapsulated bodies were soon released from their bounds, and we both started splashing and swimming along the length of the nudist beach.

As we did, we found an outcrop that was shielded from the rest of the world—a tiny sand bar that was just big enough for two. Sitting on our own little island, we savoured the peace. But then, realising nobody was close, I threw my leg over my partner who was in the sitting position.

He grasped my naked bottom firmly while kissing me passionately, searching my lips with his hot devilish tongue, and running it across my teeth. He bit my lip, making me squeal. Using his brute strength to lift me onto his ample meat muscle, he forced his way through the gateway of my labia.

I engulfed him to the hilt. My juices coated his meat as I started to ride his thrusts to meet him. Leaning back as I rode him, he took an erect nipple into his warm moist mouth. Tasting and teasing it, I could feel my quim convulsing around his piece. And as I hit my euphoric high note, my pussy gripped her steed with such strength, expelling golden juice all over my lover.

Flipping me over, my lover drove himself home once more. He crouched behind me to force himself into me with more vigour,

hammering my prone pussy with no mercy and using his thumb to tease and tantalise my exposed star.

My body was awash with sensory overload, sun, sand, sea and with uninhibited carnal lust. The orgasms rose from my feminine organs, rippling out to every nerve within my body. Covered with a sea of goosebumps, I climaxed on his determined unapologetic manhood with a shrill cry. He followed suit, pumping his cool life lustre into my tight hot confines with a bellow of accomplishment and gratification.

OLD SALT

ANONYMOUS

The whitewashed cottages were blinding white in the summer sun, and the harassed parents glanced enviously at me as I strolled unencumbered, before they turned back to their offspring, who either wanted to be on the beach or eat ice cream.

Dave had made some lame excuse about having to go back to London, and had left me with four days on my own at the cottage. I had walked into the town along the coast, ate a crab sandwich for lunch at a café and wondered how to pass the afternoon.

The narrow street was busy, so I was happy to turn up the alleyway, which led away from the crowd. A few yards into the alley, it became a path with cottage fronts on one side and the slate roofs of the street below on the other. At the very end of the row was John's Studio and Art Gallery.

I had been there several times before, and Dave and I had bought a couple of pieces, so I knew John quite well. The door was open, and at the back of the shop, John was busy at his easel. He was a typical West Country sailor; olive skinned, grey hair and beard, and dressed in just shorts with wisps of grey hair on his chest.

He looked up as I stepped into the doorway, and straight away put down his brush and reached for a sketchpad.

“Wait there a moment,” he said. His voice was soft and gentle but his tone was slightly excited.

I didn't mind being a source of inspiration, so I happily obliged. He hardly took his eyes off me as his pencil flew across the paper. I realised then that the light was behind me and that, from where he was sitting, it was shining through the thin cotton of my sundress and not leaving too much to the imagination.

After only a couple of minutes, he put down his pencil and relaxed.

“May I see?” I asked.

“Yes, but it is only a sketch at the moment.”

I walked over and stood beside him at his desk, which was littered with tubes of paint and brushes. The sketch showed me almost naked. My dress was just a vague outline, but even in the short time he had been drawing, he had captured the light and made a beautiful picture.

“Oh, did I really look as naked as that?”

He smiled. “Well, no. I did use a bit of an artist's licence, but you do have a beautiful body.”

I felt myself getting aroused, and glancing down for a moment, I realised I was not the only one.

"You make a happy man feel very old," he said with a wistful look in his eyes.

"Perhaps I could also make an old man very happy?" I replied, looking him straight in the eye.

He looked a little unsure how to react, so I turned and leaned back against his desk, my knee just touching his. He rested his hand on my thigh and stroked gently. I held his gaze as his hand moved up my thigh. His fingers found their way easily under the thin cotton of my knickers and found my now moist pussy.

"Quick, before someone comes," I said.

He stood and pulled down his shorts; his cock fully erect. He lifted my skirt, and I pulled my knickers to one side, and he slid expertly into me.

"Don't wait for me, I just want you to cum," I said.

"You might get there too," he replied. "I'm not as young as I used to be!"

He fucked me slowly as I leaned back amongst the tubes of paint, one hand supporting me, the other stroking my breasts through the thin cotton. I lifted myself to kiss him, and something in him snapped. His pace quickened and his passion became intense.

It was so erotic that I knew when he came, it would send me over the top too. I didn't have long to wait. With a strangled cry, his body went rigid as I felt him pump his cum into me. My own orgasm then

overwhelmed me. I writhed and thrusted against him, pulling him as deep into me as I could.

We stayed still for a few moments, getting our breath back. Then, without a word and with surprising strength, he lifted me up and slid something beneath me. He then withdrew, and a stream of cum dribbled out onto what turned out to be his sketch pad.

"Your lovely drawing!" I exclaimed in horror. A mixture of my juice and his cum was all over the picture he had just done.

"No," he uttered. "I did that on purpose."

I looked at him amazed.

"You have indeed made an old man very happy, but come back tomorrow and I will give you a very beautiful gift in return." He smiled at me, and the blue of his eyes made me melt all over again.

I was not sure what he meant, but it was clear he was fired up as an artist again. So, I kissed him on the forehead, straightened my dress and with a coquettish swish and backwards glance, I left him to his work.

From our cottage, I could see John's studio across the bay, and the light was on late into the evening. I slept like a log and woke the following morning feeling both relaxed and curious to see what John had burnt so much midnight oil to create.

The day was cooler but still warm and sunny as I walked back into town along the coast path. Reaching John's studio, a picture on an easel in the corner of the room caught my eye. My cotton dress was now depicted as just a sheer voile, and I was no longer standing in the studio doorway but amid boiling seascape. The juices we had contributed had

been worked into waves, reaching up to touch my body in its most intimate places, which was quite overwhelmingly erotic.

Underneath was a little label called *An Unexpected Voyage* (Mixed media. Not for sale).

John appeared through a small door at the back of the studio. "Do you like it?"

"Yes," I said. "Why can't I buy it?"

"Because it is already yours."

The picture now hangs in our flat in London. Dave loved it, but he might think otherwise if he knew how it came to be created.

For my part, I went to the West Country more often on my own now, and the pictures in John's gallery didn't feature just seascapes quite so much.

GYM ENCOUNTERS

S, 32, USA

I had always been bi-curious, but until recently, I had never acted on the urge, but just brushed it under the carpet and relished in my fantasy world when the lights went out.

I had been at the local gym for a few hours doing a mammoth workout. It had been a while, and boy, didn't I know it. Steam was evaporating off my hot moist body. My body screamed out for a cool shower, perspiring from every pore, and salty threads of sweat trickled between my big, pert breasts, tracing a salty course to my navel. My erect

perky brown nipples were barely containable through my white, sweaty sports bra. My leggings and high-waist thong had a distinct damp patch over my pussy mound I couldn't hide, accentuating my puffy cameltoe.

The gym had a big steaming walk-in communal shower with terracotta-tiled floors, wooden bench seats flanking the cool walls and a full-length mirror at each end of the room. The air was filled with refreshing steam. I peeled my leggings from my tacky body, feeling the breeze whisp across my molten exhausted body as I now stood only in my pants and bra, which both clung to my moist skin like a limpet on a smooth rock.

I heard the changing room door creaking. I knew someone was entering just out of my view as I carried on unfastening my bra to release my big firm breasts, sighing with relief as the breeze caressed them. Sliding my hands down my body, I slipped my pants off and let them fall to the floor. As I bent to pick them up, a beautiful blonde got an eyeful of my bare tanned ass and sweet, pink pussy.

As we made eye contact, we both smirked a subtle, cheeky smile.

I couldn't take my eyes off the stunning beauty that was busying herself in her gym bag, and I thought I was being sneaky until a voice said, "Do you like what you see, Chica?"

I was so surprised I answered truthfully, saying, "Yes, you're beautiful, who wouldn't?" After all, the feminine form is a thing of total beauty whether you're bi or straight, and I had always been straight.

She walked towards me, and stopping just a few inches from me, she removed her tight white gym top that emphasised her small but perfect breasts and erect nipples. She didn't need to wear a bra.

We both stood in the steamy room, her in her pants and I in my sports bra, looking at each other.

Then, she raised her hand. "What stunning hazel eyes you have," she said as she stroked my hair, tracing a finger over my parted lips in a seductive manner.

She soon replaced her finger with her mouth, and I felt myself responding instinctively. Our lips entwined, seeking out each other's tongue. I felt my pussy coming alive, tingling and fluttering.

As she kissed me deeply, she cupped my big breast and rubbed our erect nipples together. When she was sure she had bagged her prize, she gently guided me towards the benches, pushing me down on the rough wood-slatted bench. The cold wall was biting at my flesh as I leant against it. Dragging my towel from my open bag, she expertly folded it and placed it between my parted legs on the cold hard floor, where she knelt.

She went back to kissing me, but soon was tracing her lips and tongue expertly from my earlobe down to my super sensitive neck, making every sense in my body scream alive. . I had an invisible on-switch there. Working her way slowly across my firm breasts and resting at my left nipple, she took it into her eager mouth. She licked and suckled on it, pushing my boobs together and moving her attention back and forth, giving both girls equal attention. My pussy was creaming, and my legs started to quiver, as an impressive orgasm overtook me—something I had never experienced with boob play.

She urged me to lift my peachy ass off the bench, and I slipped forward, laying my gorgeous pussy bare, making it very vulnerable and totally exposed, but this Chica knew exactly what she was doing.

Kissing from my hard proud nipples, tracing a kiss trail down to my navel and descending to my sweet welcoming quim, she parted my delicate lips gently with her fingers. She found her score and greedily sucked and licked me to the most mind-blowing orgasm I have ever experienced.

It was right what they say: nobody does it like a woman.

She licked and sucked as she herself liked to be indulged. And slipping two slim fingers between my lips into my warm moist pussy, seeking my g-spot on the front wall, she expertly applied that little bit of pressure and motion and greedily devoured my clit—*Oh my God!*—I had never received cunnilingus so expertly performed.

Tidal waves of body-trembling orgasms overwhelmed every cell of my being. My pussy clinched her fingers as I held her head to my pussy, terrified she would stop.

Then, hearing voices approaching the changing rooms, the door opened.

Before the invaders could encroach, my new friend was on her feet. She walked to the steaming shower, leaving me a trembling mess on the bench and trying to act totally normal without overacting.

I was a mess but a content mess. I am now officially bisexual.

SAUCY WENCH

C, 29, UK

I have always loved period romance and historical literature. My idea of a perfect evening would include a good bottle of wine and total

solitude, hidden away in a warm, dark study, illuminated only by a sole lamp that would bring the text to life and make it possible for me to unapologetically indulge in my passion. If not, I would be in my soft, sumptuous bed, propped up by a mountainous range of duck-down, my safe space to retreat to after a manically busy day at my crazy modern office with hundreds of people coming and going every day. I would get lost in my world of a forgotten era, binge-reading until I fell into a sedate slumber.

This love for anything of a bygone era also fuelled my sexual fantasies, portraying a passionate, adventurous, idealistic and idyllic foundation for my fantasies to morph and evolve, one of which I would love to share. I hope you enjoy the following fantasy as much as I had on countless occasions over the past years as I indulged in my sordid, guilty pleasures.

At ease, knowing I was the only life form inhibiting the house, I retreated to my bedroom. Pulling back the soft, weighty quilt, I relaxed back on to my bed of eiderdown pillows. My satin dressing gown clung to my skin as cascading water clung desperately to the last crumb of earth, before tumbling into the abyss of the unknown, following every contour of my feminine form.

I allowed my finger to trace a delicate trail up and down my bare stomach as I wiggled my toes indulgently, curling the soft cool cotton sheet between them, wallowing in the total serenity and tranquillity that was not readily available with the mayhem of family life.

Tracing rhythmic circles up and down my body, then to my exposed yoni, my mind wandered into the hypnotic land of fantasy, where I can be who and what I wish. I ventured into a world I'd never dared to in real life, knowing I was totally safe doing so.

It was the 1800s. I was a lady's maid for the wife of a wealthy tobacco merchant in the Southwest. I lived in the main house in a wing just off my mistress's bedroom quarters, so I could easily assist her anytime with dressing, choosing garments, bathing, and hair and beauty. My mistress was kind and treated me well as did the master, though I rarely came in contact with him. The master was a very handsome man, tall and strong with dark hair and skin. One hot, humid Saturday afternoon, Master was called away on business; this was my usual afternoon off, to return to work fresh the next day. As Master rolled off along the gravel drive in the carriage drawn by four beautiful bay horses, the house fell silent as most of the staff took a half-day rest.

I thought I better attend to Mistress before I, too, left for my half-day treat in town, meeting up with a couple of other girls that tend the house and kitchens. Scaling the less ornate back stairs to the corridor and Mistress's chamber, I gently tapped her door, waiting to be beckoned in. But nothing came, so I presumed Mistress had also gone out to visit friends, which she often does on a weekend.

I made my way through the stunning grounds and then across the pristine back lawns. From there, I passed through the vibrant walled vegetable garden, which burst with sustenance, to the woods behind the Manor. It was a three-mile walk, but two miles if I cut through the dense woodland. With the vast emerald green canopy whispering above me and the sunlight piercing through like blazing arrows to the woodland floor, the air was warm, and the scent of the moist forest strong and enchanting.

With the forest edge in sight, I could see my favourite resting place ahead—an old fallen oak tree forming a bridge over the babbling brook that meandered through the meadow beyond. I would usually dip my toes

in, allowing my thoughts to wander for an hour. I would lay back as I straddled my grand ole friend with my feet dangling, and my skirts tucked in my bloomers unapologetically. Relishing the cool, trickling water that teased my tired, hot feet and the warm summer breeze blowing up my skirts, I closed my eyes.

I must have drifted off, and woke up with a start as a male voice greeted me, "Well, hello down there. That looks like total bliss!"

I looked up in alarm but still couldn't focus on the male presence staring down at me in all my brazen glory. When I did, I realised it was Master with a huge grin of amusement on his face.

Darting upright while fighting with my skirts, I apologised profusely. I was terrified I would be given orders, but all the Master did was laugh. He then ordered me to relax and carry on as I was; after all, it was my afternoon off, so I could please myself any way I wanted. He went on, saying he was actually going to join me.

To my surprise, I giggled.

It turned out he had been walking for five miles as one of the wheels of his coach fell off, and he hadn't the patience to hang around at the side of the road with the men, waiting for the wheelwright to come to the rescue.

Kicking off his long, black, leather riding boots and socks, he rolled up his breeches, threw off his coat and pulled his shirt up over his head.

I was presented with a view of the most beautiful male creature I had ever seen. His chest and shoulders were broad and muscular with a rug of black, curly hair that traced to his toned stomach to the V descending beyond to that secret place I had no knowledge of, and until

this moment, had never even thought about. My gasp must have told a thousand tales, without me muttering a word.

Soon, we were straddling the tree with our legs touching, chatting and giggling like lifelong friends; Master could easily be one of the village boys I grew up with.

Time had passed when Master suddenly stopped talking and looked deep into my eyes. Holding my gaze, he exclaimed how beautiful I was. He leant forward, brushing my hair off my cheek so softly, I felt a pang of desire flickered within my treasured depths.

"You are a comely wench," he whispered, his warm breath in my ear. "I want to taste your soft lips."

His breathing and manner had changed. Lust filled his piercing blue eyes, as he clasped my face, drawing me in for a warm, moist, hypnotic kiss. It was something I had never experienced before; my body was defying my confusion and reacting.

Getting to his feet, he effortlessly lifted me off the grand oak by my waist. I instinctively wrapped my bare legs around his toned, powerful torso; I had never felt a man's skin against my skin. Then, he gently lowered me onto his discarded coat to protect my soft skin from the sharp grass and meadow's herbs. With my stunning Master between my innocent thighs, I had no idea what to expect or what was expected by Master.

He tentatively undid the ribbons of my best bodice, releasing my small but pert, milky white breasts. As he did, he kissed down my neck and took one of my pink, erect nipples into his warm mouth. He suckled and nibbled each in turn, almost engulfing my whole breast with his mouth.

Something in me awoke. My skin was alive, reacting to every deliberately placed touch, kiss and lick. I was in a frenzy I had no control, scared of the events that were unfolding but also terrified the hypnotic, enchanting experience would stop.

Raising himself, he gave me a devilish smile, before kissing my readily available mouth. His gentle kiss descended from my head to my body until he descended between my virginal legs, and I shook with desire. He ran his hand up my youthful thighs under my flowing skirts. Master found the ribbon holding my bloomers up and released it, removing them completely and discarding them over his shoulder.

I was very vulnerable, but also felt masked by my skirts until Master flicked them back over my body, unapologetically exposing my downy secret to the world. Grasping my legs, he pulled me into his face, staring up at me as he darted his warm tongue over my secret button.

As a budding young woman, I had discovered quite by accident how it felt when I gently caressed my secret button, but this was something else. With Master's tongue, it was far more intense, waking up stirrings I had never felt before. It was divine, yet I felt like such a bad girl, but I wouldn't allow it to stop. I prayed for it not to stop.

Time and time again, my body released into his greedy mouth. My whole being was awash with strange feelings and emotions. A stifled whimper escaped my lips as I couldn't contain myself any longer.

Getting to his knees whilst looking down at me with a lustful, dark intrigue, he unleashed his hidden manliness—it looked enormous, strong and fleshy. As the Master placed himself between my thighs, I could feel it, nudging my secret.

"Is this the first time, wench?" he whispered as he leant further into me.

In a breathy voice, I replied, "Yes, Master."

"This is going to pain you woman, but you will come to accept and crave it. Try not to scream. Bite me if you must."

Looking me in the eyes, Master gently introduced the tip of his cock between my lips, and when he was sure he was on the mark, he used his brute strength to push through my secret entrance.

Burning pain seared through me, as I tried to stifle my cry. It felt as though I was being torn in two. Each thrust drew out a cry from me, but he drove on, kissing me to stifle my sobs. I bit his lip, and this seemed to drive him on, making his actions more forceful and determined.

As he said, the pain subsided, and pleasure started replacing the searing burn. A hot full desire engulfed any discomfort, as I started moving my hips to meet his ample thrusts. I could feel my moist secret gripping his ample weapon as I hit a delirious conclusion, and my awakened desire cascaded all over Master.

Withdrawing his member, he grasped the length of it and started working his hand up and down vigorously. Finally, with a loud bellow, his life force erupted from its tip onto my exposed belly.

I never made it to town that day nor any that followed for a long, long time.

SPLASH THE CASH
M, 37

I was with the same man for so many years. We met when I was 19 and at college. Sex was okay but never really very exciting. It was very

inhibited, and I never truly let go, but at the time, I wasn't aware I was missing out. I thought that was just how sex was, until years down the line, we split and went our separate ways.

I decided, I didn't want a boyfriend, but I yearned and fantasised about raw, unadulterated lust with a stranger, where I wouldn't be judged nor care what the other person felt or thought about the adventures we had. If we didn't gel, or it wasn't right in any way, then "next, please!" was my newfound attitude.

I found my new happy place, and life became very exciting. One of my favourite fantasies revolved around a dating app that I had learned and adapted to my needs and wants, which are continuously morphing into other ideas and kinks.

In my fantasy, I was scrolling on a highly populated dating app—left to lose and right to show interest. Milling through the never-ending desperados, I swiped left, left, left… when a very striking man caught my eye. He had chiselled, handsome features, golden blonde, wavy hair and beard with sky-blue, cutting eyes that seemed to draw you in, and a big, bright, white smile that could charm the knickers off a nun.

His profile stated he was only looking for fun and frolics with no strings, and if you had a hidden agenda of wanting a relationship, then scroll on by as he would not be the one for you.

He was brutally but refreshingly honest, and it excited and intrigued me. More than that, his candour was very alluring, causing my pussy to quiver and moisten, feeling a wave of goose pimples flooded across my body.

Curiosity had awoken this cat, and she wanted to know more, even if it was to her detriment.

I jumped in with both feet and swiped, then I waited patiently, hoping for a message. Within an hour, there was an inbox waiting for me. Palpitations thudded violently in my chest and my hands trembled as I opened the message.

There were no airs and graces, just a date and meeting destination followed by a kiss.

The day had arrived for the date, if you wish to call it that. I began getting myself ready, bathing and meticulously shaving every bristle that dared erupt from my perfect, creamy white skin. And then I moisturised and liberally applied the gorgeous scent I was given as a gift. Content with my look and makeup with my hair piled high on my head, I slipped into my flattering catsuit and strappy heels. I grabbed my cropped leather biker jacket, as I heard the taxi sound its horn outside the house. My heart skipped a beat with excitement as I slammed the front door, running to the awaiting car.

I instructed my driver to take me to the centre of the town. I watched the murmuration of bodies walking, talking and jostling about their lives and tasks as I sat nervously, daydreaming at traffic lights. I arrived at my destination—a swanky cocktail and tapas bar on the second floor of a beautiful Georgian building. Entering the vast foyer, I found my confidence and strutted through reception and the lifts. I was a high-value woman, and I would leave my mark with this handsome beast.

From the lift, I walked through a set of automatic chrome etched glass doors and was hit with the excitement of the bar. Perfumes and

aftershave permeated the air, as did the delicious scents of the vast array of tapas. Each table was laid to the highest standard, adorned with fresh flowers and burning candles. The place was alive with laughing, happy souls. All seemed to be enjoying life, from the large tables of women out in force celebrating to the intimate couples. Scanning the room, my eyes caught my date. He delighted the eye; he was everything his profile promised he was and some.

Standing, he greeted me with a kiss and guided me to my seat as a gentleman should. He then took my coat and handed it to the waitress, requesting table service.

We ordered drinks and requested a menu, and then we got chatting. He was such an articulate, friendly, interesting man. Soon, cocktails were flowing freely, and we had a vast array of vibrant, colourful food in front of us, grazing as we openly chatted,

Hours melted away, and my companion asked if I would like to spend the rest of the evening with him in his room in a nearby hotel. I knew the score and was very excited about the prospect—mentally and physically.

So, we finished our cocktails and asked the waitress to request a taxi. Heads turned as we strode down to the foyer. I had no quibble in saying we did make a handsome couple with my arm linked through his as he escorted me graciously to our awaiting car.

Arriving at the hotel, he paid and got out first. He walked around to my side and opened my door for me. As I got out, he offered me his hand so I could steady myself; I was slightly tipsy but by no means drunk.

We made our way straight up to the room. The hotel was a modern high-end place, and everything was immaculate; smiling staff greeted us as we came across them on route.

My companion opened the door to his room, and I was presented with an amazing view of the city at night through the huge windows that were shrouded in sage green drapes to compliment the furnishings. As I hung my jacket on the hangers by the door, he got to his knees and gently lifted my foot, removing my shoes one at a time. Looking up at me with his stunning eyes, he grinned and kissed a foot before placing it gently on the floor. When he got to his feet, it was my que to excuse myself to the bathroom and freshen up.

As I walked away, he was removing his shirt that masked the most amazing physique, grinning yet again as he glanced over his shoulder.

I freshened my most intimate place, flicked my panties off next to the shower along with my catsuit, released my mane of curly hair, rinsed my mouth with mouthwash and spritzed my naked body with scent. Feeling incredibly sexy and confident, I walked back to the bedroom to find my new companion completely naked. He was poised on the bed, leaning on his elbow and obviously ready to dive straight in, so to speak. It would have been rude not to oblige.

Climbing onto the bed, I squatted over his face, instructing him to admire my perfectly preened, pink appetiser. Inhaling my womanliness as he parted my lips with his tongue, he expertly darted his soft, warm, wet tongue strategically from that very sensitive, soft area between my pee hole up and over the object of every woman's desire, alternating firm and soft lapping strokes: I was in heaven, and this man was most

definitely a sexpert. Hot, spasming orgasms radiated from my pussy and arsehole.

Pausing for a moment, he lubricated his index finger with his mouth and went back to devouring his appetiser. Gently, he caressed my star with his soft, tender fingertip until I welcomed him in. The intense sensations accumulated until I violently orgasmed and released my golden nectar into his welcoming mouth; he went lapping and guzzling every drop of his prize.

Swivelling around into sixty-nine, I grasped his overtly large, veiny piece and fed him between my soft, pouty lips, taking him almost to the root and gagging lubricant over his length with every lucky dip. As I was deepthroating him most intently, my lover started rimming and licking at my star, relaxing me once more and probing my most secret place with the tip of his tongue and skilfully rubbing my love button with his thumb pad; we were both graciously giving and receiving at the same time, with our moans stifled with the other's desire.

Using his brute strength, he brought his arms around and over my loins. My companion grasped both my peachy cheeks and drew me into his greedy, enthusiastic lips. He ate me to another cataclysmic conclusion as I again released what felt like my soul into his mouth that he was unable to keep up with the deluge cascading over his face, neck and chest.

My whole body trembled to its very core; I just lay, quivering between his muscular thighs in total delirium.

Feeling an odd but delicious, warm, wet sensation on my toes, I glance back to see what my companion had in mind for me next. He was

lost in his own world, licking and sniffing my toes before sucking them; he really was worshipping them, and I can now totally relate to foot worship. It felt amazing and flicked an invisible switch in my pussy as though they were connected. Every soft, moist lick or gentle suck sent sparks flying between my legs. It was very erotic indeed.

It was clearly his thing, and he indulged himself for at least 40 minutes. Then without prompt, he lifted me around and gently lowered me onto his girthy piece. With no effort at all, he moved the pair of us as one up the bed so he was sitting, and we were chest to breast. He then bent his knees for stability as he put his big strong hands around my waist, and as I squatted on his beast, he rose to meet me. My tight wet walls gripped his tool greedily, unwilling to release him as we built a heady tempo.

We both just let ourselves be the primal animals we once were. Hedonistic, orgasmic impulses radiated through both our minds and bodies, and all rational control was lost for that split moment in time as we both allowed ourselves that gift.

I felt my pussy violently convulse around the engorged head of my mount, knowing he was ready to erupt his free-flowing lava into me. With a roar, he let go as did I.

I collapsed against his broad, manly chest as we both erratically heaved for breath, and he threw his head back against the pillows as we both let out a triumphant laugh.

We will be doing this again.

SAUCY SAFARI

F, 23, UK

In my fantasy, I was on a jungle safari with a couple of girlfriends. It was stiflingly hot and felt like sitting in a steamy sauna. Sweat trickled down our faces and necks, then pooled between our breasts. We were all wearing trousers, jungle socks and work boots provided by the tour company. Baggy T-shirts shrouded our drenched bodies, protecting us from life that thrives in the jungle and would latch and happily dine on us as a tasty treat if given the opportunity.

Glorious, vivid, green foliage and trees in every direction disorientating the less experienced of us, and tropical birds echoed above and around us and screeches and howls of primates permeated the vast jungle, alive with the smell of damp leaf litter, moss and foliage that crackled underfoot as we made our way along the trail.

Feeling something in my sock as we meandered through the trees, I sat on a tree stump to take my boot and sock off, insisting to the group to go on as I would only be two minutes and right behind them. As they descended out of view, I caught a spider ascending up my trouser leg. Panicking, I ripped my trousers off as quickly as humanly possible like a creature possessed after spotting the offending beast on my leg. Freaked out, I ran in sheer terror, trying to dislodge my newfound host and flinging my arms and legs around like a crazy creature. I realised it had been brushed off by the foliage as I danced like nobody was watching, in terror.

I could no longer hear the rest of the party nor have any idea which direction they went, as everything looked the same—a kaleidoscope of

vast, vibrant green leaves and trees. I stood still, trying to pick out sounds or movements over my erratic breathing. Terror flooded over me as I was hit with the reality that I was alone, in that vast jungle.

I started to cry as I tried to retrace my steps in the direction that I thought I came from, but in truth, I was totally disorientated. Hours passed as I tried but to no avail.

The birds scattered from the tree tops above me, as I heard leaf litter and twigs snapping and crunching, the sound seemed to be circling me. I was terrified, expecting a jungle cat or ape to lunge at me from the undergrowth that had camouflaged its form. Each crunch and crack seemed to be getting closer to me.

I closed my eyes as I cowered on the jungle floor, stifling my sobs. I sensed the animal inches from me; I could feel its breath on the back of my neck, inhaling my feminine scent from my loose blonde hair. I felt my hair gently being brushed aside as something nuzzled my loose locks. Still presuming it was an ape, I was too terrified to look, but at the same time, pleasantly surprised by how gentle it was being with me. It felt almost erotic and pleasurable.

Building up the courage to peek at my new friend, I gingerly opened my sky-blue eyes and found myself looking at a stunning tribal man. His deep ebony skin reflected the sunlight that permeated through the leaves that shielded us from the intense rays of the midday sun overhead.

Inspecting me closer, he looked me in the eye with wonderment, his green eyes meeting my blue eyes. He wore scars on his chiselled cheeks, bones protruding from both ears, and a tooth necklace adorned his strong neck draping to his toned chest.

I glanced, the length of his magnificent body, concealed only with a tiny animal skin loincloth, which clearly did nothing, it was blatantly obvious he liked the strange sight before him; he had the most impressive erection, escaping the minimal restraints. Displaying the most natural, primitive male behaviour, he stroked my face and neck as he sat down beside me, sniffing and caressing my hair and body. I could feel a warm glow emitting from between my legs as he gently teased the inside of my bare thigh.

All fear had drained away, replaced by a raw sexual intrigue. I instinctively removed my top, leaving my body totally at one with nature and exposed. My nipples were erect, and my pussy yearned for his primitive, wild touch.

It was like nothing I had ever experienced with another male. No shitty, tedious small talk or God-awful attempted foreplay that he had observed on a Porn site, just primal instinct—just sight, smell, taste, touch and pheromones.

His head moved towards my erect breast, taking a nipple into his mouth. He sucked on it so tenderly, while rolling my other nipple between his fingers.

I submitted to his advances and reclined back onto the jungle floor, allowing myself the privilege to be as vocal as I wished, with no care of being discovered. As I arched into his advances, he licked and sniffed his way to my exposed pussy. There, he tasted me as one would taste a fresh oyster for the first time, darting his pink eager tongue between my parted glistening lips. Liking his morsel, he engulfed my entire womanliness with his wild, uneducated lips, knowing instinctively how to eat me and bring me to that point of no return.

I wailed like a sea siren lost in ecstasy; my voice echoed through the jungle unapologetically.

Getting to his knees, he unceremoniously lifted me off the leaf litter, impaling me on his thick length of masculine beauty. With him deep within my moist, sweet tunnel, we started thrusting together. Over and over, he drove himself into my moistness, filling and stretching me to almost my limits.

An orgasm started to build up from deep within my feminine portal, radiating down my legs to my toes and up my torso, arms, to my fingertips. The hairs on my neck stood to attention as I felt a wave of dizzying euphoria engulf my whole being. He was so strong, fit and agile, and my pussy was gripping him firmly, locking on to him and not willing to release him until we both reached our peak.

Lifting me reluctantly from him, he flipped me around onto all fours and re-entered his new found mate, working himself to the hilt and drawing a gasp from my lips. I had to bite my lip from the shock of his immense tool. It felt so big and angry as it worked deep into my delicate, little, pink pussy. But soon, I became accustomed to the intensity and wild manner of the man driving it, and it felt divine, as I came on him over and over.

Perspiration covered our bodies. as we hammered like animals for hours. The light was dwindling, when he finally released his man milk deep within my hot, wet walls with a bellow. Collapsing on top of me, he tenderly nuzzled me into a hot, sweaty sleep on the jungle floor.

When I woke in the morning, he was gone…

My fantasy would end with him gone, and I would be alone in the jungle, wondering, "*Did I dream it all?*"

BANGING BOLDLY AND BEAUTIFUL ANONYMOUS SEXPERT(Original)

It was her time. She was no fucking longer waiting. She was done—*done*—following her parent's timeline, or their ways.

She wanted to go see Jonathan, and she would go see him. No explanation necessary.

"Meet me at Starbucks. I have my big ass truck today," his text had said.

"On the way, yay!" was her reply.

Meeting him, she asked, "Where are we going?"

"I don't know. I'm trying to find a good parking lot," he answered, laughing.

"Yes! Right in the shade," she agreed.

"You like this living room?" he asked.

"Ha ha! Yes, I do!"

"Let's put you in the back. I'll be your limo driver," Jonathan said, and she agreed, laughing.

They found a nice parking spot, and he started taking off her clothes right away.

"Ooh, easy access. I like it!" he said, discovering she wasn't wearing any bra.

"Aha!" she said. "You know it!"

He went for the girls excitedly.

"Oh my god!" she moaned. "Holy shit, baby! Where have you been my whole life?"

"Want to taste him?"

"Umm, yes, I do!" I replied naturally.

"Come on, taste him. Take him in your hands. Grab the balls. There you go, babe. Yes! Kiss him. You like how he tastes?"

"Oh, yes, baby. I so fucking do!" she said.

"Go deeper," he urged. "Ahuh! There you go. Like that. Yes, baby."

"Let me try to sit on you."

"Okay."

"Okay, baby, hold on. Let me get my leg over."

"Okay, nice and slow. Nice and slow," he encouraged her. "There you go. Shit! Is that your pussy or your ass babe?"

"I don't know."

"I think that's your ass, babe. Shit! Really? Oh, my fucking god! Holy shit! Oh my god, babe, you feel fucking incredible! Holy motherfucker!"

He kissed her soft, tight titties like she had never been sucked before.

"Oh my god, babe. I'm getting wet!" She excitedly took off her wet panties, and he started fingering her, getting her more and more excited and wet!

"Oh my god! Yes, keep going!"

"Keep stroking him babe. To get him hard again. Yes, like that! Yes!"

Soon, she was all fours on the floor…

"Oh, that's actually hot! Wow! Next time, remember, I want to see that dildo all the way in your ass."

"Oh, you do? I want to see that hard, hot cock that I can lick and suck and stroke to your pleasure until you moan so loud you cum all over my mouth. I will happily and excitedly lap it all up with my hot, wet mouth."

She continued, "You'd say 'Oh, shit!' as your body quietly quivers as you orgasm like a lightning bolt of erotic electricity moves through your body. Then you'd say again, 'Fuck yes, babe! Keep going! Don't fucking stop!' as your body bends back and you take your woman in her whole mouth."

"The girls look good," he said.

"Aww, thanks," she replied, thinking of his effect on her.

Every room he walked into, she entered with such excitement and electricity running through her whole body.

"Oh my god, you smell soooo good." He laughed, excitedly.

Then he would ask, "Are you a pole model?"

"I could be," I would answer, and asked, "Do I make a good role model?"

"You make a great pole model," he would say, making her blush

They would be standing outside, waiting to go inside the apartment, and as he stood pretty close to her, he would lightly touch and brush her arm quite secretly.

She liked that a *lot*. God, she wanted to kiss him so fucking bad! Even give him and get a peck on the cheek—she would take *anything*.

God, he looked so fucking good as he took care of business.

Once inside, she'd secretly imagine feeling, seeing and hearing the two of them fucking all over the place.

"Oh my god! My wild, hot, handsome hillbilly…" she would shout.

"Shut up!" he would say.

"Don't you fucking stop! Keep going!" she would scream.

"Yes! Shit, baby—"

"Let's go to Starbucks," Jonathan suddenly suggested, cutting into her imagination. "to talk about other options and listings and properties."

As they drove to the Starbucks, she quickly sent him a text, "This is our Starbucks, babe." and she smiled inside.

Sitting at the table, they both felt it deeply. They both smiled sweetly and almost secretly at each other.

She quietly sent him a text as they were driving to the next place: "I want to role play and be your… cunt cowgirl."

"You're so bad," he wrote back.

"You like it! You know you do."

SHORT HAUL FLIGHT
ANONYMOUS

The gangway smelt of hot aircraft engines as I walked towards the welcoming cabin crew. The steward was good-looking as usual, but they

were always gay, so what was the point in assessing him sexually? The stewardess looked like butter wouldn't melt in her mouth, but still, she was gorgeous, so the politics of envy kicked in. Not that I wasn't attractive; I've had my share of conquests.

Since it was only a short flight, the aircraft wasn't large, and there was only one other seat between my window seat in the right row and the aisle. It happened to be occupied by quite a good-looking man in a suit, who smiled as he stood to let me past. The inevitable invasion of personal space then occurred as I squeezed in front of him—very enjoyable!

What was it about airline seats? Every time I sit down in one wearing a skirt, it would ride up and show a lot of leg. This one was no different, and doing up my seatbelt pulled it still further. *What the hell?* Sorting it out would involve a contortion act, and besides, I was quite happy to let my fellow passenger enjoy the view.

As the crew prepared for take-off, the steward walked down the aisle, checking luggage and seats were in the correct position. He didn't just check my seatbelt as he looked down; maybe he wasn't gay after all.

I looked out the window for a minute or two as the aircraft was pushed back and started to taxi. Heathrow always fascinated me. There was always so much going on and bright shiny planes everywhere. The captain gave his usual welcome over the intercom and told us that, due to high pressure over Europe, we would be taking off in an Easterly direction and then making a left turn over London to put us on course for Belfast.

As I sat back in my seat, I caught my travelling companion, as he turned his head away. That gave me a thrill, thinking he had been having a sneaky look at my legs while I was looking out of the window.

Soon, the engines roared, and I felt the push as we accelerated and the nose lifted. A moment later, we were airborne. I always enjoyed take-off and sat straight in my seat to feel the sensation.

My companion must have misinterpreted my stillness, because he leaned across and asked, "Are you a nervous flyer?"

I smiled and replied, "No, I really enjoy take-off."

His eyebrows raised a touch. "Oh, I see." He seemed at a loss to know what to say next.

I must have smiled a little too broadly.

I turned back to the window. Hounslow was disappearing behind us, and the early morning sun was lighting up London in a way I had not seen before.

"London looks beautiful in this light," I commented and glanced at him.

He leaned across me so that he could admire the view, which was another invasion of personal space. His knee touched mine, but instead of moving away, I held still. He backed off for a moment and caught my eye for a second before resuming looking out of the window; his knee now firmly pressed against mine.

The aircraft banked to the left, and the physical contact extended well up my thigh.

"What a wonderful view," he commented, glancing down at my legs for the briefest moment.

"Mmm," was all I could say.

"I don't think I have ever enjoyed a take-off so much before."

"Nor have I." Not sure what to say next, I looked down at the newspaper open on his lap. "Anything interesting in the paper today?"

He grinned and said, "We can read it together if you like?"

I must have blushed, but still smiled back. "You wouldn't mind?"

"Not at all," he replied, spreading the broadsheet.

Wow, this was getting interesting! I thought.

Almost immediately, I felt his knee against mine again. I didn't move away, just enjoying the sensations that extended to the other parts of my body.

He shifted slightly in his seat, and a few moments later, I felt his hand on my thigh. Eye contact was made and held as I slid down in my seat, making my thigh available for him to stroke. It felt wonderful.

"This is a new experience for me," he said quietly.

"Me too." My pulse was racing as I wondered what to do next. Was he going to pick me up and carry me to the toilet for sex like in *Emmanuelle*? I abandoned the thought as it was impossible in a short haul plane full of business people.

God, I was horny!

Could I hear his breathing? Probably not, but the look of concentration on his face was exciting. I slid my arm as discreetly as I could over the arm of the seat onto his lap. I looked across to see if anyone was watching us, but the passengers opposite us were too wrapped up in their newspapers to notice what we were up to.

We sat there gently stroking each other's thighs, pulses racing, for a couple of minutes. I recline the seat and laid back. In this position, his hand could reach my crotch. I silently cursed the company rule that obliged me to wear tights as he got me more and more excited. I moved my hand higher up his thigh until I could stroke his now rock-hard cock through his trousers.

I wish I could continue this story with us having mind-blowing orgasms, but clothes got in the way, and the flight was too short.

The intercom crackled to life, announcing, "Cabin crew prepare for landing. Would passengers return their seats to upright and ensure their seatbelts are securely fastened."

With a sigh, we did as we were told and went back to being "normal" passengers as the aircraft swayed and turned its way along the final approach. The bump and rattle of landing followed, with the deafening roar of reverse thrust soon afterwards.

We gathered our belongings in a daze—both excited at what we had done and disappointed in its inconclusive nature. As we walked up the ramp, he asked, "Are you flying back today?"

"No, tomorrow," I replied.

"Would you like to have dinner with me this evening?"

"I'm a married woman… My husband might not approve." He looked crestfallen, and I added, "But he won't know, so I would love to! And afterwards, I hope we can finish what we started?"

He grinned broadly, gave me a very gentlemanly kiss on the cheek, and then we parted, both looking forward to some passionate sex that evening!

CHAPTER 4

DIFFERENT STROKES FOR DIFFERENT FOLKS.

FREAKY FRIDAYS

J, 45, UK

My fantasy had always been seduction and voyeur driven. I would love to watch my partner watch me. It would be based around a very drug-fuelled erotic world that could only be understood if you had lived and experienced it. Like anything, it was something like, "A little of what you fancy won't hurt you!" But in my case, I got greedy and went with "enough is never enough!"

It was Friday, and I was with my partner, who I absolutely adore, in a club. The music seemed hypnotic, beating through my veins as I was relishing my alcoholic buzz. I was feeling super sexy, and I knew I

looked captivatingly gorgeous as several men had already made eye contact with me and held my gaze, which made my pussy twinge, as I loved being watched with admiration from afar.

I would never cheat on Ben. He did something to me that I couldn't put into words. It was as if he was part of my soul. Speaking of Ben, my man was on the dance floor, lost in his own euphoric buzz and oblivious to the world around him.

I sat at the bar, sipping my ice-cold, creamy piña colada, when I felt a gentle but masculine hand on my bare right shoulder. Startled, I turned around. And there stood was the most attractive, chiselled Afro-Caribbean security guard, grinning at me in the most seductive way.

I must admit, he was an impressive example of a man. His crisp white shirt emphasised his amazing physique, confidently portraying such a charming, gentlemanly air. His skin glowed in the luminescence, radiating off his perfect colour.

Ben must have sensed the other man's intentions, for he scanned the room, looking for me in the sea of hot sweaty undulating bodies; his body language was confident and definitive. He spotted the stranger leaning in towards me, beckoning me closer to whisper in my ear over the seductively bewitching beat of the music. I saw Ben dicing his way through the crowd; his face was masked with the most unsettling, brooding frown—lips tightly pursed and his mastoid muscles contracting on the side of his face, which was a sure sign, all was not well.

As he reached me, he shook his head at the security guard menacingly and took me by the hand, at which point the security guard graciously stepped away, understanding a hidden message from my man's very masculine body language.

Ben told me it was time for us to go, and I understood what that implied. The excitement fluttered around my belly like a thousand tiny butterflies as we made our way to the pre-booked cab.

The journey home was a whirlwind in my intoxicated mind. Ben was caressing the length of my inner thigh, occasionally brushing against my yearning, twinging pussy. I chewed my lip to stop myself from responding as I naturally needed to; I could not wait to get home and descend to our bedroom, where our magic happens most freaky Fridays.

We bulldozed through the bedroom door, giggling in each other's arms. I went straight to the wardrobe and pulled out our sacred towels, we ceremonially used to protect our bed, and from the drawer, I took out my favourite vibrator, my pebble, a pink sparkling dildo, no larger than your average man's hardness, and a natural unctuous lube we both favour. I placed them all on the bed.

As I prepared for our night of pure indulgence, Ben was preparing his guilty pleasure and his pipe, which he would smoke whilst I indulged him.

After violently kicking off my shoes, I erratically peeled my clothes, then my bra and thong panties, totally exposing my shapely toned architecture. Climbing onto the bed and taking the lube, I coated my perfectly shaven, peachy pussy and my dildo. Laying back, propped up by feather pillows, I slid my fingers between my cleft, sweeping a finger over my electrically charged clitoris, and a divine feeling radiated from within.

Glancing up seductively, I made eye contact with Ben, who sat at the foot of the bed, drawing in huge swathes of intoxicating white smoke,

absorbing his drug-induced mental orgasm. For that split second, nothing else mattered to him; he was mentally suspended in his own euphoric world momentarily, as the drug encapsulated his whole being.

He came to his senses in his hazy, ecstatic world, watching me and stroking his more than ample tool as he crawled up the bed. Parting my luscious legs wide, he bent forward and paused for a minute, just breathing in my natural scent like he was analysing it within his nostrils and heaving it deep within his lungs; he loved me to smell natural and untainted. He feverishly took my glistening pussy with his welcoming mouth, centering his attention on my swollen love button. He expertly sucked and licked me to my first of many exquisite orgasms.

Before I could recover, he inserted two fingers deep within my warm, moist pussy walls to find my g-spot and made me climax again, even more fiercely this time. And as I squirted my warm liquid unapologetically, screaming as my ecstasy peaked and released, he started to lap and suck my button and hidden treasures, once more bringing me off by inserting two fingers in my overly sensitive puckered star.

I was one of the fortunate women who could have multiple orgasms, and the more I had, the more I wanted until I collapsed with exhaustion.

Ben went back to his pipe, and I caressed my sticky, swollen, electrified pussy with my pebble vibrator. The burning ecstasy was building again deep within the walls of my pussy, and soon, I was having another explosive pulsating orgasm.

I momentarily lost track of everything around me, and when I opened my eyes again, Ben was lubricating my dildo with the glistening

lube as he knelt between the parted gateway to my soul. I felt the cold tip of the rubber thalis invading my tooshie, enough to surprise and draw a gasp from my lips. My muscles suddenly allowed it to enter my tight, forbidden tunnel. As the length slid in, it sent a magnificent torrent of euphoria through my very being. And as he drove it home with no mercy, time and time again, I was demented with pleasure.

My entire being exploded with the most intense otherworldly accumulation of emotions and sensations all at once, as I violently released my triumphant shower of gold. My lover was awash with my fulfilment, and I was lost in another dimension, yet to return to reality.

My partner had always been a pleaser, and I was one very lucky girl. Ben was such an attentive partner and lover. His kryptonite was watching me getting lost in the orgasmic ecstasy he gave me. When I had had multiple orgasms—normally dozens, which was no exaggeration—I fell into a delirious slumber in his safe arms. He gently caressed me as he enjoyed the last atom of euphoria from his smoke—his guilty pleasure, and he was mine.

JAPANESE TABLE BANQUET

I, 35, USA

I had always loved to be the centre of attention—an exhibitionist, the wonder in the room. But I had no idea what past experiences it manifested itself from as a kid. I must be the one that everybody knew, heard, looked at and watched with curiosity. I thrived on the glory, and

it didn't matter if the situation was good or not—as long as I would be upfront and proud, I loved it.

My top go-to fantasy was very voyeuristic and self-indulgent. I wanted to be placed on a beautifully dressed table in the centre of a big room, covered in delicious sushi. This erotic Japanese practice was called *Nyotaimori*, which required my beautiful body as the platter used to display the food and dine from. I would be the tantalising treat, in front of a huge audience of men and women, watching with wonder and arousal.

Just the thought of this was very empowering, so here we go…

We were at a huge gathering for like-minded men and women at a private dwelling, well away from external prying eyes. The bash was held in the big pool and entertainment lounge of the property. As the night closed in, there was a subtle hum of music inside over the babbling chit-chat of couples and singletons meeting and greeting one another.

Outside was a totally different and wilder story. Naked and barely clad beauties drizzled the pool area, dancing, chatting and frolicking in the warm blue waters of the tropical lagoon pool. Champagne and cocktails flowed freely, handed to guests by men and women resembling bronzed Greek gods and goddesses with only tiny pinnies, collars and cuffs covering their modesty. A number of finely trained sommeliers graced the residence, offering the best wines in full attire in keeping with the profession. No expense had been spared, nor detail missed.

One guy and I were hired for the *Nantaimori* (male) and *Nyotaimori* (female) sushi display banquet. Making our way to the kitchen, where we had been instructed to attend an hour before dinner was served, we

were presented with what could only be described as steel catering trolleys. They were approximately six feet long, and lined with banana leaves.

I had long, dark, straight hair, small breasts with brown nipples, thanks to my ethnic mixture, and olive skin. For the occasion, I left my nails immaculate and natural. My male counterpart equated me with his black, lusty hair and creamy skin. He was also neatly groomed.

We both took our sacred ceremonial table, and the Head Japanese sushi chef instructed us to keep our eyes closed, until he said otherwise. I gently lowered myself onto the ice-cold steel, but the cold seeped through the banana leaves, biting into my flesh and causing a wave of goose pimples all over my body. I stifled a squeal as every nerve became accustomed to the stimuli it was forced to endure.

I heard the chefs conversing in their native tongue as they started busying themselves. The kitchen came to life with raised voices, banging and clattering of steel; you could hear the party in full swing in the distance.

I felt cold leaves gently but strategically placed on each erect breast and the preened flower between my legs. I could smell fresh sushi—soy sauce, ginger, lemons, wasabi and sesame—as they set expertly rolled sushi on each breast, cheeks and forehead. Another pair of hands busied around the sweetness between my legs, balancing a collection of divine fishy delights there, too. The hands moved to my legs, and I could feel a trail of self-indulgent, cool morsels being precisely placed in pairs along my toned legs and between shards of sticky ginger.

I could only imagine I looked like a food painting. Every now and again, a warm hand would brush across my nakedness, bringing pleasure

to my being. The experts at work were finally ready, as I felt dozens of petals of some form cascade across my face and caress my body.

Roses, I could smell roses.

A loud clap erupted, and the trolley started to roll, the hard coldness juddering through my body. Wheels rattled and squeaked as we hit the carpet through the double kitchen doors, to be greeted with an ear-piercing cheer, clapping and gasping in awe at the sight.

My chariot came to a standstill, and I heard tables being placed around my trolley and busy hands, placing what sounded like slate on wood and more delicate sounds of wood on wood, which must have been bowls of soy, ginger, and wasabi.

After more jostling, the Chef, who stood at my head, finally yelled, "Irasshaimase," which meant, "Welcome. Please come in."

The guests took their seats, and were soon happily conversing, their hands busied as I felt chopsticks brush varying parts of my body. Unexpectedly, I felt fingers invade beneath the banana leaves protecting my modesty, delving into the cleft of my secret, then carrying on as if nothing happened, eating, sipping, conversing… I was strangely aroused, my pussy twinging as random fingers graced my lips periodically or brushed my erect nipples, but I was forbidden from moving.

After about an hour, the Chef tapped me on the shoulder and whispered in my ear, I could open my eyes. As I did, I glanced around the room; the guests had gone back to the plush party and obviously a lot more intoxicated. Most were either naked or semi-naked, cavorting around the room, kissing and laughing.

I remembered my male counterpart and looked over to him. He, in turn, gave me a knowing smile as we were wheeled back to the kitchens. Jumping off his trolley, then rubbing his limbs vigorously, he walked over to me to assist me off my wilted banana leaf bed. Helping to rub me with gusto, he whispered in my ear, "You are coming?"

I followed him to the employee shower room, knowing we would not be disturbed, as all staff were all hands on deck mid-party and realising the invading fingers had the same effect on him as myself. We were both so aroused by our fishy, voyeuristic experience as we made for the shower.

Running the steaming, hot shower over the pair of us and warming our chilled bodies, we lathered each other's bodies to remove the fish residue. Nature took over as his hand delightfully slipped across my pert nipples. As I was facing the shower wall, I reached my soapy hand around behind me, grasping his hard, engorged weapon. My hand slid up and down his length until he was pumped and solid.

Flipping me around, he lifted me off my feet and impaled my creamy pussy onto him. Then he pressed me into the warm wall, my pussy fitting him like a glove as I wrapped my legs around him. Water cascaded over us as he pumped my welcoming vulva with such urgency, bringing me off with a scream of gratification I had never experienced before, knowing the ecstatic delirium he had given me was too much for him as he, too, let himself go, expelling his love lotion deep within me.

After we recovered our senses a little, we carried on bathing each other. Slipping into our party beachwear, we made our way poolside and partied with the elite—sipping champagne, laughing, cavorting…

What an experience! I never did find out my sushi friend's name—my bad—but I was now obsessed with food sex and voyeurism.

PUTTING ON A SHOW

G, 32, ESP

We were an attractive, young, Spanish couple, living a happy but simple life. I got my kinks from being watched and adored whilst I pleasured myself or made love with my partner. When we first got together, we used to leave the curtains open and lights on at night, knowing someone, would most definitely be watching, and the idea of that filled me with desire and lust.

I just loved the idea of people secretly watching me, and my partner would get so aroused, watching me perform for my audience; it sent him wild with passion. My fantasy had finally become a reality, and I would love to share it with you all.

My fantasy started when I was in my late teens to early twenties. I had been told I have an amazing body and always been very confident in my own skin. Even as a single, young woman, I was already tall, slim, and had long, black, straight hair with beautiful, flawless, olive skin. I had small pert breasts, a tiny waist and an ample peachy bottom.

It started in my bedroom at my parents' bungalow-style house while I was undressing. It was a stiflingly hot, Spanish summer evening. The sun had not long set, and I just had a small table lamp on my bedside table. As I removed my clothes, I heard a rustling outside my open

window; my room faced the street. Glancing up, a pair of stunning dark eyes stared back at me through a tiny slit in the wooden shutters.

My first reaction was alarm, which then changed to excitement, knowing someone, man or woman, was intrigued by me enough to watch me from the dimpsy darkness of the cobbled alley. Even not knowing the sex of that person, turned me on in a way I had never experienced before.

Who could it be?

I decided to play up to my hidden audience. I slowly undressed, and once naked, I felt very enthralled and decided I wanted to entertain my new anonymous admirer even more. Picking up my body lotion, I pumped a generous amount onto my palm and slowly rubbed my hands together seductively, before applying a silky layer along my arms. I then moved to my chest with a hand on each breast, massaging the oily lubricant into each firm mound and teasing my fingertips in tiny circular movements around my erect nipples. Hot desire started to build up between my legs in the innocent depths of my womanliness; I had this feeling before but not this intense. I wondered if they were the feelings I had been reading about.

After applying more lotion on my trim tum, I then lifted each leg in turn onto the edge of the bed, seducing my hidden fancy as I gently massaged the silky lotion into my exposed, youthful body.

Glancing up again, I saw the eyes still peering at me as I slipped my finger slowly into the depths hidden between my legs, gliding fingers over my ignited clitoris. Perching my bottom on the edge of the bed, I fully exposed my pussy to the darkness; all apprehension and fear had now wavered and been replaced by total elation and desire. I was so sexually turned on, and had never experienced anything like it.

I leaned back onto one elbow, throwing my head back as I let myself go. Massaging my lovely little rosebud, until she stood to full attention, dipping my fingers into my exposed pussy from time to time, to take full advantage of how wet my delectable, pink pussy was. It only added to the titillating experience and mind-blowing orgasm that was building within my moist walls, which soon reached its peak, giving me the most exhilarating thrill and conclusion to my life as it was.

Things had just gotten wilder and hotter since then, becoming more risqué as the years melted away, and my experience of life and sex had broadened.

Moving on through the years, I met the most amazing man who totally got me and actually found it so fucking hot watching me perform to an audience. Sometimes we would enjoy each other's bodies either in a club or party, with people watching us. But my personal favourite was via webcam and making videos, and then sending them to like-minded singles and couples. We had gone from my partner holding his phone recording me, to a full setup so he could join in if I choose to invite him to play.

My latest fantasy was making videos of myself toying and playing with my semi-hairy pussy and sharing them with favoured friends. It would start with me slipping my fingers between my fleshy lips, showing how wet I am. Then getting my toys out, I would tease myself slowly to build the tension. My partner would be massaging his big, hard length next to me, as I lubed and slipped a butt plug into my tight star, using my wand to bring myself off countless times. I would then permit him to taste my wetness. He would lap at my engorged pussy and clit, slipping his finger between my lips and then running his fingers up the front wet

wall of my pussy to my g-spot and bringing me off expertly whilst sucking my hard clit.

Then came my real treat. Rolling me onto my side and giving the camera full access to our unification, he would straddle one of my legs and place my other leg over his shoulder. He would hand-feed his member between my tight lips, stretching me to my maximum, as he slid into me to the hilt, causing me to moan in ecstasy. Skilfully, he would start pumping his member in and out of my elated pussy over and over, building tension between us. The pleasure would be so intense, I would want nothing but to remain suspended in that euphoric moment, for eternity. Time nor place would have no consequence, as we were both lost in another glorious world.

My greedy pussy would grasp him tightly as I felt the hot euphoric wave undulating from deep within my soul. I would come violently on his cock with him shortly to follow suit, withdrawing violently and releasing his milky life force across my stomach with a bellow.

Finally, I would look at the camera, giving my audience a fulfilled smile and then press, STOP.

PRENATAL URGES

E, 26, UK

My body was a whirlwind of hormones, emotions and alien sensations. Love, fear, hate and loathing. I felt like I was going batshit crazy if I was totally honest but reassured in the frequent explanation

from every woman I spoke to. It was totally normal for a 34-week pregnant woman, and "blooming" was what it was called. Blooming awful, was how I would describe it but oddly, even though I felt fatter than ever, I'd been so bloody horny. Every part of my body was super sensitive and felt mind-blowingly amazing; all I could think about was sex.

It was a normal day, with the usual daily ritual of tea, family time, kids' bedtime and finally trying to relax before bed, watching some god-awful film, but unable to concentrate on anything. Watching some scantily-clad Hollywood beauty in PVC saving the world just pissed me off more.

Uncomfortable and bored, I decided to have an early night and leave Billy to finish his film, instead of sighing and whittering through the tedious junk and ruining it for him, as he was clearly absorbed in it.

After freshening myself up and creaming every inch of my naked body, I climbed into bed, favouring being at one with my ample bareness. It was the better option than being restricted and trust up like a gammon joint in a nylon nightie. I was already uncomfortable enough with my darling little bundle, wriggling around inside of me.

My back was aching so I lay on my side, facing the wall, and hoping to drop off into my favoured fantasy land of sleep, even though I'd been having crazy dreams. Still lying there, trying to sleep, but it felt like I was sleeping with a lively Jack Russel dog. I just couldn't settle.

Billy came in 30 minutes later, asking, "Are you still awake, babe?"

"Yes, honey," I answered. "My back is killing me and little one is throwing shapes and bouncing off my bladder."

Unceremoniously, Billy stripped and dropped all his clothes, where he stood—standard! Climbing in behind me and spooning me, he wrapped his big, strong arms around us like a male safety blanket, protecting his girls from the dangers of the outside world. He felt so warm and safe, his chest against my back and toned belly against my aching loins, gently rubbing the glorious wonder he had created in my belly with love and pride.

Relaxing into each other, I felt his hand wander to one big, glorious milky boob, brushing across my huge, brown, erect nipple, most delicately, drawing a murmur from my lips. At the same time, I felt the oh-so-familiar throbbing, nestled between my ample butt cheeks, of his ever-hardening manhood. I could feel the static charge pulsing between my legs.

The yearning was like no craving I had ever experienced. The hot, pulsing ache radiating from my puffy pussy was so intense, pussy juice oozed between my ample cheeks, drooling at the very thought of being caressed or made gentle love too.

Billy helped me prop myself up on half a dozen feather pillows, before he gently moved between my parted thighs. Descending towards my big, milky breasts again and taking a big pert nipple into his warm, soft, welcoming mouth, he tenderly suckled on it. It brought on that heady, tingling feeling so familiar to them who had ever had sex during the last trimester of pregnancy, where you could literally feel your boobs come to life, colostrum triggered.

Finishing his light snack, Billy worked south, trailing moist kisses from each beautiful brown nipple to my beautiful baby bump, containing his ultimate life goal. He kissed her tenderly before descending to my

gorgeous, puffy prize, encasing his everything. Gently parting my engorged, moist lips, Billy gently took my sensitive clit between his lips, engulfing it and everything surrounding it, sucking and licking me to my first orgasm which triggered a Braxton Hicks contraction; it was a bittersweet moment.

Billy lay on his back, helping me straddle him in a reverse cowgirl, and squat onto his impressive appendage. His impressive arms took my full weight as I sank onto him, absorbing his entirety within my warm, wet magical box. He did the work whilst helping me balance. It felt wondrous, as the warm joy of his solidness slid into my accepting pouty vessel, and each thrust brought me nearer to another bittersweet conclusion.

We both groaned with pleasure as the climax rose to its heady peak. I came hard on him; a small, creamy dribble escaped down my thighs as another Braxton Hicks took hold, stealing my breath.

Letting the contraction subside with Billy's help, I relaxed back into my thrown pillow. Billy stealthily placed himself between my legs once more, taking care not to put any weight on me whilst he introduced his impressive meat to my gushing vessel, gently easing himself into me.

We kissed feverishly; our soft, warm, moist lips and tongues sparred in their pits. All the while, Billy was pumping in and out of my drowning pussy—sure and true, but with precision and skill. Time and time again, I could feel my pussy gripping his hard cock; each small orgasm building until my whole pelvic floor and pussy convulsed, determined to hold him fast as we both hit a fever pitch. I screamed in euphoric bliss as my bladder violently expelled its golden steaming contents, spraying him and everything around us.

Reaching the peak of a monumental contraction that actually took my breath, my stomach formed the shape of the bow of a boat, and I screamed as my breasts released a stream of sweet, life-preserving sustenance. Billy stayed inside of me until the contraction subsided, then gently withdrew, and brought his face down toward my now relaxing belly.

He tenderly addressed his baby girl, planting a doting kiss on her as she lay hugged in her mother's warm embrace.

CHAPTER 5

BE CAREFUL WHAT YOU WISH FOR!

JAIL BREAK

K, 27, POL

I adored being dominated by a strong man, and the danger aspect even made my pussy purr—this is one of my most enjoyed fantasies.

I was a very strong-willed, headstrong woman, so to be controlled and desired by a powerful male actually gave me power, knowing I could flip and manipulate the control switch at any time if I so wished. There was an art to being a woman; as with any craft, you learn it over time until you maximise your expertise. I lived in Tarnów, southeastern Poland, and from a Roman Catholic household, but even so, I do not practise any religion, which I had to be clear about because of what I wanted to share.

I was walking home from a long shift at the railway station, where I work the ticket office. It was well after 10 p.m. and almost deserted, as I wearily ambled home. Walking down a dank, dark alley beside an old, abandoned church, I decided to stop for a crafty cigarette before I took the main road, where I stood a chance of being seen by a family member or a friend.

Many moons ago, I played here as a kid, so it was a safe, familiar friend. Even though ivy grew on it now, the doors had graffiti, and windows were boarded up. I perched on the old church doorsteps as I had a thousand times as a child. It seemed a lifetime ago as I was 24 now, but still my family frowned on me smoking. This way it was less grief and peaceful. I sat in the dimpsy dark, savouring my Smoky forbidden treat, memories danced in the darkness as I allowed my mind to wander through time unchecked.

Lost in my own world, I was taken by surprise as I was physically lifted backwards, by the waist. A strong hand clasped my mouth, preventing my screams from being heard, as someone dragged me into the bowels of the dark, abandoned ruins of the once church.

Terrified, I tried to fight and scream, to no avail; my captor was just too strong. I could smell his natural, masculine scent. As he slammed me onto an old pew, I got a glimpse of him. There was something vaguely familiar about the dark figure. In his husky voice, he whispered to me not to scream and that he just wanted to feel the warmth of a woman, as it had been so long.

"I won't hurt you," he growled.

Our eyes connected in the dark, and I could see something very vulnerable about my assailant. He then threw off a huge woollen donkey

jacket, revealing his stunning toned physique as the chink of light behind him illuminated him. He was clearly a man in his prime, and still, I felt I knew him, but how?

He firmly instructed me to remove my clothes, which I did obediently, knowing I was no match for him and had nowhere to run. I thought if I gave him the attention he craved he would soon let me go. After all, I was not a virgin.

Standing before my captor, totally naked, I shivered from the cold and fear.

"You know who I am!" he whispered as he approached me again.

My brain whirled, trying to rationalise what he had just said as he pulled me into his now bare chest. Grabbing a handful of my hair, he started kissing my vulnerable neck passionately; my carotid artery violently pulsated within, as he licked and nipped. As his kiss descended to my vulnerable, exposed, erect nipple, he gently took it into his mouth, devouring it hungrily.

I could feel my pussy coming to life, which shocked me, and I tried to resist, but it was no use. He looked up at me with big piercing green eyes that seemed to catch every stray chink of borrowed light. *I knew those eyes.* They reminded me of a boyfriend I had as a teenager. My family disapproved of him and forbade me from seeing him. He left town, and we lost touch.

Placing both hands on my butt cheeks and drawing me towards him, he devoured my neatly trimmed pussy, forcing his determined tongue between my musky moist lips. Instinct took over as I opened my legs, giving him full access to the inner gates of his desires. He was lapping

me feverishly, bringing me to a resentful, heady orgasm, which I almost felt guilty for. Lowering me onto his jacket and my discarded clothes, he took up full residence between my thighs and skilfully used his fingers to find my g-spot. He then sucked my clit, until I was delirious, and I wrapped both my legs around his head, terrified he would stop. Waves of cascading ecstasy radiated through my body to another glorious conclusion, as my tight pussy gripped his fingers.

I didn't want him to stop now as I couldn't get enough of him, and he seemed to know it. As he lifted himself from between my trembling thighs and stood towering over me, he gave me a dirty, devilish smirk, light glinting off his teeth.

Dropping his jeans and kicking them to the side, he stood between my thighs with his massive meat piece pointing to the vaulted ceiling. Then he got to his knees, and effortlessly lifted me. As I entwined my legs around his torso, he sank me deeply onto his cock with no resistance, my pussy greedily sucked him to the hilt.

We feverishly fucked as lost lovers would. I could feel every ridge of him as we worked together, both gasping for breath and beads of sweat showering each other, as our desperate union peaked. Over and over again, using each other as an anchor as we rode each other to a boiling, wet, thunderous conclusion. I climaxed once more with an impressive convulsion, squirting all over his piece, and as I did, he grabbed my hair and growled my name.

As I lay on the pile of damp clothes, it suddenly became clearer why he was familiar. He was indeed my forbidden boyfriend from way back. He had broken out of jail, and instinct brought him home. Fate did the rest.

BLACK AND WHITE

R, 24, UK

It was a very normal day. It was raining outside, and I was on the sofa, trying to watch some TV, but nothing held my attention. I started to drift off into my own little fantasy world, drumming up never-ending sexual scenarios; this one was one of my favourites.

I wanted to send an email to my partner, stating in black and white as follows:

Samuel,

For one week only, I give you my FULL PERMISSION to do with me—mind, body and soul—as you please. You don't need my permission to fuck me in any way you please. You can gag, bind, slap me, and just humiliate and degrade me. Even if I cry and beg you to stop, I want you to assert your dominance and punish me harder, longer and basically brutalise me in every way possible.

Later, I was in the kitchen, tidying and washing up from dinner, as the house had fallen silent. The kids were in bed, and I was in a world of my own, getting on with my chores, so I could relax. Ben was working late at the garage, and I knew he would be in a vile mood when he got in, as he had to stay on, which he had done a lot lately.

I heard the key in the door, and instantly, my heart palpitated in anticipation of the agitated mood Ben would be in. As he walked into the kitchen, I saw a distinctive, lusty look in his eyes, but he was also scowling, which confused me.

Ben lurched at me violently and grabbed a handful of hair, making me scream so loud. But, he told me to shut my mouth, and that I was only getting what I deserved. I struggled as he was hurting me, but with the brute force of a pent-up man, he forced me face down onto the worktop, crushing my face onto the cold, hard surface whilst ripping at my leggings with his other hand.

I was starting to regret my email but it was too late; he had my full permission in black and white, and he knew it.

As I struggled, he kicked my legs apart to gain easier access to the musky softness between my legs. I braced myself for what was to come as he was amply endowed, and sex could be painful, even when he was at his most tender. I felt his engorged length nudge between my delicate petals, and once he was sure of his mark, he thrust home, making me scream out in agonising pain.

The pain slowly turned to pleasure as his warm, hard cock drove me to the hilt, and I started to relax, involuntarily letting out a stifled moan. I could feel my climax building and licked my fingers before slipping them over my now engorged clit. As our orgasm and tempo built up, his breathing deepened. He then bellowed like a rampant bull, emptying his load deep into me and collapsing on top of me.

As he steadied himself against the worktop, he ordered me to get down on my fucking knees and clean up the mess I had made. I did so gladly, licking and sucking every bit of our juices from his now flaccid length.

As I finished cleaning him up, I stood, and he kissed me on the lips.

"Sorry, love," he said.

I smiled. After all, I did give him my permission. I did not reach my heady goal, but I knew there would be other opportunities in the coming days.

Lesson of the day: be careful what you wish for!

FREYJA

V, 37, SWE

I had been watching far too many Viking series of late. I loved the whole Viking thing; it did something to me. Dear Lord, what I would do to harness that raw manliness in today's man. But they are few and far between, and my fantasy was far hotter than any life experiences I ever had to date.

But never say never. We can all dream.

In my fantasy, I was a young Viking woman with no husband. When I was a young girl, my village was attacked by a rival clan, and I was stolen away from my family. Most of the men were murdered while the women and girls were taken as slaves by my now Clan warriors in a fight for lands.

I grew up as one of the Queen's handmaidens, in the main longhouse. The longhouse was a big wooden structure built of conifers and pine, the roof was turfed, and at the centre of it was a huge fire pit, which was kept always burning. Scattered around the longhouse were wooden benches and tables, sheepskins sprawled and draped over benches and handcrafted cushions and pillows adorned the floor.

I was busying myself around the village, collecting and trading, and replenishing our vegetable stores. The men of the village were away, fighting and leading raids, so the only people left were the Queen, her house staff, mothers and children and the elders—the infirm of the village.

It was a beautiful, warm day—mid-spring, flowers bloomed, birds sang, and animals reproduced. Life was a joy once more, after a tough, desperate winter.

Back at the longhouse, I was tending my Queen in her bedchamber in preparation for supper. I was braiding fresh flowers into the long trestles of her golden hair that cascaded down her tattooed back, as she sat before me in her bodice and skirts. The Queen was a fine woman with firm breasts, a tight waist and unchallengeable natural beauty, framed with golden waves that washed over her shoulders and breasts.

As I was fixing the combs in her golden locks, we heard some commotion, shouting and screaming from every direction. Before I had the chance to react, a group of men came bursting through the chamber door, wielding swords and daggers, covered in blood.

I did not know these men as they addressed our queen; aggressively, but holding herself strong and noble, she stood to address them back. They had been instructed not to harm her, but take her alive to a rival clan's village, which was a three-day ride through the hills.

She demanded to dress for the journey, and stated they would not take her alive unless allowed to do so.

I hurried to dress my queen for her dangerous venture, with fur and skins. Her knitted upper garments over an elaborately detailed leather

bodice and a vast fur cape with a hood to protect her from the elements on the dubious journey, shrouding her entire person. Still standing proud, flanked by warriors, she was escorted from the longhouse.

I was left scared for my life, with one strong, captivating form of a warrior. He was too perfect an example of man to be the cruel, bloodlust-fuelled monster that I remembered. The one who took me as a child under his arm after cutting down my parents and siblings.

Caressing me with his eyes and a sure grin, he took a step towards me, grasping me by my arm and drawing me to him firmly. He wrapped both his arms around me, bringing me to him, breast to breast, calmly whispering in my ear he was expected to service the goods and it could be as sensual, or rough as I wished. He was giving me a choice, to comply and enjoy as a husband and wife would, or he would take me by force.

I begged him as I knew if he did as ordered, I would surely end up with a child, knowing how my feminine cycle had finished seven days and nights ago. He just grinned at me, stating he would have to take me as a wife if it did.

Terrified, I slipped my belt from my middle, slipping my tunic and bodice to the floor. I stood fully exposed and shaking with fear of my would-be attacker, but I chose to comply. I had seen what happened when you did not as a child to the other women from my former life.

Tears started trickling down my cheeks as my lip quivered, and I tried to stifle a sob. Brushing my hair away from my face as it stuck to my salty tear-stained cheeks, my assailant seemed to have become quite tender and gentle.

"You will be craving my touch by the time I finish ravishing your body," he whispered in my ear in a low, husky voice.

He stepped forward and dropped his weapons and cloak. placing both hands on my face, tenderly cupping it and kissing both tear-soaked eyes. Then his soft lips moved to mine as he teased them so lightly. This was not how I remembered it as a child; it was very brutal and bloody.

Lowering me gently onto the Queen's bed, he fully de-robbed and kicked off his fur boots. I lay staring at him in awe as I had never seen a fully naked man, so beautiful. His braided mohawk and body hair that caressed every cut of muscle, the weapon he concealed between his powerful thighs, and the tribal tattoos decorating his god-like body, gave me feelings I had never experienced before. My most feminine secret started fluttering, and my nipples hardened with pure excitement.

Noticing, he said, "Your eyes are defying your virtue, woman." Climbing on the soft, fur-covered bed next to me and resting on one elbow as if savouring the sight before him, he traced an invisible path to my erect nipple, brushing over it as a feather may.

Again, a sharp gasp escaped my lips as he leant forward and took my firm nipple into his mouth, and his natural, masculine scent filled my nostrils as I took deep breaths. He sucked and licked my nipples hungrily.

I tried to defy my body and resist, but I couldn't; I didn't want him to stop.

As he suckled one nipple, he traced an invisible, meandering path to my navel, then on to my secret flower after teasing his way through the forest of coarse hair that guarded the prize. He paused and removed his

hand. Bringing it to his mouth, he coated his fingers with spit. He slipped a finger between the secret cleft nestled at the base of that dense forest where the foot of two mountains met, gently running over the pleasure button I had not long discovered for myself, making tiny circular motions. Then, losing the full length of his fingers into the wetness, they plundered over and over again until waves of pleasure overcame my body.

As these new sensations enveloped my body, he climbed between my thighs and gently eased his lethal weapon between the petals guarding my treasure. Pinning my arms to the bed, he drove himself into me with desperate desire and vigour, causing me to scream in piercing agony, straining against his pain-causing tool.

He held me fast and drove on time and time again, until the pain dissolved to ecstatic pleasure once more. One hand had my buttock as he mounted his pace, and the other clasped around the back of my neck.

Now working with him to meet his merciless thrusts, I felt hot waves of godly pleasures flooding over me, arching my back in sheer ecstasy as we became one. With a warrior cry, he allowed his man milk to flood the permitted channel, totally unrestricted.

Collapsing on top of me, he kissed my breasts as he heaved air into his lungs. After a few moments of recovery, he exclaimed he was keeping me, just in case I bore him a male heir.

I was now his and his alone to do as he wished. I had been chosen by Freyja, the Goddess of war. I had a duty to the Gods.

CONSENSUALE NON-CONSENSUALE (CNC)

R, 46, USA

I had always been into CNC or Consensual Non-consent. It was one of my biggest fantasies. Basically, it was a rape fantasy, but as its name stated, it would be consensual. More importantly, it involved my husband, Tim.

My husband and I were at a beautiful national park, having a picnic for our anniversary. It was a scorcher of a day as the sun beat down on us. But the sky was a stunning clear blue, with the birds singing in the trees in our spot. We were at a very secluded part of the park, tucked away, a hidden gem in the madness of life. We could hear children laughing and squealing nearby, and a dog yapping periodically a good mile or so away. Everything was so still.

It was a lovely romantic setting, instigated by Tim. He prepared a picnic basket, a cute posey of daisies in a small blue vase, a good well-chilled bottle of prosecco—cool, crisp, bubbly, which was perfect for today—a couple of wine glasses, a vast array of cheeses, biscuits, grapes, tapas, fresh breads, and champagne and strawberries for after, enough to feed four people.

Everything was laid out on a huge picnic blanket under a huge weeping willow tree in its full glory, sunbeams teasing its thousands of tiny leaves that, as a collective, acted as an impermeable parasol from the sun.

We had come here a few times over the years; it was very remote, and I could almost guarantee we would not be disturbed. It was our anniversary, so who knew what could be on the cards.

We had been there for about an hour eating, laughing, and just loving and enjoying each other's company as we always had, when I saw a group of bikers approaching. As they got closer, it was plain they were planning to pull in by us, interrupting our romantic day.

We were apprehensive, to be honest, as they were all men and there were six of them. They were young, fit and their muscular bodies were covered in tattoos, which only made them look more intimidating. Their body language and bravado with each other also made it perfectly clear, they were not going to be saints and looking for trouble.

They pulled up, climbing off their machines, shouting and jostling with each other as they circled us, commenting on our picnic. Then their attention turned to me, saying how pretty I was, that I needed a good cock, and their pal was just the guy to do so.

Tim and I stood, declaring we were leaving, abandoning our picnic, literally! We walked away, but one of the guys lunged for me, grabbing me and pulling me into him violently.

Tim tried to defend me, but one of the guys punched him in the jaw; he was fighting with three of them. My husband did work out and was a strong guy, but they overpowered him. They roped him like a steer and tied him to a tree, gagging him with one of my good napkins to stifle his protest.

The men all turned their attention to me, and no matter how much I protested or struggled, I couldn't get away. I had a good idea of what was coming and started to sob with terror. They only laughed at my turmoil, pushing me around and toying with me for a reaction.

I was hissing and spitting like a wild cat, every time one came too close. One big, strong guy roughly grabbed my arm, forcing me to my

knees and holding my arms behind my back. It dawned on me what they were going to do. The first man was handsome with black hair, brown eyes and olive skin. He wore a black biker jacket over a grubby T-shirt, blue jeans and a pair of brown cowboy boots.

I looked up at him, pleading with my eyes, and he stared at me directly in the eyes as he released his huge, towering cock from his jeans. Grabbing my hair, he forced his offending weapon roughly between my tight lips and gritted teeth.

Tim was roaring with rage but stifled by his gag, unable to do a thing to save me. He was striving to free himself, but was totally helpless.

As the first guy was finishing ramming my face with his cock, the next stepped up, repeating the process while the rest squabbled for the next spot. They all fucked and gagged me with their cocks, slapping my face and relishing my reaction every time I retched as an offending cock hit the back of my throat, and laces of drool seeped from either side of my tormented mouth; tears were streaming down my cheeks.

I was struggling for breath being slapped and deemed a whore until the last one in the pecking order was done. Thankfully, he was a small man, and it was clear he didn't really want to do this but had no choice or would have suffered the wrath of the gang.

Dragging me off the floor roughly, they pushed me around again, groping at my breasts and spitting in my face. Worse, they were shouting at my husband, declaring what a whore I am and loving it, and how I am enjoying them instead of his boring, little cock and what a pussy he was. I could see the tears rolling freely from Tim's eyes and down his cheeks.

Pushing me to the ground again, the big, ugly guy pinned me by the shoulder as the handsome guy ripped my wet knickers off. In one sharp

movement, he rammed his angry cock between my pussy lips, ramming it to the hilt over and over again; it was a bittersweet moment.

Just before he was about to shoot his load, he dragged himself off me as if he wanted to wait and savour the moment.

They took in turns once more, fucking me harder and more aggressively than I had ever been fucked in my life, as they laughed and jeered each other on. They choked me and rubbed dirt on my face, throwing me around like a fuck puppet until the little one led me over to my husband and told me to kneel next to him, which I did, hoping it would soon be over.

They all stood around us, wanking and grimacing until finally, they all shot their loads over us both. Their final insult was to force me to sweep some cum off my tits and rub it in my husband's mouth, at which point he retched. Then they made me kiss him passionately, which I did gladly.

Finally, they pulled their jeans up, mounted their bikes and rode off, jeering and laughing, leaving me to untie Jim.

It didn't happen exactly how I fantasised it, but it was something.

CHAPTER 6

BITTERSWEET STING OF TOUGH LOVE

BURNING DESIRE

K, 24, UK

I was well aware of my life traumas that moulded the woman I had become. I loved fetish and had some very hot, kinky fantasies that mostly revolved around control, manipulation and degradation, and pleasure and pain.

This story was one I wished to share, and hopefully, it got you as hot as it did me telling it.

My partner, who we would call C, and I. were away on a short break at a delightful four-star hotel in the city. The hotel was upmarket and classy with a 1930s theme, striking colour combinations of golds,

oranges, blues and monochrome. The interior was designed with bold, geometric patterns, parquet flooring and various metalwork fixtures and fittings. The atmosphere was very upbeat, warm and welcoming.

We had been looking forward to this break for a long time.

After a fun-filled evening of dinner, drinks and dancing, we returned to our room. C had packed a whole travel case of sexual paraphernalia for us to fully indulge ourselves whilst away. There was 100 percent trust between us, so I always let him have free rein in the proceedings, and he never disappoints.

He instructed me to remove my dress and panties, and after, I sat on the side of the bed, tentatively waiting and tingling with arousal. C opened his case of tricks and produced a set of handcuffs. He then went to work, securing one of my wrists to the bedpost, instructing me to move back onto the bed and make myself comfy against the plush pillows.

I relaxed back with one arm cuffed above my head and the other hand free.

His eyes caressed my bronzed nakedness as he grinned at me, drawing another toy from his case. This time, it was a telescopic spreader that he secured around my ankles, forcing my legs apart with any tiny resistance, it triggered. As I stayed totally motionless, he only had a peek of my tender treat hidden between my lithe legs.

Next, he pulled out a ball gag, and making his way around the bed, he gently placed the ball between my partially open lips, securing the strap over my ponytail with a buckle. It would obscure any sound I make to a dull grumble so it would not permeate the surrounding walls for unpermitted ears to hear, ensuring us total privacy.

He placed two candles on either side of the bed, and the room had a very flattering ambient glow. My partner was a picture of god-like masculine beauty in the candlelight. My pussy throbbed in anticipation of what was to come; I could feel how wet I was as I moved my thighs together. But in turn, the telescopic rod forced my legs open a fraction more, exposing the glint of moisture between my pussy lips.

He positioned himself between my parted legs and gently teased my pink bud with the moist pad of his thumb, drawing a stifled moan from my limited lips. Again, my legs involuntarily opened another few inches as my body undulated in response to his touch. Seeing this, he carried on manipulating my pink exposed bud, peeping from beyond the pink shroud as my body responded eagerly.

C then turned his attention to my brown, erect nipples. He firmly tweaked both quite hard, causing me to scream and fight to escape the searing pain from the ankle cuffs biting into my flesh as it forced my legs further apart.

Firmly gripping my throat, he leant forward and said, "Dirty whore! Squeal and writhe for me. I want to see your pussy in her full unprotected glory!"

I gasped for air as he bit my pussy lip hard, drawing another muted scream from and drool escaping from the corners of my lips.

Leaning over me, he picked up one of the candles and trickled molten wax across my comely, buxom breasts from nipple to nipple. It stung with such intensity I felt a tear trickled down my cheek. I was now totally exposed and helpless to his twisted desires.

Sensing I was slightly anxious, he moved his attention back to my pussy as a way of reward. He expertly flicked and toyed with my gapping

pink prize until I was at the point of orgasm before going back to his candlework, dripping his hot lava on the length of my quivering body.

My legs were barred open to the maximum, and he was giving me a knowing glance with his lust-filled eyes. It filled me with excitement, fear and apprehension. He poured searing wax all over my exposed pussy and star, making me scream in bittersweet agony. Then waiting a few seconds, he massaged the molten exude into my overstimulated, electrically charged pussy.

As the sex wax dissolved into a warm, gooey lubricant, he positioned himself between my legs. He suddenly drove his merciless weapon into me to the hilt, thrusting over and over again. He would slap my face if I dared make a sound, whispering obscenities into my ear as he grasped my restricted throat.

Abruptly pulling out of my tight embrace, he used his brute strength to flip me over into the doggy position. I held myself firmly with my free arm as he slapped my bare stinging ass and drove into me once more. As he worked into me, he spit on my exposed asshole and slipped two fingers into my puckered secret place, drawing another agonising squeal from my smothered lips.

Driving his manhood so deep, I could feel him buffeting my cervix. He was like a man possessed, filling my tender pussy to her physical limits.

Using my free hand, I started delicately massaging my super charged clit as the intense feelings started to blend into a very fierce orgasm, manifesting deep within the walls of my quim. As it peaked, I felt every nerve explode as my pussy released her hot nectar with a

violent cascade, gripping her amorous guest firmly, reluctant to release him.

Roughly grabbing a handful of my hair and wrenching it from its ponytail restraints, he forced my head back violently, causing me to scream. He came with gusto, letting out a low, guttural growl of satisfaction as I felt his entire being convulse with orgasmic pleasure. He collapsed on top of me, knocking the wind out of me.

We lay for what seemed like an eternity, coated in cool sweat and calming the fire in our lungs.

MUMMY ISSUES

S, 28, UK

I had always had a dominant, sadistic, dark personality. I used to feel shame about it, but as I got older, I fully embraced it and found it a place in my life. I loved to express it in the bedroom, or wherever the heck it took my fancy, within reason, of course!

I had to admit I got bored easily with men, so I didn't keep them around long. Men served a purpose to me—sex and gratification only. Some would say I'm a slag, but I'd say I re-con my men, and when they reached their full potential and knew their place, I moved them into a new home with that little bit more knowledge of themselves and the world.

Oh, and what women wanted and needed started with mental de-masculinization.

My current boyfriend was a "car guy" and part of the racing and drifting world, cocksure and full of bravado. We were at a car meet, and my man was all pumped around his friends. I could sense he was desperately and quite pathetically showing off for his fellow boys and the young lovelies that follow them around. He was trying to be seen and fit in, but his arrogance and disrespect were grating on my very soul.

He needed to be put in his place.

We got in a pristine BMW E30, where all you can smell was leather, polish and one of those very potent, very masculine dangling air fresheners, which smelled like your nan's outhouse toilet that burned the lining from your nose. On our route home, I gave my partner a sharp, disapproving, flitting glance.

He was beginning to understand there was a certain behaviour I did not accept. He knew the repercussions and what was expected of him in penance to be paid in due. Not a word was uttered nor needed as we travelled back home; we pulled in the driveway in silence.

Making straight for the bedroom, I asked him if he had emptied himself today.

"Yes Mistress," he replied submissively.

I instructed him to strip and go freshen up, and whilst he was busying himself in the bathroom with his allotted chores, I was getting into my sexy PVC bra and high-waisted pants. I completed my attire with my strap-on belt, latex stockings and my favourite red 6-inch high-heeled stilettos. I had a huge selection of toys of which I could amuse myself for hours.

As he entered the room, he climbed onto the bed and assumed the doggy position. I stroked him gently along the entirety of his naked, muscular back. I ran my hand from the nape of his neck to the crack of his beautiful ass, and he let out a subtle purr of appreciation. I was considering roping his hands behind his back but decided it was more of a kink to have him stay, of his own free will and endure his punishment. I opened the drawer to select my toy of choice; I was torn between my big, red Jel-oh with ribs and girth and beaded prober, which is kinder.

I chose the Big Red due to the total disregard he showed me in front of his friends; he needed to be punished. Attaching Big Red, I started by massaging lube onto the length of his lovely, girthy cock, telling him his punishment would be kinder on him if he relaxes and accepts it, gracefully.

As I was getting him worked up, I slipped a finger into his asshole, making him moan. I applied a bit of pressure to his love gland just inside his asshole, and he grunted. Which I decided was enough pleasure for him.

I lubed Big Red, stroking the impressive column of rubber, and nestled it against his now slightly relaxing anus. Without warning, I thrust it home, sure and true, making him scream in pain. I could feel my pussy creaming as I thrust Big Red into him again and again.

He screamed, begging me to stop, but I was just warming up my boy. As I upped the rhythm, it got harder and faster. With each thrust, he would scream and beg me to stop but stayed submissive; he didn't move even though every nerve in his body was screaming for me to stop.

I was pumping into his ass feverishly now, until he screamed, "Mummy, help me! Please Mummy!" which is what I wanted to achieve.

My desire was to send him home to his Mummy, with Mummy issues and total confusion about why he called for his Mummy, whilst engaging in such a lurid act.

CASTLE OF COMFORTS

G, 30, UK

The night sky was dark and ominous. With not so much as a chink of moonlight glistening through the almost biblical, black blanket stealing every trace of natural light, it was as if it was angry. Thunder rumbled and growled in the far distance, as the storm prepared to unleash its wrath. The trees violently tossed around, dispersing their valuable leaves and blossoms recklessly with no conscience. Deep within the majestic castle walls, I resided for the night, away from prying eyes.

The bedchamber walls held a thousand secrets within its solid granite solander. A huge mahogany four-poster bed dominated the warmly illuminated room. The canopy and curtains were deep rouge and black with matching throws, bolsters and pillows. A glorious fire roared in the grate of the inglenook fireplace, helping to illuminate the room with two deep piles of scatter cushions on either side of the hearth. Lastly, the floor was scattered with superbly thick sheepskin rugs.

I stood in front of the fire, relishing the warmth being radiated onto my semi-naked skin, dressed in a tiny little black fishnet bodysuit, thong-backed, and with only just enough material to conceal my pink

vulnerable pussy. Black tape crisscrossed my nipples, and around my neck was a black leather collar.

He stood in front of me, the vision of his oiled, tattooed chest, arousing my every nerve ending and desire igniting my pussy. He forced me onto my knees to clip a chain onto the collar. As he did, he leant forward, pushing his hungry lips against mine before sinking his teeth into my plump bottom lip, sending waves of excitement through me.

As he stood back up, grasping the cold steel chain in his right hand, he set his rock-hard cock free, which I instinctively took in my mouth. My eyes water, as he thrust his member unmercifully deep into my throat.

He began reaching his climax and pulled himself away from me, resisting the instinctive urge. He pulled the chain up sharply, forcing me to stand. Staying dominant and in control, his hands began exploring my body, sliding his fingers between my legs and finding me wet and ready. His hands gripped my ass, and he kissed me with so much fucking passion, my already wet pussy was aching for him to touch it.

One hand moved from my ass, reaching between my legs. He forced two fingers inside of me, caressing my g-spot and making my entire body pulse with pleasure. He then pushed me backwards, and I fell onto the bed, using his body as an anchor. Leaving the chain free, he held my wrists down to the bed, as he forced his big, hard cock deep inside of me.

I was completely slave to his advances.

He fucked me hard, but it wasn't enough; he didn’t want this night to end. Sliding his piece out of me, he leant over me and gently bit my bottom lip.

Then everything slowed. He gently caressed my body, far more tentatively than before, gliding his fingers over me, following my feminine silhouette. So gently it sent my senses wild. Slowly, the passion intensified.

He stood over me once more, but this time, rolling me onto my front, breasts firmly against the bed but lifting my ass enough for his cock to find its way, deep inside me again. His hands gripped my body, his fingers digging into my flesh. His breaths were heavy, and his moans were subtle as his pleasure encapsulated.

Every thrust took my breath away. My hands gripped the flowing satin, entwining my fingers. My moans lost in the moment, growing louder as I grew ever closer to the most incredible climax of my life. We came in unison, our bodies collapsing in a heap of naked ecstasy.

I came to my senses as a bolt of lightning flashed, followed by a terrifying roar of thunder.

TO LOVE A BRAT

T, KWT

I would love to be sexually dominated and ravaged by my Master (my husband R). Surrendering to his demands that others, my girlfriends, said they would most definitely disobey and challenge him. But even though we chatted openly as women, they were not part of my lifestyle and did not understand the dynamics of the lifestyle that my husband and I both adored. As an emotionally bonded couple, this kind of lifestyle worked perfectly for us.

I had to be dominated; anything less would not work for me, and would mentally and emotionally bore me. I was a powerful woman in my own right in everyday life, spending most of my workday instructing others as a superior, so when I stepped through that front door at the end of my crazy day, I wanted my man to be just that—*the man*—and took full control in every aspect of our home and love life.

I wanted to share this fantasy that had become a reality for us.

It was the weekend, and all I could think about was relaxing and having a lazy few days, expecting no visitors. You know ladies, one of those pj's and no bra and knicker weekends, just slobbing it out in front the TV, watching movies and eating absolute junk.

R came into the room naked, his masculine, toned presence striding towards me with a purpose. He instructed me to get on my knees and lick his semi-engorged anaconda to full glory. Standing inches from my face, his menacing member demanded my attention. But I really just wanted to relax and do nothing; sex was as far from my thoughts as was work.

I was just taking pleasure in just being.

Taking me by the hair close to my scalp so as not to cause pain, R pulled down my pj shorts and tore the buttons off my top, exposing me in all my feminine glory. He introduced his magnificent length into my pursed lips, forcing them apart, again instructing me to lick his glorious member as if licking an ice cream.

Begrudgingly, I tried to resist, but the strength in his toned arms and the fierce presence of his member left me no choice. But I wouldn't play with his balls and lick as instructed.

Getting impatient with my obstinacy, R forcefully introduced his engorged length deeper into my mouth, nudging my unprepared tonsils and making me gag on him violently. This was my warning to do as instructed.

Wavering, I complied with R's instruction, licking and sucking his angry beast as he demanded how fast I ran my tongue over his engorged helmet, lapping, licking and sucking as if I was greedily devouring a melting ice pop.

When R was satisfied, I was then complying fully, sucking and licking him with all my might. Pulling from my greedy grasp, R lay back on the luxurious New Zealand sheepskin rug, instructing me to straddle his perfect male physique and take him deep within the tight, moist walls of my feminine.

As I slowly lowered my pussy onto him, he allowed a groan to escape his lips. When I swallowed him within my womanly embrace, I uttered in a very low whisper, "Thank you, Master." For our rules state I must thank my Master for allowing me to impale my moist desires and absorb every last inch and sensation.

"I can't hear you! Louder, brat!" he demanded, giving my exposed derriere cheek a sharp blow, causing a scream to escape my lips.

"Thank you, Master!" I repeated with urgency.

I was instructed to ride his glorious, well-oiled pole to the rhythm of his heartbeat. I placed my right palm just under his left nipple, teasing my fingers through the glorious rug of hair, to get to his skin, and there I found his heartbeat and started to rise and fall simultaneously. as his flute played in unison with my viola, and my viola with his increasing heartbeat.

The faster his heart tempo, the faster I was permitted to rise and envelop his ample beast, but not the joy of orgasm. I was ordered I must not come until permitted by my Master. If I disobeyed, there would be consequences for my subordination.

My pouty pussy was screaming for a release, but I dare not. R's heart rate was around 100 beats a minute, and I rose and fell, impaling him deep within me with every contraction of his strong heart.

We were feverishly fucking like a pair of wild rabbits on a warm spring afternoon. There was nothing romantic about it. It was just pure carnal desire as I rode my Master harder and faster than I thought possible, desperate to let go.

My Master, still not satisfied with my efforts, unceremoniously flipped me and discarded me onto the floor beside him.

Chastising me, he said, "You are disappointing me! I must bind you and show you!"

He demanded I kneel as he pulled some ribbon from the coffee table. Then ordering me to place my hand behind my back, he firmly and painfully bound my wrists together. He pushed me forward, exposing my ass and pussy with no way of resisting. I wasn't a fan of anal, so my nerves kicked in as did a tiny bit of panic at being so exposed and vulnerable, knowing I had displeased my Master.

Prone and anxious, my Master exuded saliva onto my butt crease and his monstrous anaconda, telling me if I was a good girl, he would be gentle, but if I resisted, I would suffer his wrath.

Spitting more to lubricate his serpent, Master lined it up with my forbidden treasure. Knowing I must obey, I tried to relax and ease the

experience by pushing out with my inner muscles, opening that sacred door to ease the delivery.

Master gently eased the tip in, and I gasped and soaked up the intense sensations. He ventured further until he was deep within me, quietly allowing me to get accustomed to the intrusion. He pulled out only to go forth with more vigour, making me scream and strain against my restraints, ribbons cutting into my delicate flesh.

As the allegro tempo increased, so did the rising pleasure, to my surprise. I could feel every internal muscle screaming as the swells of tempo undulated through the nerves in my being.

A hard slap landed to my derriere, signalling I could orgasm. As we both released our souls to the cosmos, we lost ourselves for that short period of eternity.

That was my first introduction to being creampied, and it most certainly would not be my last; I aimed to disobey more often, as it was so worth it.

Master, even forgot I never thanked him; he was so self-absorbed in the glory of his serpent spitting its venom.

Shhh!

CHAPTER 7

TAKE A WALK ON THE WILD SIDE

HOGTIED

C, 22, UK

From the dawn of my sexual awakening, it became clear to me that what was termed as normal sex didn't really appeal to me. I found it quite tedious and more of a chore.

As I got older and more confident with my desires, I made it perfectly clear to my partner of six years what really turned me on. It was not for the faint-hearted and would send most women running for the hills. I loved being bound, ball-gagged and whipped, enjoying the euphoria intense pain gave me, to the degree that couldn't be too much punishment.

My fantasy would start with my partner and me in our bedroom. The room was warm, comfortable and private, with the blackout blinds down

and the door locked from inside; there was no chance of being disturbed. To have such a sexual experience safely, you must have total trust in your partner and have a safe word that would be adhered to for emergencies; mine was "Pineapple," but I had yet to use it.

Totally naked, I stood before my partner, Malcolm, watching him intently whilst he towelled his steaming body dry from our hot cascading, sensual shower. We just took together, as we always did as part of our bonding process before the degradation.

Malcolm ordered me to lie on the bed, face down, as he struggled to pull the pandora's box of sexually orientated bric-a-brac out from under our divan bed, where we stored it away from prying eyes in an old leather suitcase.

As I lay on my belly obediently, I heard him open the suitcase, and the clanking sound of the steel chain followed. Drawing my hands behind my back in a police officer fashion, I braced myself for the cutting ice-cold steel, that would take my breath away once it touched my skin.

Malcom wrapped the chain securely around both of my wrists and padlocked them; the cold steel links pinched my skin, making me wince every time I made even the subtlest of movements. He then pushed both of my legs up behind me, securing one leg to each wrist and exposing my vulnerable, freshly shaven, pink pussy; I was hogtied like a suckling pig ready for the spit.

From behind, Malcolm ordered me to open my mouth and slipped a ball gag between my luscious lips. He then secured the buckle at the back of my head, so tightly that warm laces of drool hung like glistening crystal stalactites, almost beautiful, representing my vulnerability.

Descending into the case again, he pulled out a short, broad paddle whip. It looked like the type you see Jockeys use on their steeds to wake them up, but caused no pain, serving as a reminder of who was riding, so to speak.

With a sharp flick, my sleeping clit stood to attention. Malcolm then gently caressed her as a reward for being a good girl, and 15 minutes of delirious déjà vu followed until my clitoris almost resembled a tiny thallus, pink and erect, standing to attention for her master, as golden nectar seeped between my glistening lips.

Bracing a handful of my beautiful hair, I let out a stifled scream as Malcolm licked my neck and nibbled my ear. Releasing me, he stroked the indents of my rib cage, sweeping across them with such delicacy, I whimpered an approval. He sank his teeth into my succulent loin as if he was biting a ripe pear, assuring me what a good little bitch I am being.

Dropping to my engorged, meaty pussy, he engulfed her with his entire mouth, driving his tongue deep within her walls, bringing forth the most justly earned, leg-trembling orgasm; my warm, wet tunnel convulsed, and I sprayed golden nectar into his waiting mouth, which he gulped greedily.

Rising to his knees, he forced his huge colossus member between my cheeks, causing me to lurch forward with agonising delirium; his monster was unprepared with only her natural juices to ease the way. The burning pain began to subside as waves of ecstasy welled in my belly, ready to explode. His lengthy driven strokes impaled my deepest desire, which, in turn, embraced his tool with tremendous force, he also let out an animalistic, guttural cry. As we convulsed as one, he withdrew his monster and released the buckle of the ball-gag.

Crawling up the bed like a spectre in the night, he again wrenched at my head, taking a handful of my hair. He then ordered me to suck and lick every last trace of me off his cock and balls, which I did gracefully. When he was content I had done my job to the best of my ability, Malcolm got back between my thighs and started lapping every last trace of himself from my relaxed, twinkling star. He licked, rimmed, and probed my star with his powerful tongue deep within her tunnel, bringing on a thunderous finale, he had to start cleaning me up yet again. Then he gave me a sharp smack on my peachy bottom for daring to make such a mess again. If I wasn't so exhausted the cycle could go on and on.

On finishing, he released my now totally numb arms and legs, rendering me immobile. He climbed under the sumptuous fur throw that was on the chair at the end of the bed and nursed me in his arms, caressing me until the tingling subsided in my limbs, and I drifted off into a deep contented slumber.

BLOODLUST

ALI

My fantasies hinged on personal, spiritual, chemistry, connections and things of that nature. My type, along with my fantasies, involved men who were incredibly masculine. My friends branded me a lumber-sexual because big, burly, strong, bearded men were who I fawned over. Although, it was not because I wanted to be treated ultra-feminine in the bedroom setting. Sure, I'd love to feel special, sexy and pampered, but in a way, also be dominated. I loved pain because sex and love were

bland without some sprinkling of naughty spice, hair-pulling, scratching, smacking, grabbing and even cutting—all consensual, of course.

All these actions and interactions added to the spiritual bonding process of wild, animalistic sex. Let this be a warning though that my fantasy was not for everyone, and some might even find it triggering. But all of these things wrapped together, encompassing every aspect to complete the final image in my mind's eye.

One of my fantasies went like this…

I wanted my lover to take me to an environment where I can openly submit to his primal desires. We walked a good mile or so from the car we left parked in a gravel car park just off the main road. As we descended to the lower path, we entered into a woodland. With the ancient oaks towering above us, it was easy to imagine any era we could be in; it felt like I had been transported back to the 1400s.

The trees whispered in the warm breeze with birds hurrying about their business. An odd squirrel scurried up a tree, startled by us as we approached. The air smelled warm and fresh with the dank smell of leaf litter. and the pungent smell of a fox emitted from the disturbed leaves and ancient soil they masked, as we walked through.

We finally reached a small clearing. enveloped by beautiful trees, their leaves glistening in the sunshine. With no warning, my lover took me by the hair and pulled me down onto the bare, hard soil, kissing me feverishly. The shock and excitement stole my breath, and I let out a gasp as his locked lips released me.

As I collapsed back on the hard ground, my big, bearded brute mercilessly ripped at my beautiful bodice, releasing my youthful firm

breasts. Bending to take one erect, pink nipple in his mouth, he gave the other a hard nip, making me squeal as the pain, as lusty pleasure radiated through my entire being.

Flipping my skirts back over my shoulder, he descended between my beautiful, toned inner thighs. He forced my legs apart to reveal I was totally naked and at his mercy. I could feel the warm breeze caressing my pouty, swollen lips as his captivating mouth reached my most secret place. He delicately parted my softness with his tender tongue strokes and started to lap at my love button, driving me crazy with want and need.

From feverishly lapping at my now deliciously coated pussy, he took a deep lusty breath and looked up at me with his captivating stare, holding my gaze; he had the most beautiful hazel eyes, framed by the most luxurious, black lashes that any woman would die for.

His stare bored into my soul with obvious desire; the same yearning radiating from my pussy was almost unbearable to the point, the ache was almost physical.

He reached into his shirt pocket, which hung on his shoulders as there was no time to discard it, and drew out a very beautiful and ornate silver penknife. Full of want, need, fear, lust, trust and doubt with a glimmer of terror—a perfect concoction of good versus evil—he threw me an animalistic glare, like that of a dog when it had its sights set on a rabbit; nothing was going to deter him from his quarry.

Grasping the back of my neck firmly, he slit my ivory skin, just below my collar bone. The searing pain was so immense, I almost passed out.

As I was coming to my senses, I glimpsed him putting his knife in his pocket. He then leant towards my vulnerable, heaving chest; my life force was trickling between my cleavage. My lover started lapping at me feverishly, sucking and licking the ribbons of blood dripping into the clef, between my beautiful breasts.

An immense pleasure started welling up in my loins, deep within the warm, wet chamber of my pussy as I dug my nails into the muscular, tanned flesh of his back. He fought to discard his trousers, exposing his well-defined thighs, aggressively forcing home his magnificent, warm throbbing appendage, deep within my captivating sweet wetness.

An utterly divine sensation rippled through me as he entered me. I could feel my intoxicating orgasm, manifesting within. I had no control of my mind, body nor soul. My legs shook as waves of ecstasy undulated over my entire being.

With the tempo rising, we both threw ourselves passionately together for the ultimate carnal union, the reward with us both embracing the other in a wild, feverish finale. He thrust into my loving embrace, and my wetness tightly and involuntary embraced his manhood, as we both responded, hearing an invisible drum beat. The rhythm built up, until we reached our orgasmic heights, there was no coming back from, and he released his life sustaining nectar into me. As he did, he let out an animalistic, otherworldly bellow, like that of a wounded animal, which echoed through the forest, sending the birds to flight and animals scurrying for cover.

Our bodies collapsed together, profusely sweating and panting in a delirious pile of wanton flesh on the ground. My lover swiped my blood from his mouth with the back of his big strong hand, before leaning in

once more, to kiss my lips. I could taste an oddly familiar, metallic hint in his mouth. I licked my lips, as we both rolled onto our backs on the cool soil, absorbing the most exquisite sensations we were both left with, from our primal, almost sadistic encounter.

I didn't mean this to be ritualistic nor harmful to anyone but myself. I was not sure why I fantasise about my lover cutting me and lapping my blood with his tongue in a vampish way, but boy, it got me every time.

BABY BULL

V, 22, CHE

I had been clucking like a broody hen lately. My maternal clock was going mad, and I was craving to have a baby. A lot of my friends had had babies of late, and I just felt now was the right time for us, too.

My partner, S, was very keen on us getting pregnant. When we started dating, I was not on the pill, which led us to situations where I would always make him pull out to come. This led to some frustrations on his end, as masturbating was the only way I would allow him to ejaculate. And yet somehow, I started getting turned on by the power and control this gave me over him. S had older children, almost my age from his previous relationship.

With his ex, S had offered her as a "Hot Wife" to other guys. She enjoyed getting fucked by other men, often "BBC," but from what I understood, this was not at all a Cuckold relationship where she had the upper hand in the bedroom. Instead, she was the sub, or "Slut" as he called her, acting out being a slut in front of him. He confessed he had

always been completely comfortable with his ex having sex with younger, fitter, more muscular guys.

I thought I could combine his interest in watching his partner having sex with other men, with my interest as a Dominant. But for this, I had to find an element that would make him jealous.

I was 5’5” and petite. I had brunette hair, small but perky breasts, and an amazing derriere. With me being 22 years old, S was 20 years older. He was tall and slim, and what people described as a silver fox. He was a very attractive older man with the most amazing physique, endless stamina, charm, a playful brain and a very dirty mind, with an uncanny skill of reading women’s desires.

If I was going to make him jealous, I would have to play differently.

Firstly, I would decide when I would have sex with other guys, then select and invite them, making it much more of a cuckolding situation.

The first guys to have sex with me were wearing condoms. S would encourage me to seduce and undress for the guys: I personally tended to dress to provoke. I preferred leather and PVC such as knee-high PVC boots and leather miniskirts. It would be a kind of fuck-me look to accentuate and unmask as opposed to wearing next to nothing, choosing to tease and tantalise as I removed items of clothes, as if unwrapping a magical gift.

As the game went on, I would like to take control and make S sit patiently, watch and listen. I would have him tied and on occasion, my bull and I would make him watch restrained to a chair. I would love to expose his cock to see if he was getting hard as I was being passionately

taken by my bull; there would be sessions where I put his cock in a cage to stop him getting an erection whilst watching us.

S was 100 percent straight, but I was set to push his boundaries, making him clean the bull's cock after having sex with me. Later, I would demand he makes the bull hard, wearing a collar and leash, licking and sucking the bull hard and introducing my bull's cock to my pussy and moving to my engorged clit and sucking her.

The play always happened at our place, where I was most comfortable and safe. Not only that it added kink and spice fucking in the conjugal bed, but sometimes, I only allowed S to listen to me having sex in our bed.

My girlfriends were all mothers now, and I wanted to get pregnant, too. So far, I hadn't allowed S to come inside of me, even after 18 months of being together. He already had kids, so this was where I decided I wanted to show him I was the one dominating. I wanted to take it a step further and make him watch another man fuck me and cum inside of me, completing the concept of cuckolding him, and showing him the other guy is allowed to do something he was not permitted to do. Making him suck before and clean after, made my fantasy even better.

S simply had to watch me getting fucked and sexually ravaged by other big, strong lads or "bulls," whether he was into it or not.

Arrangements had been made, but I kept S in the dark about it. I had to be ready around 6 p.m. as the Bull was due to arrive at 7pm. I had a glorious bubble bath and shaved my legs and pussy as for me that was just manners—you wouldn't dine from a dirty plate now, would you?

A couple bottles of bubbly on ice, of course, three flutes, and a huge bowl of red succulent strawberries. When 7 p.m. arrived, as did the tap

on the door. Opening it, I was greeted by a gorgeous, Italian man with green eyes and rose-pink lips, framing his perfect, white teeth.

"Hey, I'm Joel from the ad. You are expecting me," he said, licking his lips as he grinned.

"Hi, there. Lovely to meet you. Do come in," I responded and gestured to the bedroom. "My partner is just through there, if you care to go in."

I watched our handsome guest, as he walked past me. He wore fitted trousers, tan pointed loafers and a casual T-shirt under a suit jacket. He looked clean shaven and wore Aventus, which is one of my favourite men's fragrances that I bought for S last Christmas.

On entering the room, I was amazed how well the two men were getting along. I turned to S, ordering him to sit as I removed my red PVC dress. Underneath, I was wearing a black suspender and crotchless pants and black stockings with black PVC high-heeled fuck-me boots, which accentuated my toned legs and pert bum. My hair was loose, as I knew S liked it up.

I approached S, taking him by surprise when I grabbed him by the hair, giving him a sadistic smile as I strutted to the bed.

"I want a child, so we are going to get one on my terms," I said to him.

I gestured to his new friend, who was obviously aware of his job because he was already half-naked with only his trousers hugging his finely tuned legs and arse, unzipping as he strode over.

I lay on my back across the bed, knowing I was going to be deepthroated by a very enthusiastic man.

S was clearly immersed in desire, lust and frustration with slight disdain as it should be him impregnating his bitch. He was giving me what I wanted and knew he had no choice but to pander. Still, there was a hint of resentment in his actions and expression, I could feel it.

Oh, I could feel it, but it gave me power!

I whispered to the bull to present his flaccid cock to S to suck to magnificence before presenting it to me, which he willingly did so to S's initial discomfort as he was a straight man.

I positioned my head back over the edge of the bed as my new friend stood above me. What a sight I had as his big, meaty weapon got released from its restraints and hit me in the mouth with some force. I started to greedily suck him until his manliness soon stood even prouder and more menacing as he introduced it to my restricted throat with a low growl.

S knew his place and sat back obediently. Deepthroat was one of my favourite sexploits, and knowing how big this bull really was, I gagged as it found its happy place with each thrust. The fullness was so intense I tried to scream out, but could not due to my fleshy gag.

Both men were lost in their own sexual motives; one not giving me a thought but fulfilling his primal needs, and the other could do nothing but think of me with another man's sweet treat buried deep to the root.

As I gagged stomach juices over my new friend's meaty weapon with each thrust, it encouraged him as he gripped one of my tits firmly as an anchor point. Tears streamed down my face, as I wretched and gasped for stolen air when possible.

S was not permitted to show any emotion, allowing himself to just be. After all, bittersweet was always the best.

Bull picked me up so I was straddling him. Usually, my bull conquests would wear a condom, but on this occasion. I wanted maximum impact, so bareback it was, and how divine it felt. Wrapping my thighs tightly around his solid toned torso and sliding his mammoth weapon between my untainted pussy lips, I absorbed him into me, letting gravity do its magic. He felt so good as I slowly became impaled on him.

Using his brute strength, he effortlessly lifted me to meet his thrusts, and I was in heaven. My pussy gripped him so tightly as if she was holding on for life, terrified of losing him at that moment in time. That was our bonding moment, just he and I staring into each other's eyes, as we got lost in our feelings and time.

Stepping back, he lowered himself onto the bed with me firmly seated on his cock. I felt so complete, as he pounded me ferociously. After a few minutes of getting used to the intense sensations, it started to feel glorious, bringing me orgasm after orgasm, each one building to a new higher level of gratification. Wave after wave of pleasure overrode my every sense, peaking in a screaming glory of juice as I squirted all over my bull's cock as he still battered my pussy.

Riding on once more and savouring the delicious waves of gratification, my bull and I kept thrusting together, for that one life-changing, ultimate conclusion, which I so deserved, but not been permitted as I usually insisted on condoms.

The orgasm was like none I had ever experienced. My pussy knew exactly what was needed of her, as I relished the sensations of every last thrust, until my bull released his man milk deep within my convulsing, warm, wet walls.

S's facial expression told a thousand tales, and I loved it. I instructed my bull to release and allowed S to impale my prone pussy, giving him the opportunity to feel what my bull had felt impregnating me, but still not allowing him to cum inside of me. He knew the rules.

Before I allowed S to relax, he was ordered to clean my bull baby daddy's cock clean with his tongue, and only then could he join us to relax .

Minutes later, I lay cradled by both men, as we let Mother Nature do her thing, drifting off into a content slumber surrounded by my protective man flesh.

And yes, it worked.

INCUBÓ

J, 42, UK

I had long had an interest in otherworldly things, and it manifested in my fantasy over the years and developed into my kink. My fantasy was based around a very ancient demon, Incubus. He was not a malevolent entity at all as folklore seemed to imply, but he drew his energy from the unrequited love the female devotees developed for him, that no previous nor future lover in the woman's life would ever compare. So, from then on, her life purpose hung on her next illicit encounter with the demon.

The demon seducer took the form of a stunningly beautiful man, smart, handsome, alluring and charismatic. It was believed he emitted a

tantalising odour the woman wanted, needed and craved to the point of obsession. His sole goal was to ravish his prey, and feed off her feminine sexual energy.

My fantasy would start with me lounging in an indulgent bubble bath, the bubbles teasing my skin as the warm water washed over me in tiny waves, as I made the smallest of movements. Scented candles illuminated the hot, steamy bathroom, casting enchanting shadows that were dancing up the walls.

I lay back and let my body totally relax in the silence of the room, dissolving away the day's grind.

Soon, a good 40 minutes had passed as I lost track of time. It was getting late, so I begrudgingly roused myself from the tantalising water and patted my steaming body dry with the gorgeous, toasty warm, Egyptian cotton towel draped on the heated towel rail. Then, I opened the cut glass trinket bowl, where I kept my talc and puff, and liberally dusted my body to absorb any moisture left, before I retired to my bed, which at this point was extremely inviting. My bed was my go-to emotional security blanket, that I absolutely loved and needed in this crazy world.

There was nothing quite like climbing into a freshly laundered bed at the end of a crazy day, after a bath; it was like pressing the reset button on life. I was so relaxed and cosy I could barely find the energy to press the touch lamp, which was only inches from my hand, but forced myself . I drifted into that in-between world where you were just drifting off but still semi-aware of what was going on around you, and the small creeks of the now settling building, as it relaxed for the night once more.

Feeling someone caressing my hair very gently and stirring me from my deep slumber on my stomach, I started to wake. I could hear breathing in my ear. I could sense the presence was male. There was an intoxicating odour I could smell, as I drew air silently into my nose. The only way I could describe it was when you were with someone you really loved and physically attracted to, and you just adored their natural odour, it did something to you—pheromones, I guess.

I was fully conscious; I had no partner nor pets in my apartment, so I was a little baffled, but oddly, not fearful whatsoever. I could feel the warm breath on my cheek, as he drew in my scent and delicately kissed my face and neck, gently nibbling just below my ear.

Then, I felt him leaning over my naked body ever so gently, tracing his hands across my loins to my buttocks. I had to confess, I could feel the sexual excitement building, as I felt my pussy start to radiate that unmistakable warm desire from within. I couldn't stifle the small purr that escaped from my lips.

I had to look; I needed to know who he was. I slowly turned my face, until I found myself locked eyes with the most enchantingly handsome man. He had blonde hair, a little facial hair and piercing, crystal blue eyes. The moonbeams just emphasised his impressively carved physique.

He gave me a lustily grin, and my heart melted and just wanted him. *I must have him!* I turned over, and he started to kiss my lips with ravenous urgency, tracing his tongue over my teeth and lips. Then, he proceeded licking and kissing down my neck to my breasts, which he took one in each hand, tracing his lips and tongue from one to the other, suckling on them greedily.

Moving down my body effortlessly, he licked my navel while still using his hand to play with my erect nipples. His hands caressed the length of my entire body and put one on the inside of each of my thighs and gently teased them open, giving him full access to my most private, but divine secret that all women possessed.

Descending between my thighs, he skilfully ran his erect tongue between my moist lips and found his goal. He kept lapping and sucking me to my ultimate reward. As my whole body convulsed with pleasure, he lifted his magnificent being from between my legs until we were nose to nose. Breathing deeply, he pressed his soft, determined lips to mine, kissing me passionately as he drove his huge column into the sweet depth of my entire being, making me arch my back to welcome him.

His stamina unfettered as he drove into me, over and over. Unrestrained rivers of nectar wept from within me as I orgasmed to a higher plane. As we fulfilled our carnal needs in unison, my mind was whirling as I absorbed all the sexual energy…

I woke in the early hours to the birds singing their dawn chorus; bewildered, exhausted and craving my new lover. But where did he come from? Would I see him again? I could still smell him on my body. I needed him.

DEEP-ROOTED

S, 32, UK

I had always had a domination fantasy going on, well veiled from the world. I had no idea where it stemmed from, but all I did know is it was deep-rooted and had been with me since I discovered men and sex.

My partner Simon was such a big, strong, rugged specimen of a man, and was everything a woman could wish for in a mate. But my fantasy involved being in total control of him and for him to experience being weak and vulnerable. I would love to watch him grovelling and pleading. I wanted to unapologetically watch the urgent expression on his face, when he realised he was not in control and at my total mercy.

It was like taming a wild beast, knowing at any time, if I pushed him too much, he could combust with fear, rage or wild Neolithic, uneducated lust and overpower me without a thought and take me with all that primal lust pent-up in his loins.

Simon and I had a very important business dinner with clients. I had my full face on, and I felt fantastic and very sexy. I was wearing my gorgeous, new undies—a delicate tiny black high-waisted thong that barely shrouds the captivating mysterious, succulent clef, between my legs and a beautiful push-up bra, which made my mediocre breasts look decidedly ample and full. I had my back to John, but could feel his eyes boring into me, as I zipped up my seductively stimulating over-the-knee heeled boots. Running my hand up the inside of my stockinged thigh to just below my groin.

I glanced up at him, knowing full well he had been staring at me. Looking him in the eye, I saw a look only true lovers could identify. I felt a deep yearning twinge in my most secret place, a hot tingling desire that took my breath away.

The man looked so powerful, dominant and determined with his brooding, lusty stare and broad, hairy chest with beautifully carved toned arms; his hands entwined in the satin sheet on either side of him, trying to mentally restrain himself.

I had other ideas; Simon needed to earn the right to fuck me. I took my opportunity to straddle him, kissing him passionately and feverishly. I slipped my hand down next to him, I grasped his tie, then commanded him to put his hands together, tying them firmly and instructing him to hold the bedpost, as I secured him firmly to it.

I stood and demanded he lie on his belly, which he did very gingerly, so as not to hurt his swollen manhood. I gave him a devilish stare and saw the alarm building in him, not knowing what was about to happen but was aware it was out of his general comfort zone as a hot-blooded man.

Opening the draws at the end of our bed, I took out a pair of gloves I used for tanning my body and brought out our chosen lube—coconut oil, as it was edible, and felt and smelled divine. I profusely oiled my hands and started rubbing the glistening oil all over his length of hot, pulsating flesh, lulling him into a false sense of security.

I positioned myself behind him and told him in a low, husky voice, I loved him and wouldn't hurt him.

I liberally oiled his tightly puckered hole and with gentle, trickling movements ran my fingers over it, to his soft, warm sack and gently back again, as he started to relax. I slipped a finger into his clenched arsehole, which his tight sphincter very gladly accepted; I was stroking his member with my left hand and yes, I was right-handed.

I introduced a second finger, working it tenderly, relaxing his sphincter, for what was about to come. Feeling the texture of the front wall of his rectum, I could feel his walnut-sized prostate and as I put a little pressure on it, with the two fingers inside of him, he let out a low growl.

He was loving it; his body was defying his head and his arsehole was gladly welcoming my fingers, so I reached down with my left hand and scooped up another glistening glob, and massaged it around his now relaxing hole. His anus engulfed my fingers willingly.

Rhythmically, I massaged his pleasure gland, and his hole was slowly inviting me in. Suddenly, pleasure turned to pain; his asshole completely absorbed my hand, as his sphincter gave in, allowing me in.

After the initial start, I let him settle into the new full feeling. When he did, I started slowly working my hand around, paying attention to his gland. As I built up a steady circular rhythm, Simon was getting to the point of no return and making very primitive, low, groans like a wild silverback. And with a monstrous roar, he had a monumental bawling climax, jacking his milk everywhere. I could feel his sphincter contracting around my wrist, as he collapsed forward on the bed, moaning and uncontrollably quivering.

I gently extracted my hand from him and kissed him on the back of the head. Peeling my gloves off, I excused myself to the bathroom, to wash my hands and freshen up and perfect my makeup, once again.

As I walked back into the room, Simon had this rosy glow of joyous bewilderment, on his precious face. I released him from his bounds as the tie was cutting into his flesh; he vigorously rubbed his raw wrists back to life.

Now, I was ready for my night out, and Simon knew his place.

HIS GUILTY CONFESSIONS

(A taster from a man's point of view)

MY FANTASY: FORBIDDEN FRUIT (A TRUE STORY)

J, 35, UK

It all started when I was around 18, 19 years old. I worked with an older woman who seemed a lifetime older than me, even though she was a mere 29 years old. And I had to add—married.

What started off as cheeky workplace banter soon grew to blatant flirting and risqué behaviour. She was clearly very unhappy with her husband and moaned about their stale marriage and about him constantly, how she was so unsatisfied. She was thinking of leaving him, which had crossed her mind numerous times over the 10 years they had been married.

I thought nothing of it and just told her politely if she needed to talk about anything, she could talk to me. We exchanged numbers, and that was it for a few weeks.

One night, out of the blue, I was at home—I still lived with my parents and was saving for my own place—sitting in the living room, as my family was busying around me doing their thing, I received a text from her.

"Hi, X!" was all the text said.

We exchanged a few texts, and she confessed her husband had fallen asleep in the chair. She was feeling really neglected and frustrated mentally and physically—he didn't satisfy her needs.

My phone pinged again with another message from her. Opening it, I was confronted with the most amazing, perfectly formed, bouncing boobs with the most astonishing pink, erect nipples—34DD, I would've guessed.

The caption said, "I wish he would play with these."

My mind went wild. Knowing someone could glimpse at my phone at any moment, I pardoned myself and headed to my bedroom. I had never for one second thought she would go this far, so it really did fill me with an element of surprise.

I replied, saying, "I would," in a cheeky, cocksure manner as most 19-year-old lads would, but truth be told, I was well and truly out of my comfort zone. I felt slightly exhilarated, but apprehensive and nervous of the new situation I was stepping into, with no prior experience.

Pulling a young bird in the club while I was out with mates, was a totally different kettle of fish than this scenario. I felt slightly *out-womanned*, so to speak, but excited, to say the least.

My courage grew the more I looked at her picture. By this time, my enormous length was growing to an extent it had never experienced before. It was a different, more intense arousal than I had previously encountered, but I liked it.

The nervous tension added to it until I started caressing my impressive column in long, firm strokes. It felt so wrong yet

so amazingly right, in a devilish kind of way. My bulbous head looked so shiny and impressive. I took a picture and sent it to her.

But to my surprise and slight disappointment and confusion, I heard nothing more from her that night. Needless to say, my next shift with her was one I would never forget. That, I was sure of.

The next day was business as usual, but I was worried I had overstepped last night by sending her a picture of my cock. I was so anxious about seeing her; my nerves welled in the pit of my stomach.

That shift, we were put in the warehouse, stocktaking together. *Great!* I thought to myself, feeling very tense, not knowing what was to come. *Here goes nothing!*

As I walked through the door, I tried to act normally. I noticed subtle changes in her right away. Her hair was done differently, and she had a full face of makeup on. She was actually a very beautiful woman and not the plain Jane I was used to seeing on a daily basis. She was glowing.

I approached her and started to make small talk. As we were alone and working, she seemed very vacant and pre-occupied, making me slightly uncomfortable. I leant back onto the cold metal warehouse wall, and she started to approach me, locking her mesmerising eyes into mine. She then pushed me back in quite a dominant, aggressive manner.

"Be quiet or this won't happen again!" She firmly instructed me.

Before I could utter a word, she dropped to her knees and undid my trouser button. She glanced up at me as she slid my zipper open, exposing my naked manliness.

Releasing my proud cock, she watched my face as she enveloped my total length into the depth of her warm, moist throat. I had never

experienced fellatio so deep, intense and expertly executed. My mind was going crazy.

She went faster and deeper, more driven to achieve her goal. She thrust deep within her, making herself gag, which only increased the sensations that were sending me wild to a euphoric height I couldn't control any longer.

Then it happened. I felt an unforgettable, orgasmic tidal wave flood through my whole being, releasing an explosive wetness deep within her throat. I let out an involuntary groan, which I had to stifle, not only to protect us both but on our mutual understanding that it was the unnegotiable rule she had set for me to claim my reward.

As she released me, she gave me a grin that Lucifer would be proud of. Getting to her feet, wiping her mouth with the back of her wedding hand, she put a finger to my lips and said, "Shhh." Nothing more.

That was the start of my infatuation with older, married women, which is all I fantasise about now. They are my thing as they were so accommodating and knowledgeable—dirty girls and forbidden fruits.

ISBN 978-1-332-15456-2
PIBN 10291987

PART 1.

THE MANUFACTURE OF SOAP.

The first part of this thesis deals with the manufacture of soaps and the production of the waste liquor from which glycerine is recovered as a by-product, and this recovery is dealt with in part 11. Before describing our experimental work upon this subject we will discuss soaps in general, their properties, both chemical and physical, their source, formation, and the machinery necessary for their manufacture.

In its strict acception, a soap is the compound of an alkali, either potassium or sodium, with the higher fatty acids, especially with oleic($C_{18}H_{34}O_2$), palmitic ($C_{15}H_{31}COOH$), and stearic ($C_{17}H_{35}COOH$) acids. However, the insoluble compound of a fatty acid with a heavy metal is also termed a soap. For example, there is the lead soap or lead plaster of the pharmavy, iron and chromium soaps used in dyeing and in the printing of textiles, alumina soap used as a thickner of lubricating oils, and many other such. Potassium or potash soaps are usually soft, and are known as soft soaps, while sodium or soda soaps are hard and come into the market under the name of compact, cut , or filled soaps.

Commonly considered, soap is, according to its quality and the use for which it is intended, a

PART I.

THE MANUFACTURE OF SOAP.

The first part of this thesis deals with the manufacture of soaps and the production of the waste liquor from which glycerine is recovered as a by-product, and this recovery is dealt with in part II. Before describing our experimental work upon this subject we will discuss soaps in general, their properties, both chemical and physical, their source, formation, and the machinery necessary for their manufacture.

In its strict acception, a soap is the compound of an alkali, either potassium or sodium, with the higher fatty acids, especially with oleic($C_{18}H_{34}O_2$), palmitic ($C_{15}H_{31}COOH$), and stearic ($C_{17}H_{35}COOH$) acids. However, the insoluble compound of a fatty acid with a heavy metal is also termed a soap. For example, there is the lead soap or lead plaster of the pharmacy, iron and chromium soaps used in dyeing and in the printing of textiles, alumina soap used as a thickener of lubricating oils, and many other such. Potassium or potash soaps are usually soft, and are known as soft soaps, while sodium or soda soaps are hard and come into the market under the name of compact, cut , or filled soaps.

Commonly considered, soap is, according to its quality and the use for which it is intended, a

mechanical mixture of the above mentioned compounds, with varying proportions of water, with soluble alkali compounds of the rosin acids, with sal soda, with sodium silicate or soluble glass, or with other inert, detersive, or odoriferous agents, incorporated for the purpose of cheapening the product, improving its appearance, increasing its detersive action, or overcoming its natural odor with an agreeable perfume. Among the adulterants benefiting or harming a soap, are, ochre, ultramarine, sodium aluminate, borax, gelatine, resin, vermillion, copper arsenite, alcohol, vaseline, tar, sugar, champhor, petroleum, phenol, naphthalene, bran, starch, etc. Therefore, commercial soap is a mixture of pure soap with a dilutent, as water, with body imparting substances, as talc, starch, or petroleum residue; or with detersive agents in aqueous solution/ as sodium carbonate, borax, or sodium silicate. These additions may all be present in a single soap but the nature and amounts of the addition present depends upon the character of the soap itself and the purpose for which it is intended.

Soaps may be divided into three general classes viz.- laundry or household soaps, generally containing an excess of alkalies in the form of either sodium carbonate or sodium silicate, or free alkali, and resin; toilet or medicated soaps, the best grades of which are free from impurities and free alkali, or contain

mechanical mixture of the above mentioned compounds, with varying proportions of water, with soluble alkali compounds of the rosin acids, with sal soda, with sodium silicate or soluble glass, or with other inert, detersive, or odoriferous agents, incorporated for the purpose of cheapening the product, improving its appearance, increasing its detersive action, or overcoming its natural odor with an agreeable perfume. Among the adulterants benefitting or harming a soap, are, ochre, ultramarine, sodium aluminate, borax, gelatine, resin, vermillion, copper arsenite, alcohol, vaseline, tar, sugar, champhor, petroleum, phenol, naphthalene, bran, starch, etc. Therefore, commercial soap is a mixture of pure soap with a dilutent, as water, with body imparting substances, as talc, starch, or petroleum residue; or with detersive agents in aqueous solution\ as sodium carbonate, borax, or sodium silicate. These additions may all be present in a single soap but the nature and amounts of the addition present depends upon the character of the soap itself and the purpose for which it is intended.

Soaps may be divided into three general classes viz.- laundry or household soaps, generally containing an excess of alkalies in the form of either sodium carbonate or sodium silicate, or free alkali, and resin; toilet or medicated soaps, the best grades of which are free from impurities and free alkali, or contain

medicinal agents; and commercial soaps, also termed industrial soaps, which may be subdivided into (a) soft soaps, and (b) hydrated or hard soaps, as has already been mentioned.

The common fats and oils contain the fatty acids in combination with glycerine, termed glycerides, and it is from these that soaps are generally made. Saponification is the term applied to the process of decomposing the glycerides and forming a soap, and this can be effected in the following ways:-

Aqueous Saponification. This is the most simple and convenient method for the hydrolysis of the glycerides except when alkalies are used for the saponification. The operation may be expressed by the equation: $C_3H_5(C_{18}H_{35}O_2) + 2H_2O = C_3H_5(OH)_3 + 3C_{18}H_{36}O_2$, the mixture being subjected to the action of water or steam at high temperatures or pressures. If the water is acidulated with a dilute mineral acid, the hydrolysis may be accomplished at a much lower temperature, for the acid serves as a catalyzer and accelerates the reaction between the water and the glycerides of the fat. This method is employed chiefly for the manufacture of candle stock, and the preparation of glycerine.

(2) By the action of lime, termed lime saponification. This method may be illustrated by the equation: $2C_3H_5(C_{18}H_{35}O_2)_3 + 3CaO + 3H_2O = 3Ca(C_{18}H_{36}O_2)_3 + 2C_3H_5(OH)_3$. The stock, usually tallow, is melted and

medicinal agents; and commercial soaps, also termed industrial soaps, which may be subdivided into (a) soft soaps, and (b) hydrated or hard soaps, as has already been mentioned.

The common fats and oils contain the fatty acids in combination with glycerine, termed glycerides, and it is from these that soaps are generally made. Saponification is the term applied to the process of decomposing the glycerides and forming a soap, and this can be effected in the following ways:-

Aqueous Saponification. This is the most simple and convenient method for the hydrolysis of the glycerides except when alkalies are used for the saponification. The operation may be expressed by the equation: $C_3H_5(C_{18}H_{35}O_2) + 2H_2O = C_3H_5(OH)_3 + 3C_{18}H_{36}O_2$, the mixture being subjected to the action of water or steam at high temperatures or pressures. If the water is acidulated with a dilute mineral acid, the hydrolysis may be accomplished at a much lower temperature, for the acid serves as a catalyzer and accelerates the reaction between the water and the glycerides of the fat. This method is employed chiefly for the manufacture of candle stock, and the preparation of glycerine.

(2) By the action of lime, termed lime saponification. This method may be illustrated by the equation: $2C_3H_5(C_{18}H_{35}O_2)_3 + 3CaO + 3H_2O = 3Ca(C_{18}H_{35}O_2)_3 + 2C_3H_5(OH)_3$. The stock, usually tallow, is melted and

then run into the digester together with the lime that has been previously thoroughly mixed with water. The quantity of unslacked lime commonly used for the saponification is from 2 to 4 percent of the weight of the tallow, for, although 8.7 percent is theoretically required, the above amount has been found to be sufficient in practice. The charge, having been added, the digester is closed and the steam turned on, and maintained at a pressure of fram 8 to 10 atmospheres for a period of from 4 to 10 hours, or until saponification is complete, whereupon, the contents of the digester are blown into wooden tanks. After a time the mass resolves itself into two layers, the supernatant lime "rock" consisting of lime soap and fatty acids, and the "sweet" water, in which is dissolved the glycerine, liberated as shown in the above equation. This glycerine solution is allowed to flow to the glycerine plant where it is treated as described in part 11.

93- Acid Saponification. The melted raw material is run into a lead lined tank and treated with 4 to 12 percent of concentrated sulphuric acid, and the mixture is subjected to the action of superheated steam. After the acidification the liquor is removed and the fatty acids washed free from all traces of the acid. The following equation illustrates the process:-

$C_3H_5(C_{18}H_{35}O_2)_3 + H_2SO_4 = C_3H_5(SO_3OH) + 3(C_{18}H_{36}O_2)$.

94- By the action of caustic alkalies:-

then run into the digester together with the lime that has been previously thoroughly mixed with water. The quantity of unslacked lime commonly used for the saponification is from 2 to 4 percent of the weight of the tallow, for, although 8.7 percent is theoretically required, the above amount has been found to be sufficient in practice. The charge, having been added, the digester is closed and the steam turned on, and maintained at a pressure of from 8 to 10 atmospheres for a period of from 4 to 10 hours, or until saponification is complete, whereupon, the contents of the digester are blown into wooden tanks. After a time the mass resolves itself into two layers, the supernatant lime "rock" consisting of lime soap and fatty acids, and the "sweet" water, in which is dissolved the glycerine, liberated as shown in the above equation. This glycerine solution is allowed to flow to the glycerine plant where it is treated as described in part ll.

93- Acid Saponification. The melted raw material is run into a lead lined tank and treated with 4 to 12 percent of concentrated sulphuric acid, and the mixture is subjected to the action of superheated steam. After the acidification the liquor is removed and the fatty acids washed free from all traces of the acid. The following equation illustrates the process:-

$C_3H_5(C_{18}H_{35}O_2)_3 + H_2SO_4 - C_3H_5(SO_3OH) + 3(C_{18}H_{36}O_2)$.

94- By the action of caustic alkalies:-

$C_3H_5(C_{18}H_{35}O_2)_3 + 3NaOH = C_3H_5(OH)_3 + 3C_{18}H_{35}O_2.Na$. This equation represents the reaction employed in ordinary soap making, and will be treated more in detail farther on. The caustic unites with the fatty acid radical to form the soap, and the glycerine is formed as a by-product which is recovered from the waste soap liquor.

The first three of these methods are used mainly for the production of fatty acids, the last for soap making. In a general way these four methods illustrate the methods of the formation of a soap and the chemistry envolved. If the tallow is choosen as the raw material, the yield of solid fatty acids by the lime saponification is from 44 to 48 percent; while the aqueous saponification admits of a slightly higher yield, that is, about 50 percent. Acid saponification yields upwards of 55 percent of fatty acids, and alkali saponification yields about 50 percent. With lime saponification practically all of the glycerine, upwards of 10 percent, is obtained, and the same may be said for the alkali saponification; while with the acid saponification not more than 3 percent is recovered.

" The chemistry of saponification was first explained by Chevreul, who attributed the cleansing action of soap to the free alkali formed by the decomposition of the soap when brought into solution. Krafft and Stern confirm this, and hold that in the hot dilute soap solution, part of the soap is dissociated into

$C_3H_5(C_{18}H_{35}O_2)_3 + 3NaOH = C_3H_5(OH)_3 + 3C_{18}H_{35}O_2.Na$. This equation represents the reaction employed in ordinary soap making, and will be treated more in detail farther on. The caustic unites with the fatty acid radical to form the soap, and the glycerine is formed as a by-product which is recovered from the waste soap liquor.

The first three of these methods are used mainly for the production of fatty acids, the last for soap making. In a general way these four methods illustrate the methods of the formation of a soap and the chemistry envolved. If the tallow is choosen as the raw material, the yield of solid fatty acids by the lime saponification is from 44 to 48 percent; while the aqueous saponification admits of a slightly higher yield, that is, about 50 percent. Acid saponification yields upwards of 55 percent of fatty acids, and alkali saponification yields about 50 percent. With lime saponification practically all of the glycerine, upwards of 10 percent, is obtained, and the same may be said for the alkali saponification; while with the acid saponification not more than 3 percent is recovered.

" The chemistry of saponification was first explained by Chevreul, who attributed the cleansing action of soap to the free alkali formed by the decomposition of the soap when brought into solution. Krafft and Stern confirm this, and hold that in the hot dilute soap solution [illegible]

free acid and free alkali, but on cooling, the free acid unites with some of the undissociated neutral soap, to form insoluble bi-palmate, bi-stearate, or other bi-salt, leaving the free alkali in solution. The turbid appearance of the solution may be due to oily drops of the free fatty acids."

Amonge the raw materials used for the manufacture of soaps are: tallow, grease, and bone stock. These classes may occur in various grades, and in determining the quality, buyers as a rule, depend on the simple tests of color, odor, and grain, supplemented by the titer or hardness test, the percentage of moisture, melting point, and the percentage of free fatty acids. The raw materials are not necessarily of animal stock as described above, but may be of vegetable origin, as cotton-seed oil, coconut oil, palm oil, palm-kernel oil, corn oil, olive oil, red oil, etc., and in their many modifications.

In the preceeding discussion of the raw materials used in soap manufactures, we have considered those bodies which carry two compounds, viz., a glyceride and a caustic alkali, which, when in chemical combination, form a soap. Therefore, soap boiling consists essentially in bringing a fatty body and a caustic alkali in aqueous solution in contact under suitable conditions, whereby a simple chemical reaction ensues

with the formation of an alkaline salt of a fatty acid and the liberation of glycerine. The chemical properties of the various glycerides which constitute the various fats and oils employed in soap manufacture determine their behavior in the soap kettle and the variation in the amount of alkali absorbed by any particular fat or oil is due to the difference in the composition of the glycerides themselves and from the varying proportions in which the glycerides occur in any particular stock. As the molecular weight of the glyceride increases the amount of alkali necessary for saturation decreases, hence, those commercial fats and oils in which the glycerides of low molecular weight occur possess the highest alkali absorption in proportion to their weight. The greater quantity of salt required for graining the soap made from such stock is due to the presence of those glycerides of low molecular weight whose greater solubility in brine of the sodium salt is a marked characteristic. As the glycerides increase in molecular weight, the solubility in brine of the soap obtained therefrom diminishes, hence, less salt is required for graining.

The manner of effecting the combination or chemical reaction between a fatty body and a caustic alkali and the conditions under which the reaction is completed gives rise to three general classes of soap manufacturing processes, viz.- boiled, semi-boiled, and cold process, whereby soap, to which the same des-

criptive terms may be applied as well, are produced. This classification is arbitrary and is not based on any essential chemical differences in the processes. The division is more mechanical than chemical and has reference chiefly to the time required, the artifical heat employed, andthe mechanical apparatus necessary to a satisfactory operation of the process.

A cold soap is one made by the direct combination of the materials in the proportion in which they are to remain in the finished soap, the combination being effected without the aid of heat other than that required to bring the ingredients to the requisite temperature and that heat evolved by the chemical reaction.

Boiled soaps, also called settled soaps, are those which in the process of manufacture have been subjected to changes whereby the soap is purified and the glycerine separated.

A semi-boiled or run soap, is one containing all the materials added to the kettle but has not been subjected to the graining process.

The manufacture of a settled soap is accomplished in the following steps: (1) saponification; (2) graining and settling; (3) crutching; (4) framing; (5) slabbing; and (6) drying, pressing, etc. These soaps

are the most important and constitute the class most generally manufactured and used. All household soaps are made by this process as well as the base for toilet soaps, and it is this class of soaps that we produced in the laboratory.

Three stages are required for the complete formation of glycerine and the combination of the alkali with the fatty acids, by the saponification of the glyceride stock, and each stage manifests itself in certain characteristic conditions, viz.- the emulsion formed on admixture of the stock and lye, the pasty mass obtained on continued boiling, and lastly, the final condition resulting from boiling the pasty mass with an amount of alkali sufficient for complete saponification. These three successive stages of saponification may be represented by the chemical formulas:

Raw Materials:

Stearin (tallow) $C_3H_5(C_{18}H_{35}O_2)_3$ Caustic soda: $3NaOH$

1. Emulsion $C_3H_5OH(C_{18}H_{35}O_2)_2$ Soap: $C_{18}H_{35}O.NaO$
   Caustic soda: $2NaOH$

2. Pasty mass $C_3H_5(OH)_2(C_{18}H_{35}O_2)$ Soap: $2C_{18}H_{35}O.NaO$
   Caustic soda: $NaOH$

3. Glycerine $C_3H_5(OH)_3$ Soap: $3C_{18}H_{35}O.NaO$

Graining. The purpose of graining is to separate the soap from the superfluous water with which it is associated, and which, forming the menstrum for

for the salt, glycerine, lye, impurities in the stock, etc., constitutes the soap lye. The salt is added either as the dry salt or as a saturated brine, in small quantities at a time, to the quietly boiling contents of the kettle and thoroughly boiled with it until a portion taken on a paddle coagulates or separates so that waste lye runs from it. The waste lye should be clear, of a salty taste, and should not contain free alkali in excess of 0.4 percent. This amount of free alkali in waste soap lye is not perceptible to the taste. The more concentrated the salt solution in contact with the soap the less water will be retained by it. In boiling this character of a soap the stock lye should not have a greater density than 13 degrees Baume', and should contain from 7 to 10 percent of salt. This is the lowest density that will remove the soap completely from solution, while the stock lye is the clearest and least discolored, and is the most valuable, owing to the high percentage of glycerine present. When the desired grain has been obtained the soap is boiled up to the top of the kettle, the steam turned off, and the contents allowed to rest until the following morning.

Settling. Fitting or settling the soap is the term applied when weak lye or water is added to the soap to

for the salt, glycerine, lye, impurities in the stock, etc., constitutes the soap lye. The salt is added either as the dry salt or as a saturated brine, in small quantities at a time, to the quietly boiling contents of the kettle and thoroughly boiled with it until a portion taken on a paddle coagulates or separates so that waste lye runs from it. The waste lye should be clear, of a salty taste, and should not contain free alkali in excess of 0.4 percent. This amount of free alkali in waste soap lye is not perceptible to the taste. The more concentrated the salt solution in contact with the soap the less water will be retained by it. In boiling this character of a soap the stock lye should not have a greater density than 13 degrees Baume', and should contain from 7 to 10 percent of salt. This is the lowest density that will remove the soap completely from solution, while the stock lye is the clearest and least discolored, and is the most valuable, owing to the high percentage of glycerine present. When the desired grain has been obtained the soap is boiled up to the top of the kettle, the steam turned off, and the contents allowed to rest until the following morning.

Settling. Fitting or settling the soap is the term applied when weak lye or water is added to the soap to

thin it to the desired consistency. The strengthening lye from the preceeding change is withdrawn and the soap boiled up with live steam to the top of the kettle and it is then allowed to stand for five days, during which time the contents of the kettle, because of the different specific gravities, resolve themselves roughly into two portions, viz.- the finished soap carrying about 30 percent of water, and the niger, which carries considerably more water than does the supernatant soap, as well as the impurities and coloring matter settled from it. The niger constitutes from 20 to 25 per cent of the volume of the settled soap in the kettle.

The detergency of soap is greatly increased by the addition of certain substances called fillers, in aqueous solution, while the soap is still in the fluid condition. The substances used as fillers have already been mentioned, and the nature and amount of the filler determines whether the soap is heavily or lightly filled.

Crutching. For the incorporation of the filling material into soap, the belt driven crutcher is generally employed. There are three types of this machine each possessing their several points of excellence, but we will attempt to describe only one of them. This

thin it to the desired consistency. The strengthening lye from the preceeding change is withdrawn and the soap boiled up with live steam to the top of the kettle and it is then allowed to stand for five days, during which time the contents of the kettle, because of the different specific gravities, resolve themselves roughly into two portions, viz.- the finished soap carrying about 30 percent of water, and the niger, which carries considerably more water than does the supernatant soap, as well as the impurities and coloring matter settled from it. The niger constitutes from 20 to 25 per cent of the volume of the settled soap in the kettle.

The detergency of soap is greatly increased by the addition of certain substances called fillers, in aqueous solution, while the soap is still in the fluid condition. The substances used as fillers have already been mentioned, and the nature and amount of the filler determines whether the soap is heavily or lightly filled.

Crutching. For the incorporation of the filling material into soap, the belt driven crutcher is generally employed. There are three types of this machine each possessing their several points of excellence, but we will attempt to describe only one of them. This

consists of a cylindrical vessel in which is mounted a vertical shaft carrying a series of horizontal paddles which rotate entirely within the body of the soap, which remains practically stationary. With this type it is impossible to incorporate air into the mass of the soap as the mixing is done entirely within the body of the soap. The capacity of the crutcher is about 1200 pounds. The liquid soap is transferred to the crutcher by means of a pump, generally of the Tabor, Hersey, or Johnson rotary type.

Framing. The soap frame consists essentially of an uncovered box having a capacity of about 1200 pounds and supplied with removeable sheet-steel sides, and ends of wood or sheet steel set on a wooden bottom, which is mounted on truck wheels. The soap from the crutcher is emptied into the frame and allowed to remain there until it has hardened, whereupon the sides are removed and the soap allowed to rest on the bottom for several weeks or until the soap has cured, that is, until it has dried. This operation requires a great deal of floor space and is objectional for that reason, and although this method of curing has so many disadvantages it is still used almost entirely by soap manufactururers. A better method, and the one used by the more up to date plants is the following: The liquid

consists of a cylindrical vessel in which is mounted a vertical shaft carrying a series of horizontal paddles which rotate entirely within the body of the soap, which remains practically stationary. With this type it is impossible to incorporate air into the mass of the soap as the mixing is done entirely within the body of the soap. The capacity of the crutcher is about 1200 pounds. The liquid soap is transferred to the crutcher by means of a pump, generally of the Taber, Hersey, or Johnson rotary type.

Framing. The soap frame consists essentially of an uncovered box having a capacity of about 1200 pounds and supplied with removeable sheet-steel sides, and ends of wood or sheet steel set on a wooden bottom, which is mounted on truck wheels. The soap from the crutcher is emptied into the frame and allowed to remain there until it has hardened, whereupon the sides are removed and the soap allowed to rest on the bottom for several weeks or until the soap has cured, that is, until it has dried. This operation requires a great deal of floor space and is objectional for that reason, and although this method of curing has so many disadvantages it is still used almost entirely by soap manufacturers. A better method, and the one used by the more up to date plants is the following: The liquid

soap is run to the upper story of the building into a large vat or tank. From this tank it flows by gravity over a system of steam heated rollers, seven in number, and each a little closer than the preceeding one. The soap is spread over the roller in a thin layer or film, from which it is taken by the next roller and so on, until it reaches the last, from which it is removed by means of a scraper which breaks it up into thin strips or shavings. These shavings fall onto a belt moving very slowly and which enters a dryer, which is simply a wooden box about 10 feet high, 8 feet long, and 5 feet wide, supplied with glass windows by means of which the interior can be seen. This dryer is supplied with steam pipes, and as the soap travels back and forth on the belt within it it is dried and cured. The whole process requires about an hour. The shavings leaving the dryer fall into a basket, which when full, is carried to the press, and the chips pressed into large slabs, similiar to those coming from the frames. Slabbing. The slabber is a machine for cutting the slab of soap into smaller slabs, and consists of a frame work having a series of horizontal parallel wires at a distance apart corresponding to the width or height of the unpressed bars of soap. The slab of soap mounted on a truck is pushed along under the frame of the

soap is run to the upper story of the building into a large vat or tank. From this tank it flows by grav-ity over a system of steam heated rollers, seven in number, and each a little closer than the preceeding one. The soap is spread over the roller in a thin layer or film, from which it is taken by the next roller and so on, until it reaches the last, from which it is re-moved by means of a scraper which breaks it up into thin strips or shavings. These shavings fall onto a belt moving very slowly and which enters a dryer, which is simply a wooden box about 10 feet high, 8 feet long, and 5 feet wide, supplied with glass windows by means of which the interior can be seen. This dryer is sup-plied with steam pipes, and as the soap travels back and forth on the belt within it it is dried and cured. The whole process requires about an hour. The shavings leaving the dryer fall into a basket, which when full, is carried to the press, and the chips pressed into large slabs, similiar to those coming from the frames.

Slabbing. The slabber is a machine for cutting the slab of soap into smaller slabs, and consists of a frame work having a series of horizontal parallel wires at a distance apart corresponding to the width or height of the unpressed bars of soap. The slab of soap mount-ed on a truck is pushed along under the frame of the

slabber and as the soap comes into it it meets the taut steel wires and is cut into smaller slabs. These slabs are then removed to the cutting table, where each is cut into bars.

Each slab is lifted onto the cutting table and pushed lenghtwise through one or two wires held in the cutting head, by means of which, it is cut into two or more narrower slabs as wide as the single bar is long. These slabs are then cut at right angles by another attendant to the dimensions corresponding to the width and thickness of a single bar. The individual bars are then slightly separated from one another so that the air may circulate freely around them. When the truck is full of these bars it is removed to the drying room.

The purpose of the drying room is to hasten the evaporation of the water from the surface of the bar so that there may be formed a thin crust of comparatively hard soap which serves to retard further evaporation from the interior of the bar, and which allows the bar to be pressed and stamped without the soap adhering to the dies. Now there is an unequal equilibrium of moisture content between the exterior and interior parts of the bar, a partial explanation of the

sweating to which soaps are universally susceptible. This accumulation of moisture does not develop until after the bar is wrapped and packed. With the soap wrapped and packed in a box the conditions are naturally different. The tendency for the moisture to pass from the interior of the bar to the drier surface remains, but further evaporation from the exterior of the bar is checked. Here the moisture accumulates and softens the soap, which in turn adheres to the wrapper. The drying room is either furnished with ventilating fans or steam or cold air pipes, or both. The requirements for the drying room are that a large volume of air must be furnished at the required temperature and be maintained in rapid circulation. A temperature of 80 to 100 degrees F. is productive of the best results.

When the soap comes from the drying room it is ready for pressing. This consists in pressing the cakes of soap into the desired shape and volume, and stamping them with the trade marks etc. The automatic steam-power soap press is the one universally used at the present time and they have a guaranteed capacity of from 60,000 to 75,000 cakes per day of 10 hours.

The semi-boiled soap as has already been mentioned is primarily a cheap method of soap manufacture, with economy in fuel, labor, and time. It is best,

however, to give the soap a simple purification by graining it sharply, thus prolonging the time consumed in its manufacture by one day. The process in outline is similiar to that just described, and is the method used exclusively for the manufacture of soft soaps.

The production of soap by the cold process far surpasses all other methods in the economy of every element entering into the cost of production, but it possesses certain paramount disadvantages, which re-strict its use to a very limited field. The mechanical equipment required consists simply of tanks containing the fat, oil, and caustic lye, a crutcher in which the ingredients are mixed, and frames to receive the mixture and in which the chemical reaction of saponification continues, if under favorable conditions, to completion. Although this process varies in most of its details from the manufacture of laundry soaps as we have already described, we shall not attempt to go farther into the discussion of this method, nor shall we give in greater detail the method we have just described, concerning the various modifications, alterations, etc., which the different manufactururers use, for we have covered briefly all the essential points to be observed in the production of a soap in our general outline of their manufacture.

The method employed in the making of a soap by us in the laboratories of Armour Institute Of Technology was exactly similiar to that which we have outlined under the heading, the manufacture of boiled orsettled soaps, with the exception that our apparatus was crude, on a smaller scale, and that we added cotton-seed oil when the saponification had reached the pasty state.

Trirty five pounds of tallow, having a saponification number of 195, was placed in a kettle and melted by means of a steam coil placed in the bottom thereof. When the tallow was in the liquid condition we added 20 pounds of our caustic alkali solution containing 6 percent of NaOH and then boiled the mixture. After about 10 hours boiling the emulsion stage was completed, that is, the first third of the alkali was then in combination with the tallow (stearin). At the end of the next 15 hours boiling we judged that the pasty state was completed, that is, two-thirds of the caustic was in combination with the stearin, and at this point we added 15 pounds of cotton-seed oil having a saponification number of 137, and 20 pounds more of the lye. The boiling was then continued for another period of six hours, whereupon the saponification was complete, that is, all the alkali was in combination with the s

stearin, for the solution on top boiled very quietly, was frothy and smooth, and the stock would slide from the paddle in large transparent flakes, and when a small portion was rubbed between the fingers it curled up smooth and dry, without any indication of grease.

The saponification being complete, the stock was ready for the graining. While the mixture was boiling quietly we added a little salt, NaCl, but this small addition soon threw so much soap out of solution that our kettle would not hold it. To overcome this difficulty we removed all the soap from the kettle and made up a brine solution which we heated to boiling in the kettle and then added a little of our soap solution and continued the boiling until it was all thrown out of solution, whereupon we allowed it to settle and solidify, and then removed it, leaving the brine in the kettle for the next lot, adding a little salt each time to make up for that used. Our kettle being small, as the soap was thrown out of solution and solidified, it filled the entire kettle, so that it held a large proportion of water mechanically, because of its expansion. So when the soap came from the kettle it was extremely soft and contained 80 percent of water. The entire lot of soap having been treated in this way weighed 190 pounds, which calculated to a 30 percent

stearin, for the solution on top boiled very quietly, was frothy and smooth, and the stock would slide from the paddle in large transparent flakes, and when a small portion was rubbed between the fingers it curled up smooth and dry, without any indication of grease.

The saponification being complete, the stock was ready for the graining. While the mixture was boiling quietly we added a little salt, NaCl, but this small addition soon threw so much soap out of solution that our kettle would not hold it. To overcome this difficulty we removed all the soap from the kettle and made up a brine solution which we heated to boiling in the kettle and then added a little of our soap solution and continued the boiling until it was all thrown out of solution, whereupon we allowed it to settle and solidify, and then removed it, leaving the brine in the kettle for the next lot, adding a little salt each time to make up for that used. Our kettle being small, as the soap was thrown out of solution and solidified, it filled the entire kettle, so that it held a large proportion of water mechanically, because of its expansion. So when the soap came from the kettle it was extremely soft and contained 80 percent of water. The entire lot of soap having been treated in this way weighed 190 pounds, which calculated to a 30 percent

moisture basis, that being the average moisture content of such a soap, made the yield 50 pounds of soap, or 51 percent of the raw materials used.

Because of the small size of our kettles and the expansion of the soap when thrown out of solution quite a quantity of the waste soap liquor was taken up mechanically, so that we did not attempt to measure this part, but we had to eliminate it from the soap. To do this we made up a brine solution and washed the soap with it, so that it finally contained very little free alkali as will be seen from the analysis which concludes part 1 of this thesis. Now the mass of soap was a soft slimy mixture and it had to be dried, but because it contained so much water it was impossible to use the temperature of boiling water (100 degrees C.) because the water being in such excess of the soap formed a fluid which ran through the containing vessel, so we had to resort to air drying. As the soap became dryer we cut it up into small pieces and spread them out on screens. When it became dry and hard we pressed them together into cakes.

It was very difficult for us to find a good method for analyzing soaps, for each text book and soap chemist advised a different method, and we could not get good checks on our analysis, that is, checks that

satisfied us. However, we finally came across a satisfactory method given in bulletin 109, of the United States Agricultural Department, which we used except for a slight modification which we introduced.

As we have already mentioned the moisture content of the outer layer of a bar of soap may be very different from that of the interior of the cake. We took a portion of each lot of soap, mixed it, and pressed it into a cake, and after allowing it to cure for some time, we cut it in two in a diagolal direction and cut from one of these fresh surfaces, in thin layers, a sufficient quantity for all determinations, taking care to cut entirely across so as to get a fair sample and proportion of the outer and inner portions.

Moisture. Heat two grams of the finely shaved soap for two hours in an oven at 105 degrees cantigrade. The loss is considered as water, though of course, this is not accurate, as volatile oils may constitute a part of the loss, and on the other hand, all water may not be driven off, and if the soap contains free alkali carbon dioxide may be absorbed from the air.

Insoluble Matter. Dissolve 5 grams of soap in hot water (use about 75 c.c.). Filter on a Gooch or weighed paper and wash with hot water; dry at 105

degrees C., weigh, and calculate the percentage of mineral matter.

Total Fatty Matter. To the filtarte from the insoluble matter add 40 c.c. of half-normal sulphuric acid, heat on the water bath until the fatty acids have collected in a thin layer on top, cool in ice water then heat again with water, cool, remove fatty layer, wash with ice water, dry with filter paper, unite the acid liquids, transfer to a separatory funnel, and shake out with two portions of 50 c.c. each of gasoline, wash the gasoline twice with 20 c.c. of water. Evaporate off the gasoline, add the cake of fatty acids, etc., dry at 100 degrees centigrade and weigh as total fatty matter.

Total Alkali. Heat the acid liquid from the determination of total fatty matter to drive off traces of gasoline, cool, add methyl orange, and titrate the excess of acid with a half-normal NaOH solution. From this titration calculate the amount of acid neutralized by the alkali in the soap and figure to percentage of sodium monoxide. A more rapid method is to ash the soap, dissolve the ash in water, and titrate.

Free Alkali. Treat the freshly cut surface of the soap with a few drops of phenolphthalein; if it does not turn red it may be assumed that free caustic

alkali is absent. If free alkali is present, dissolve two grams of the soap in 100 c.c. of neutral alcohol, filter from the undissolved sodium carbonate etc., wash with alcohol, add phenolphthalein, titrate with standard acid, and calculate to percentage of free alkali as NaOH. Should the alcoholic solution be acid instead of alkaline, titrate with standard alkali and calculate the percentage of free fatty acids as oleic acid. Washtthe portion insoluble in alcohol with water add methyl orange to the washings, and titrate with half-normal sulphuric acid. Calculate to percentage of sodium monoxide present as the carbonate, or possibly as the borate or silicate. If borax is present boil off the CO_2 after neutralizing exactly to methyl orange; cool, add mannite and phenolphthalein, and titrate the boric acid with standard alkali.

Unsaponified Matter. Dissolve 5 grams of soap in 50 c.c. of 50 percent alcohol; if any free fatty acids are present add just enough standard alkali to neutralize them and wash into a separatory funnel with 50 percent alcohol. Extract with 100 c.c. of gasoline (B.P. 50-60 degrees). Wash the gasoline with water, evaporate, and weigh as unsaponified matter. This may consist of fat that has not been converted into soap or of hydrocarbons.

Glycerine. Dissolve 20 to 25 grams of soap in hot water, add a slight excess of sulphuric acid, and heat on the water bath until the fatty acids separate in a clear layer. Remove the fatty acids and filter the acid solution into a graduated flask. Remove the chlorides and the soluble fatty acids by adding crystals of silver sulphate, cool, make up to mark, mix, allow to settle, filter through dry paper, take an aliquot portion corresponding to five grams of soap, and determine the amount of glycerine by Hehner's bichromate method, as described in part 11. This mathod cannot be used when sugar is present as it also would reduce the bichromate.

Soap.	Ivory.	Ours.	American F.
Moisture.	18.25	29.92	16.98
Dry Basis.			
Total Alkali Na_2O	9.23	9.86	9.50
Free Alkali NaOH	1.48	1.59	1.21
Na_2O as Na_2CO_3	0.42	0.00	0.36
Total Fatty Matter	87.64	86.92	87.57
Unsaponified "	1.22	1.63	1.36
Glycerine	0.00	0.00	trace

arate in a clear layer. Remove the fatty acids and filter the acid solution into a graduated flask. Remove the chlorides and the soluble fatty acids by adding crystals of silver sulphate, cool, make up to mark, mix, allow to settle, filter through dry paper, take an aliquot portion corresponding to five grams of soap, and determine the amount of glycerine by Hehner's bichromate method, as described in part II. This method cannot be used when sugar is present as it also would reduce the bichromate.

Soap.	Ivory.	Ours.	American P.
Moisture.	18.25	29.92	16.98

mix, allow to settle, filter through dry paper, take an aliquot portion corresponding to five grams of soap, and determine the amount of glycerine by Hehner's bi-chromate method, as described in part II. This method cannot be used when sugar is present as it also would reduce the bichromate.

Soap.	Ivory.	Ours.	American F.
Moisture.	18.25	29.92	16.98

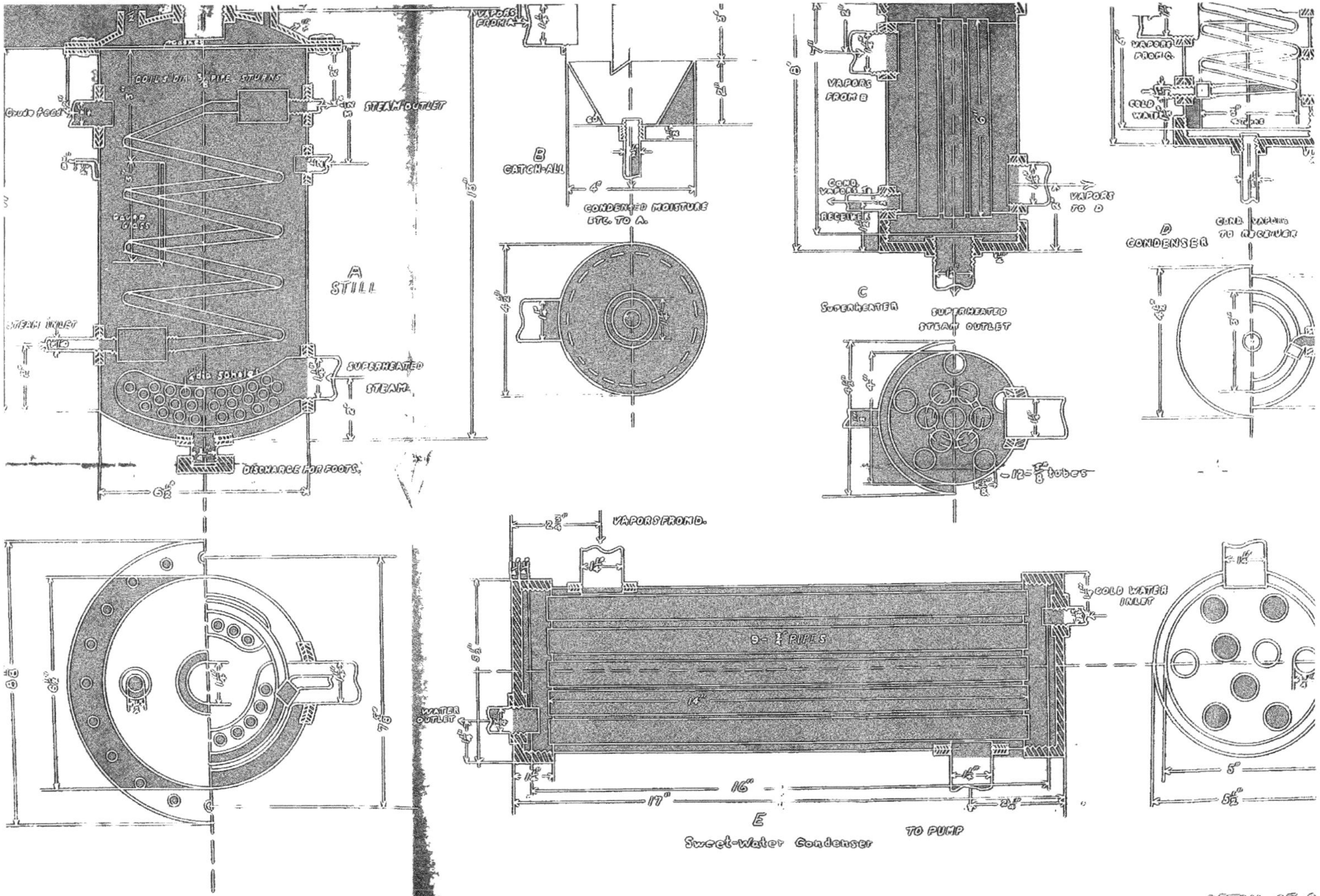
A
STILL
STEAM OUTLET
Crude feed
STEAM INLET
SUPERHEATED STEAM
DISCHARGE FOR FOOTS.
B
CATCH-ALL
VAPORS FROM A
CONDENSED MOISTURE ETC. TO A.
C
Superheater
VAPORS FROM B
COND. VAPORS
RECEIVER
VAPORS TO D
SUPERHEATED STEAM OUTLET
12 - 5/8" tubes
D
CONDENSER
VAPORS FROM C.
COLD WATER
COND. VAPORS TO RECEIVER
E
Sweet-Water Condenser
VAPORS FROM D.
9 - 1" PIPES
COLD WATER INLET
WATER OUTLET
TO PUMP
17"
16"
DETAIL OF S

PART 11.

THE RECOVERY OF GLYCERINE.

In the discussion of the manufacture of settled soaps in part 1, we traced the progress of a boil of soap with the formation of the various lyes. These lyes contain all the glycerine which the natural oils and fats are capable of yielding, and may contain as much as five to eight percent of pure glycerine; but usually the percentage is lower, about three percent. Besides this, the lyes contain varying amounts of common salt, sodium hydroxide, sodium carbonate, and sodium sulphate, contaminated by more or less soap in suspension, and soma mucilaginous matter or animal tissue remaining with the stock when rendered. This often foul-smelling liquor, a by-product with the soap maker, now becomes the raw material of the glycerine refiner.

The specific gravity ofthe waste soap liquor varies from 1.07 to 1.14 according to the amount of sodium chloride in solution. Since, in the recovery of glycerine, the impurities must all be gotten rid of, the value of the lyes depends on the percentage of glycerine and on the freedom from free sodium hydroxide and sodium carbonate.

PART 11.

THE RECOVERY OF GLYCERINE.

In the discussion of the manufacture of settled soaps in part 1, we traced the progress of a boil of soap with the formation of the various lyes. These lyes contain all the glycerine which the natural oils and fats are capable of yielding, and may contain as much as five to eight percent of pure glycerine; but usually the percentage is lower, about three percent. Besides this, the lyes contain varying amounts of common salt, sodium hydroxide, sodium carbonate, and sodium sulphate, contaminated by more or less soap in suspension, and some mucilaginous matter or animal tissue remaining with the stock when rendered. This often foul-smelling liquor, a by-product with the soap maker, now becomes the raw material of the glycerine refiner.

The specific gravity of the waste soap liquor varies from 1.07 to 1.14 according to the amount of sodium chloride in solution. Since, in the recovery of glycerine, the impurities must all be gotten rid of, the value of the lyes depends on the percentage of glycerine and on the freedom from free sodium hydroxide and sodium carbonate.

One method of purifying the lyes is the purification by the removal of the fatty acids, rosin acids, and other organic impurities. The liquor then contains the pure glycerol and salt in solution. The latter is removed by heating the liquor to the "salting-point" in fire heated vessels or tube heated evaporators. The "salting-point" is reached when the liquid has acquired the specific gravity of fourty-four degrees Twaddell at fifteen degrees Centigrade. If the evaporation is carried on farther, salt will be deposited, while the specific gravity and percentage of glycerol will rise. Consequently, the vessels in which the evaporation is carried on beyond the salting point must be provided with stirring and scraping arrangements to re- the salt as it separates, since all tube evaporators are liable to incrustation with salt and the gradual stopping up of the heating tubes. The finished crude glycerine which comes from the evaporator has a specific gravity of about 1.3, and contains about eighty percent of glycerole, ten percent of salt, and the remainder of water and small amounts of impurities. The methods of purification do not differ much, hence, the method taken up in detail farther on is sufficient to illustrate the general plan of procedure during purification and concentration.

One method of purifying the lyes is the purification by the removal of the fatty acids, rosin acids, and other organic impurities. The liquor then contains the pure glycerol and salt in solution. The latter is removed by heating the liquor to the "salting-point" in fire heated vessels or tube heated evaporators. The "salting-point" is reached when the liquid has acquired the specific gravity of fourty-four degrees Twaddell at fifteen degrees Centigrade. If the evaporation is carried on farther, salt will be deposited, while the specific gravity and percentage of glycerol will rise. Consequently, the vessels in which the evaporation is carried on beyond the salting point must be provided with stirring and scraping arrangements to re- the salt as it separates, since all tube evaporators are liable to incrustation with salt and the gradual stopping up of the heating tubes. The finished crude glycerine which comes from the evaporator has a specific gravity of about 1.3, and contains about eighty percent of glycerols, ten percent of salt, and the remainder of water and small amounts of impurities. The methods of purification do not differ much, hence, the method taken up in detail farther on is sufficient to illustrate the general plan of procedure during puri-

It might be said here that crude soap-lye glycerine containing a considerable quantity of thio-sulphates, sulphides, and sulphites, are almost valueless to the refiner of crude glycerine.

There are many different systems of apparatus used for the recovery of glycerine from the waste soap liquor, and before going into our experimental work upon this subject and the design of our plant, which is given in detail in the accompanying blue-prints, we will describe the method and apparatus used by Armour and Company.

The waste liquor from the soap works, which has a specific gravity of 16.5 degrees Baume' and contains 3.5 percent of glycerine, and 0.5 percent of sodium chloride, is run , by means of pipes, to the waste lye tanks, situated in the upper story of the works. These tanks are lead lined, nine feet long, six feet wide, and twelve feet deep. Here 60 degree Baume' sulphuric acid is added until the liquor is neutral. The mixture is then agitated by means of compressed air entering through pipes at the bottom, and the albuminous matter precipitated by the addition of aluminium sulphate, although basic sulphate of iron may be used.

The liquor is then passed through a filter press, employing eight-duck canvas as the filtering

It might be said here that crude soap-lye glycerine containing a considerable quantity of thio-sulphates, sulphides, and sulphites, are almost value-less to the refiner of crude glycerine.

There are many different systems of appara-tus used for the recovery of glycerine from the waste soap liquor, and before going into our experimental work upon this subject and the design of our plant, which is given in detail in the accompanying blue-prints, we will describe the method and apparatus used by Armour and Company.

The waste liquor from the soap works, which has a specific gravity of 16.5 degrees Baume' and con-tains 3.5 percent of glycerine, and 0.5 percent of sodium chloride, is run , by means of pipes, to the waste lye tanks, situated in the upper story of the works. These tanks are lead lined, nine feet long, six feet wide, and twelve feet deep. Here 60 degree Baume' sulphuric acid is added until the liquor is neutral. The mixture is then agitated by means of com-pressed air entering through pipes at the bottom, and the albuminous matter precipitated by the addition of aluminium sulphate, although basic sulphate of iron may be used.

The liquor is then passed through a filter press, employing eight-duck canvas as the filtering

medium, under a pressure of 45 pounds per square inch. The precipitate is useless and is sent to the dump. The filtrate is run into another tank which is 15 feet wide, 50 feet long, and 14 feet high, and is now somewhat acid. In this tank enough caustic soda is added to neutralize the acid, and the liquor is then run into another tank, about the same size as the one just described, where it is stored until desired for further treatment.

The next step is the evaporation of the liquor andthis is done in a triple effect evaporator. In each effect are steam coils and the steam enters the first at a pressure of 75 pounds per square inch, and leaves the last at a pressure of 15 pounds per square inch, thus passing through the whole three effects. The first effect is maintained at a vacuum of five inches of mercury and the lye enters it at 15 degrees Be'. and leaves it at 18 degrees Baume'. From here it passes to filter box which is six feet long, four feet high, and four feet wide, holding a 36 mesh screen, and maintained at the same vacuum as the first effect, that is, five inches of mercury. This vacuum sucks the liquid through the screen, andthe salt is retained by it. The filtrate is then run into the second effect which is kept at a vacuum of 15 inches and where it is con-

medium, under a pressure of 45 pounds per square inch. The precipitate is useless and is sent to the dump. The filtrate is run into another tank which is 15 feet wide, 60 feet long, and 14 feet high, and is now somewhat acid. In this tank enough caustic soda is added to neutralize the acid, and the liquor is then run into another tank, about the same size as the one just described, where it is stored until desired for further treatment.

The next step is the evaporation of the liquor andthis is done in a triple effect evaporator. In each effect are steam coils and the steam enters the first at a pressure of 75 pounds per square inch, and leaves the last at a pressure of 15 pounds per square inch, thus passing through the whole three effects. The first effect is maintained at a vacuum of five inches of mercury and the lye enters it at 15 degrees Be'. and leaves it at 18 degrees Baume'. From here it passes to filter box which is six feet long, four feet high, and four feet wide, holding a 36 mesh screen, and maintained at the same vacuum as the first effect, that is, five inches of mercury. This vacuum sucks the liquid through the screen, andthe salt is retained by it. The filtrate is then run into the second effect which is kept at a vacuum of 15 inches and where it is con-

centrated to 22.5 to 23 degrees Baume'. It is again run to a filtering box exactly similiar to the first one, with the exception that it is maintained at a vacuum of 15 inches of mercury. From here the liquid, at 23 degrees Baume', is sent to the third and last effect, where it is concentrated to a specific gravity of 34 degrees Baume' and again filtered free from the salt as before, the vacuum in this case being the same as that of the last effect, viz.- 26 inches of mercury. The vapors from all three effects pass through condensers on the roof of the plant, where they are condensed and run to the sewer.

When the liquid leaves the last evaporator, all the water has been removed from it and it is two-tenths of one percent alkaline. Enough 74 percent NaOH is then added to it to make its alkalinity five-tenths of one percent which is done in a tank, and after it has been so treated it is ready for the distillation.

It is, therefore, run into the glycerine still which is an asbestos coxered cast iron cylinder, nine feet high and four feet in diameter, and contains a one-inch copper coil through which steam, at 40 pounds pressure, is passed. The steam enters at the top of the still through a one-inch pipe, and also leaves it at the top through the same sized pipe which leads to a

centrated to 22.8 to 25 degrees Baume. It is again run to a filtering box exactly similiar to the first one, with the exception that it is maintained at a vacuum of 16 inches of mercury. From here the liquid, at 25 degrees Baume, is sent to the third and last effect, where it is concentrated to a specific gravity of 34 degrees Baume, and again filtered free from the salt as before, the vacuum in this case being the same as that of the last effect, viz.- 26 inches of mercury. The vapors from all three effects pass through condensers on the roof of the plant, where they are condensed and run to the sewer.

When the liquid leaves the last evaporator, all the water has been removed from it and it is two-tenths of one percent alkaline. Enough 14 percent NaOH is then added to it to make its alkalinity five-tenths of one percent which is done in a tank, and after it has been so treated it is ready for the distillation.

It is, therefore, run into the glycerine still which is an asbestos covered cast iron cylinder, nine feet high and four feet in diameter, and contains a one-inch copper coil through which steam, at 40 pounds pressure, is passed. The steam enters at the top of the still through a one-inch pipe, and also leaves it at the top through the same sized pipe which leads to a

coil in the superheater. The crude glycerine enters the still through a two-inch line at the top and enough of it is allowed to flow in to keep the still about three fourths full. The still is maintained at a vacuum of 27 inches of mercury. The glycerine vapors pass off through an 18-inch goose-neck to the superheater. From here they pass to two receivers, each eight and one half feet high, and three and a half feet in diameter, which are arranged in a line with the still. The heavier vapors fall into the first receiver, while the lighter ones fall into the second, which is the farther from the still. Neither of these receivers is under a direct vacuum.

The vapors which do not condense in either one of the receivers pass to a third vessel, from where, the so called "sweet-water" is pumped to the superheater, giving up some of its heat. The liquid in the first receiver has a specific gravity of 22.5 degrees Baume', while that in the second receiver is about 16 degrees Baume'. The still contains 180 pounds of glycerine to an inch in height, thus having a capacity of about 15,000 pounds of the crude liquid. The glycerine in the second receiver is either put back into the still, or stored until there is a large amount on hand, in which case it is evaporated down to 29

coil in the superheater. The crude glycerine enters the still through a two-inch line at the top and enough of it is allowed to flow in to keep the still about three fourths full. The still is maintained at a vacuum of 27 inches of mercury. The glycerine vapors pass off through an 18-inch goose-neck to the superheater. From here they pass to two receivers, each eight and one half feet high, and three and a half feet in diameter, which are arranged in a line with the still. The heavier vapors fall into the first receiver, while the lighter ones fall into the second, which is the farther from the still. Neither of these receivers is under a direct vacuum.

The vapors which do not condense in either one of the receivers pass to a third vessel, from where, the so called "sweet-water" is pumped to the superheater, giving up some of its heat. The liquid in the first receiver has a specific gravity of 22.5 degrees Baume', while that in the second receiver is about 16 degrees Baume'. The still contains 180 pounds of glycerine to an inch in height, thus having a capacity of about 15,000 pounds of the crude liquid. The glycerine in the second receiver is either put back into the still, or stored until there is a large amount on hand, in which case it is evaporated down to 29

degrees Baume' in another still under a vacuum of 25 inches of mercury, and a steam pressure of 15 pounds per square inch, and sold as P.Y. (pale yellow) glycerine.

The glycerine from the first receiver is run into a tank and purified by dilution with water to a specific gravity of 15 degrees Baume'. To every thousand pounds of this liquid is added one-quarter of a pound of 66 degree Baume' sulphuric acid and an equal amount of 74 percent sodium hydroxide to neutralize the acid, and 20 pounds of bone black to bleach the glycerine. The whole is then agitated by means of compressed air, run through the filter press at a pressure of 45 pounds per square inch, neutralized with soda ash, one pound in excess, and again filtered as before to remove the soda. The glycerine is then fed to a concentrator under a 25 inch vacuum, where it is evaporated down to 29.75 degrees Baume'. It is then fed for a second distillation under the same conditions as before. Each still has a separate pump, andthe action is the same throughout with the exception that theglycerine now has a strength of 30.5 degrees Baume', and the second receiver contains steam coils to concentrate the glycerine therein to the same gravity as that in the first receiver. It then goes to a tank for bleaching, for which

degrees Baume' in another still under a vacuum of 25 inches of mercury, and a steam pressure of 15 pounds per square inch, and sold as P.Y. (pale yellow) glycerine.

The glycerine from the first receiver is run into a tank and purified by dilution with water to a specific gravity of 15 degrees Baume'. To every thousand pounds of this liquid is added one-quarter of a pound of 66 degree Baume' sulphuric acid and an equal amount of 74 percent sodium hydroxide to neutralize the acid, and 20 pounds of bone black to bleach the glycerine. The whole is then agitated by means of compressed air, run through the filter press at a pressure of 45 pounds per square inch, neutralized with soda ash, one pound in excess, and again filtered as before to remove the soda. The glycerine is then fed to a concentrator under a 25 inch vacuum, where it is evaporated down to 29.75 degrees Baume'. It is then fed for a second distillation under the same conditions as before. Each still has a separate pump, andthe action is the same throughout with the exception that theglycerine now has a strength of 30.5 degrees Baume', and the second receiver contains steam coils to concentrate the glycerine therein to the same gravity as that in the first receiver. It then goes to a tank for bleaching, for which

purpose 25 pounds of bone-black are added to every thousand pounds of the glycerine. It is then filtered and sent to the storage tanks ready for shipment. The P.Y. glycerine is bleached by adding eight pounds of bone black to every thousand pounds of the liquid.

Hence, there are two products of the plant, the P.Y., or commercial glycerine, and the C.P. or glycerine used for medicinal purposes. Pure glycerine is a colorless, oily liquid, having a sweet taste, and miscible in all proportions with water and alcohol, but insoluble in ether. When cooled to a low temperature glycerine solidifies, but the crystals thus formed do not melt below 17 degrees Centigrade. It boils at 290 degrees, and has a specific gravity of 1.265 at 15 degrees Centigrade.

The waste lye which we used in our experimental work, came from the soap works of Armour and Company, in a large galvanized iron cylindrical tank containing about 100 gallons. The following teste were made on it:

(1) Specific Gravity.

(2) Total Alkali as Sodium Hydrate.

(3) Free Alkali as sodium Hydrate.

(4) Combined Alkali as Sodium Carbonate.

(5) Sodium Chloride.

purpose 25 pounds of bone-black are added to every thousand pounds of the glycerine. It is then filtered and sent to the storage tanks ready for shipment. The P.Y. glycerine is bleached by adding eight pounds of bone black to every thousand pounds of the liquid.

Hence, there are two products of the plant, the P.Y., or commercial glycerine, and the C.P. or glycerine used for medicinal purposes. Pure glycerine is a colorless, oily liquid, having a sweet taste, and miscible in all proportions with water and alcohol, but insoluble in ether. When cooled to a low temperature glycerine solidifies, but the crystals thus formed do not melt below 17 degrees Centigrade. It boils at 290 degrees, and has a specific gravity of 1.265 at 15 degrees Centigrade.

The waste lye which we used in our experimental work, came from the soap works of Armour and Company, in a large galvanized iron cylindrical tank containing about 100 gallons. The following tests were made on it:

(1) Specific Gravity.

(2) Total Alkali as Sodium Hydrate.

(3) Free Alkali as sodium Hydrate.

(4) Combined Alkali as Sodium Carbonate.

(5) Sodium Chloride.

(6) Glycerine.

The method of analysis was as follows:

Specific Gravity. Determined by means of the Westphal balance.

Total Alkali as Sodium Hydrate. Ten c.c. of the waste lye, filtered free from suspended impurities, was placed in a beaker and diluted to about 150 c.c. with distilled water. A few drops of methyl orange was then added and titrated with half-normal sulphuric acid. Calculate the amount of alkali neutralized by the sulphuric acid to NaOH.

Free Alkali. Use ten c.c. of the lye and dilute as before, add phenolphthalein as the indicator, and titrate to the discharge of the red color with half-normal sulphuric acid. Calculate to percentage of free sodium hydrate.

Combined Alkali as Sodium Carbonate. To find the combined alkali, express the difference in amounts of sulphuric acid in the two previous titrations in terms of sodium carbonate. This figure divided by the weight of the lye used in each case gives the percent.

Sodium Chloride. Use ten c.c. of the lye and dilute as before, then make slightly acid with nitric acid, and heat to about 60 degrees. Add suffic-

(6) Glycerine.

The method of analysis was as follows:

Specific Gravity. Determined by means of the Westphal balance.

Total Alkali as Sodium Hydrate. Ten c.c. of the waste lye, filtered free from suspended impurities, was placed in a beaker and diluted to about 150 c.c. with distilled water. A few drops of methyl orange was then added and titrated with half-normal sulphuric acid. Calculate the amount of alkali neutralized by the sulphuric acid to NaOH.

Free Alkali. Use ten c.c. of the lye and dilute as before, add phenolphthalein as the indicator, and titrate to the discharge of the red color with half-normal sulphuric acid. Calculate to percentage of free sodium hydrate.

Combined Alkali as Sodium Carbonate. To find the combined alkali, express the difference in amounts of sulphuric acid in the two previous titrations in terms of sodium carbonate. This figure divided by the weight of the lye used in each case gives the percent.

Sodium Chloride. Use ten c.c. of the lye and dilute as before, then make slightly acid with nitric acid, and heat to about 60 degrees. Add sulfo-

ient silver nitrate solution to precipitate all the chlorine as silver chloride, and boil until the precipitate has coagulated and the supernatant liquid is clear. Filter on a weighed Gooch crucible by the aid of suction, wash, dry at 105 degrees Centigrade, and weigh. The increase in weight gives the weight of silver chloride from which the percentage of sodium chloride can be calculated.

Glycerine. Place enough of the lye in a 500 c.c. graduated flask, to correspond to about one gram of glycerine, dilute slightly, add silver oxide, allow to stand for ten minutes, and then add a slight excess of lead acetate. Make up to volume, filter, and place 25 c.c. of the clear filtrate into a beaker, then add 40 c.c. of the standard bichromate solution (each c.c. of which has a certain value in glycerine), and 15 c.c. of strong sulphuric acid. Cover the beaker and heat on the water bath for two hours, cool, and titrate back the excess of bichromate with a standard ferrous ammonium sulphate solution. From these results calculate the percentage of glycerine. This reaction may be illustrated by the equation: $C_3H_8O_3$ $3O_2$ $C_2H_2O_4$ CO_2 $3H_2O$.

Using the above methods, the waste soap liquor analyzed as follows:

lent silver nitrate solution to precipitate all the chlorine as silver chloride, and boil until the precipitate has coagulated and the supernatant liquid is clear. Filter on a weighed Gooch crucible by the aid of suction, wash, dry at 105 degrees Centigrade, and weigh. The increase in weight gives the weight of silver chloride from which the percentage of sodium chloride can be calculated.

Glycerine. Place enough of the lye in a 500 c.c. graduated flask, to correspond to about one gram of glycerine, dilute slightly, add silver oxide, allow to stand for ten minutes, and then add a slight excess of lead acetate. Make up to volume, filter, and place 25 c.c. of the clear filtrate into a beaker, then add 40 c.c. of the standard bichromate solution (each c.c. of which has a certain value in glycerine), and 15 c.c. of strong sulphuric acid. Cover the beaker and heat on the water bath for two hours, cool, and titrate back the excess of bichromate with a standard ferrous ammonium sulphate solution. From these results calculate the percentage of glycerine. This reaction may be illustrated by the equation: $C_3H_8O_3$ $3O_2$ $C_2H_2O_4$ CO_2 $3H_2O$.

Using the above methods, the waste soap liquor analysed as follows:

Specific Gravity	1.073
Total Alkali as NaOH	0.25
Free Alkali as NaOH	0.12
Combined Alkali as Na_2CO_3	0.18
Sodium Chloride	7.27
Glycerine	3.07

The determination of the amount of sulphuric acid necessary to neutralize a given amount of soap lye, and the amount of aluminum sulphate necessary to precipitate the albuminous matter in a given amount of the liquor, was the first step. We used the lye in ten kilogram lots, andthe amount of acid necessary to neutralize this amount was calculated as follows: By means of a pipette we placed 25 c.c. of the lye in a beaker, and added enough half-normal sulphuric acid to neutralize it, using methyl orange as an indicator. It required 3.4 c.c. of the acid to neutralize this amount of the lye, and, since 1 c.c. of half-normal sulphuric acid contains 0.049 gram of H2SO4, 3.4 c.c. contain 0.1666 gram of H_2SO_4. The weight of 25 c.c. of the lye is 25 x 1.07 or 26.75 grams. Therefore, since 26.75 grams of the lye required 0.1666 grams of sulphuric acid to neutralize it, 10 kilograms, or 10,000 grams require 10,000 / 26.75 x 0.1666 or 62.14 grams of sulphuric acid. The acid used to neutralize the

Specific Gravity	1.073
Total Alkali as NaOH	0.25
Free Alkali as NaOH	0.12
Combined Alkali as Na_2CO_3	0.18
Sodium Chloride	7.27
Glycerine	3.07

The determination of the amount of sulphuric acid necessary to neutralize a given amount of soap lye, and the amount of aluminum sulphate necessary to precipitate the albuminous matter in a given amount of the liquor, was the first step. We used the lye in ten kilogram lots, andthe amount of acid necessary to neutralize this amount was calculated as follows: By means of a pipette we placed 25 c.c. of the lye in a beaker, and added enough half-normal sulphuric acid to neutralize it, using methyl orange as an indicator. It required 3.4 c.c. of the acid to neutralize this amount of the lye, and, since 1 c.c. of half-normal sulphuric acid contains 0.049 gram of H2SO4, 3.4 c.c. contain 0.1666 gram of H_2SO_4. The weight of 25 c.c. of the lye is 25 x 1.07 or 26.75 grams. Therefore, since 26.75 grams of the lye required 0.1666 grams of sulphuric acid to neutralize it, 10 kilograms, or 10,000 grams require 10,000 / 26.75 x 0.1666 or 62.14 grams of sulphuric acid. The acid used to neutralize the

liquor was that having a specific gravity of 1.84, 1l c.c. of which contains 1.715 grams of H_2SO_4. Therefore, the amount of acid necessary to neutralize ten kilograms of the waste liquor is 62.14 / 1.715 or 34.1 c.c. of the 1.84 acid.

The necessary amount of aluminum sulphate was determined as follows: one hundred c.c. of the lye was placed in a flask, and to it was added, drop by drop, from a burette, a solution of aluminum sulphate, 25 grams per 200 c.c. After the addition of each drop the solution was allowed to settle, and the addition was continued until a precipitate was no longer formed. Ten cubic centimeters were thus required to precipitate all the albuminous matter in 100 c.c. of the soap liquor. This volume was equivalent to 1.25 gram of aluminum sulphate, and since 10 kilograms are equal to 9345 c.c. (10,000 / 1.073), the amount of the sulphate necessary to coagulate the albuminous matter from ten kilograms of liquor is 9345 / 100 x 1.25 or 116.2 grams.

We next placed 10 kilograms ofthe liquor in a kettle and added the necessary amounts of acid and aluminum sulphate as calculated above, and boiled the mixture for a few moments so as to thoroughly mix the contents, and then placed the mass in a galvanized can and allowed it to settle for twenty-four hours. We

ume of the waste liquor is 62.14 / 1.715 or 34.1 c.c.
the 1.84 acid.

The necessary amount of aluminum sulphate
determined as follows: one hundred c.c. of the
was placed in a flask, and to it was added, drop
drop, from a burette, a solution of aluminum sul-
te, 25 grams per 200 c.c. After the addition of each
p the solution was allowed to settle, and the addit-
was continued until a precipitate was no longer form-

Ten cubic centimeters were thus required to pre-
itate all the albuminous matter in 100 c.c. of the
p liquor. This volume was equivalent to 1.25 gram
aluminum sulphate.

FIGURE 1.

repeated this operation eight times, thus having treated 90 kilograms of the waste soap liquor. This amount required 327 c.c. of sulphuric acid having a specific gravity of 1.84, and 2.25 pounds of the aluminum sulphate.

After allowing the albuminous matter to settle, we filtered the liquor through the filter press (see figure 1) at a pressure of 50 pounds per square inch. The filtrate was then run into a Swensen evaporator (see figure 2) and boiled under a vacuum of 27 inches of mercury and a steam pressure of about 20 pounds per square inch. The evaporation was continued until the liquid was reduced as far as possible, that is, the volume was reduced to 26 liters.

The liquid here was somewhat acid, and, as it had to be neutral before continuing the evaporation our next step was to make it so. We determined the acidity in the same manner as already described, and found that 97.05 grams of NaOH were required to neutralize the 26 liters of lye. Upon the addition of this amount of alkali a further precipitation was brought about which we removed by means of the filter press as before.

The liquid was then ready for further evaporation, and this was done in an evaporator smaller

(see figure 1) at a pressure of 50 pounds per square inch. The filtrate was then run into a Swenson evaporator (see figure 2) and boiled under a vacuum of 27 inches of mercury and a steam pressure of about 20 pounds per square inch. The evaporation was continued until the liquid was reduced as far as possible, that is, the volume was reduced to 26 liters.

The liquid here was somewhat acid, and, as it had to be neutral before continuing the evaporation our next step was to make it so. We determined the acidity in the same manner as already described, and

FIGURE 2.

than the one previously used (see figure 3). The vacuum was 25 inches of mercury, the temperature 140 degrees Fahrenheit, and the steam pressure was ten pounds. We noted that as new liquor was added to that already in the evaporator the vacuum went up to al most 27 inches. This was due to the fact that the new cold liquid condensed some of the vapors in the evaporator.

Having treated the 90 kilograms of waste soap liquor in this manner we withdrew the concentrated liquid from the evaporator, and held it until the next lot was ready. The second lot consisted of 110 kilograms, treated exactly as in the first case. When this second lot was withdrawn from the first evaporator and neutralized and filtered,it was added to the first lot and the whole put into the second evaporator (see figure 3). When the liquid was finally taken from this evaporator, after it had been concentrated down as far as possible, it was allowed to cool and settle, whereupon the salt which had been thrown out of solution, settled to the bottom, and was separated from the supernatant liquid by filtration through cloths.

Since we were unable to filter the solution several times during the evaporation as explained in the preceeding pages, because of the too large capacity of the evaporators, it was a very difficult matter to

neutralized and filtered, it was added to the first lot and the whole put into the second evaporator (see figure 3). When the liquid was finally taken from this evaporator, after it had been concentrated down as far as possible, it was allowed to cool and settle, whereupon the salt which had been thrown out of solution, settled to the bottom, and was separated from the supernatant liquid by filtration through cloths.

Since we were unable to filter the solution several times during the evaporation as explained in

FIGURE 5.

to separate the salt from the liquid, for the salt was in an excess and the liquid was thick and syrupy, and we could not use a vacuum. The filtrate now had a very sweetish and not unpleasant odor, was thick, and of a yellowish color. Before going farther we had to make this filtrate slightly alkaline, which we did by adding sodium hydrate to the filtrate. The liquid was then ready for purification by distillation in the still and apparatus, which is shown in detail in the blue-print at the beginning of part 11, together with an assembled drawing of the same, and the specifications from which the small model was made. Figure four shows this minature plant, as designed from the aforesaid blue-prints, just before the steam and water connections were made.

At intervals during the above treatment, we took samples of the liquid at various stages of the process, determining the specific gravity of each and the amount of glycerine contained therein. The results were as follows:

Sample.	% Glycerine	Specific Gravity.
At Start.	3.07	1.073
After 1st. filtration	3.14	1.087
After Concentration	63.71	1.364

The operation and description of the appara-

to separate the salt from the liquid, for the salt was in an excess and the liquid was thick and syrupy, and we could not use a vacuum. The filtrate now had a very sweetish and not unpleasant odor, was thick, and of a yellowish color. Before going farther we had to make this filtrate slightly alkaline, which we did by adding sodium hydrate to the filtrate. The liquid was then ready for purification by distillation in the still and apparatus, which is shown in detail in the blue-print at the beginning of part II, together with an assembled drawing of the same, and the specifications from which the small model was made. Figure four shows this miniature plant, as designed from the aforesaid blue-prints, just before the steam and water connections were made.

At intervals during the above treatment, we took samples of the liquid at various stages of the process, determining the specific gravity of each and the amount of glycerine contained therein. The results

FIGURE 4.

tus which we designed for the purpose of refining the glycerine after leaving the evaporator will now be explained in detail. The letters used refer to the blue prints.

A, is the still proper. It consists of a brass body, at the upper end of which is bolted a brass flanged cover. This cover carries a vacuum gauge and an oil cup in which a thermometer may be placed. The still contains a copper coil, at the lower end of which live steam is admitted and at the upper end of which the steam isexhausted. Into the still at the bottom runs a pipe which terminates in a piece full of small holes, by means of which superheated steam passes.

The liquid from the evaporator was run into the still until it was a little more than half full,as judged from the gauge glass. The steam was then allowed to enter the coil, and as the liquid became heated, the glycerine vapors were evolved. These vapors leave the still at the tôp, and enter the catch-all, B, while at the same time superheated steam enters the still by means of the perforated pipe at the bottom and helps the vapors to leave the still, and at the same time tending to increase the vacuum by their condensation,

tus which we designed for the purpose of refining the glycerine after leaving the evaporator will now be explained in detail. The letters used refer to the blue prints.

A, is the still proper. It consists of a brass body, at the uppor end of which is bolted a brass flanged cover. This cover carries a vacuum gauge and an oil cup in which a thermometer may be placed. The still contains a copper coil, at the lower end of which live steam is admitted and at the upper end of which the steam isexhausted. Into the still at the bottom runs a pipe which terminates in a piece full of small holes, by means of which superheated steam passes.

The liquid from the evaporator was run into the still until it was a little more than half full, as judged from the gauge glass. The steam was then allowed to enter the coil, and as the liquid became heated, the

as the superheated steam hits the cooler liquid within the still. As the volume of the liquid in the still decreases more is added so that the still was always about half full. The liquid is added by suction, that is, the vessel containing it is held to the feed pipe near the top of the still and the cock opened. The vacuum within sucks the liquid up into the still.

Those vapors condensing on their way to the catch-all, and in the catch-all, run back to the still by means of the pipe connected from the bottom of the catch-all to the still. Those which do not condense pass out through the top into the superheater C. This superheater is also made of brass. Steam which enters at the top and passes down through vertical copper tubes superheats the glycerine vapors coming from the catch-all, thus preventing them from possibly condensing, and so not passing over into the condenser D. However, the very heaviest vapors do condense in spite of this precaution and run into a receiver, not shown in the blue-prints but clearly shown in figure four. The steam which has given up some of its heat to the glycerine vapors passes out at the bottom of the superheater, and enters the still A, at the bottom, after being superheated by means of a Bunsen burner placed at the pipe half way between the still and the superheater.

as the superheated steam hits the cooler liquid within the still. As the volume of the liquid in the still decreases more is added so that the still was always about half full. The liquid is added by suction, that is, the vessel containing it is held to the feed pipe near the top of the still and the cook opened. The vacuum within sucks the liquid up into the still.

Those vapors condensing on their way to the catch-all, and in the catch-all, run back to the still by means of the pipe connected from the bottom of the catch-all to the still. Those which do not condense pass out through the top into the superheater C. This superheater is also made of brass. Steam which enters at the top and passes down through vertical copper tubes superheats the glycerine vapors coming from the catch-all, thus preventing them from possibly condensing, and so not passing over into the condenser D. However, the very heaviest vapors do condense in spite of this precaution and run into a receiver, not shown in the blueprints but clearly shown in figure four. The steam which has given up some of its heat to the glycerine vapors passes out at the bottom of the superheater, and enters the still A, at the bottom, after being superheated by means of a Bunsen burner placed at the pipe half way between the still and the superheater.

The glycerine vapors, after being superheated by passing around and amonge the steam pipes of the superheater, pass to D, the condenser proper. This is a brass shell containing a copper coil through which cold water is continually circulating. Here all but a small proportion of the vapors, and those the lightest, are condensed and run into a receiver similiar to the one attached to the superheater, as shown in figure four. The lightest vapors, which do not condense in the condenser, pass to the "sweet-water" condenser E, in which they are condensed by passing around and among vertical copper pipes through which cold water is constantly circulating. The water enters at the bottom and leaves at the top. The condensate is drawn off by the pump which is connected to the lower end of the condenser. If it is desired to save the sweet water, a small receiver can be placed near the condenser in the pipe leading to the pump. The pump is placed at the end of the system to furnish the necessary vacuum, which is increased by the condensation of the superheated steam and vapors, as has been desdribed. The minor details of the apparatus can be readily understood by consulting the drawings.

In practice it has been advisory to place a valve in the pipe leading from the bottom of the catch-

the glycerine vapors, after being superheated by passing around and among the steam pipes of the superheater, pass to D, the condenser proper. This is a brass shell containing a copper coil through which cold water is continually circulating. Here all but a small proportion of the vapors, and those the lightest, are condensed and run into a receiver similar to the one attached to the superheater, as shown in figure four. The lightest vapors, which do not condense in the condenser, pass to the "sweet-water" condenser E, in which they are condensed by passing around and among vertical copper pipes through which cold water is constantly circulating. The water enters at the bottom and leaves at the top. The condensate is drawn off by the pump which is connected to the lower end of the condenser. If it is desired to save the sweet water, a small receiver can be placed near the condenser in the pipe leading to the pump. The pump is placed at the end of the system to furnish the necessary vacuum, which is increased by the condensation of the superheated steam and vapors, as has been described. The minor details of the apparatus can be readily understood by consulting the drawings.

In practice it has been satisfactory to place a valve in the pipe leading from the bottom of the catch-

all back to the still. This valve is kept closed until the catch-all contains a certain amount of aondensed vapors, consisting principally of liquid whcih has been carried over mechanically, whereupon the valve is opened and the liquid allowed to run back to the still. This eliminates any traces of salt in the final distillate, for it has been found that this was mechanically carried over in solution through the pipe from the still to the catch-all.

The reason for elways evaporating glycerine in vacuo is due to the fact that when glycerine is heated to its boiling point under atmospheric conditions it decomposes.

When we treated and purified our crude glycerine as above described, we obtained a slight precipitate in the distillate from the réceivers. This was due to the passage of some of the crude glycerine from the still to the catch all through the pipe just under discussion. As before said, this could be remedied by placing a valve in the pipe. The precipitate formed in the crude glycerine was probably due to a deterioration of the liquid at some step in the process because of the long intervals which had to elapse between each step. With the pump alone we obtained a vacuum of 25 inches of mercury, when the still was in

all back to the still. This valve is kept closed until the catch-all contains a certain amount of condensed vapors, consisting principally of liquid which has been carried over mechanically, whereupon the valve is opened and the liquid allowed to run back to the still. This eliminates any traces of salt in the final distillate, for it has been found that this was mechanically carried over in solution though the pipe from the still to the catch-all.

The reason for always evaporating glycerine in vacuo is due to the fact that when glycerine is heated to its boiling point under atmospheric conditions it decomposes.

When we treated and purified our crude glycerine as above described, we obtained a slight precipitate in the distillate from the receivers. This was due to the passage of some of the crude glycerine from the still to the catch all through the pipe just under discussion. As before said, this could be remedied by placing a valve in the pipe. The precipitate formed in the crude glycerine was probably due to a deterioration of the liquid at some step in the process because of the long intervals which had to elapse between each step. With the pump alone we obtained a vacuum of 25 inches of mercury, when the still was in

operation we obtained a 27 inch vacuum. The temperature at which the distillation was conducted was about 175 degrees Fahrenheit.

When the process of purification was complete, we removed the distillates from the receivers, united them, treated them with sulphuric acid and caustic soda as described in the preceeding pages, mixed it with bone black, and filtered the resulting mixture. We did not carry the purification beyond this point, as the amount of glycerine was too small to warrent further treatment, as the rest of the process is purely mechanical. The glycerine as finally obtained had a specific gravity of 1.239, and contained 90.07 percent of glycerine by analysis.

There remains to be considered the black residuum left in the crude glycerine still. All the organic matter not removed in the preliminary treatment of the lye accumulates in the still and forms this black, viscous residue, which if the distillation be carried too far, becomes so hard as to be removed from the still only with great difficulty. To facilitate its easy handling and the recovery of the considerable quantity of glycerine retained by it, the distillation is checked at that stage beyond which there is danger

[illegible]

of contaminating the distillate with entrained matter from the still. The quantity of glycerine present depends on the concentration and is about 50 per cent. This substance is known as foots.

While yet soft and comparatively fluid, the foots is transferred to a tank and neutralized with oil of vitriol, and then filtered. This product is then concentrated, forming crude glycerine from foots; this is then distilled, and the glycerine thus obtained constitutes the dynamite glycerine of commerce. It is of a pale straw color and requires only subsequent distillation and filtration through bone black to become water-white, chemically pure glycerine of the pharmacopoeia.